dear ADAM

KELSEY WHITNEY

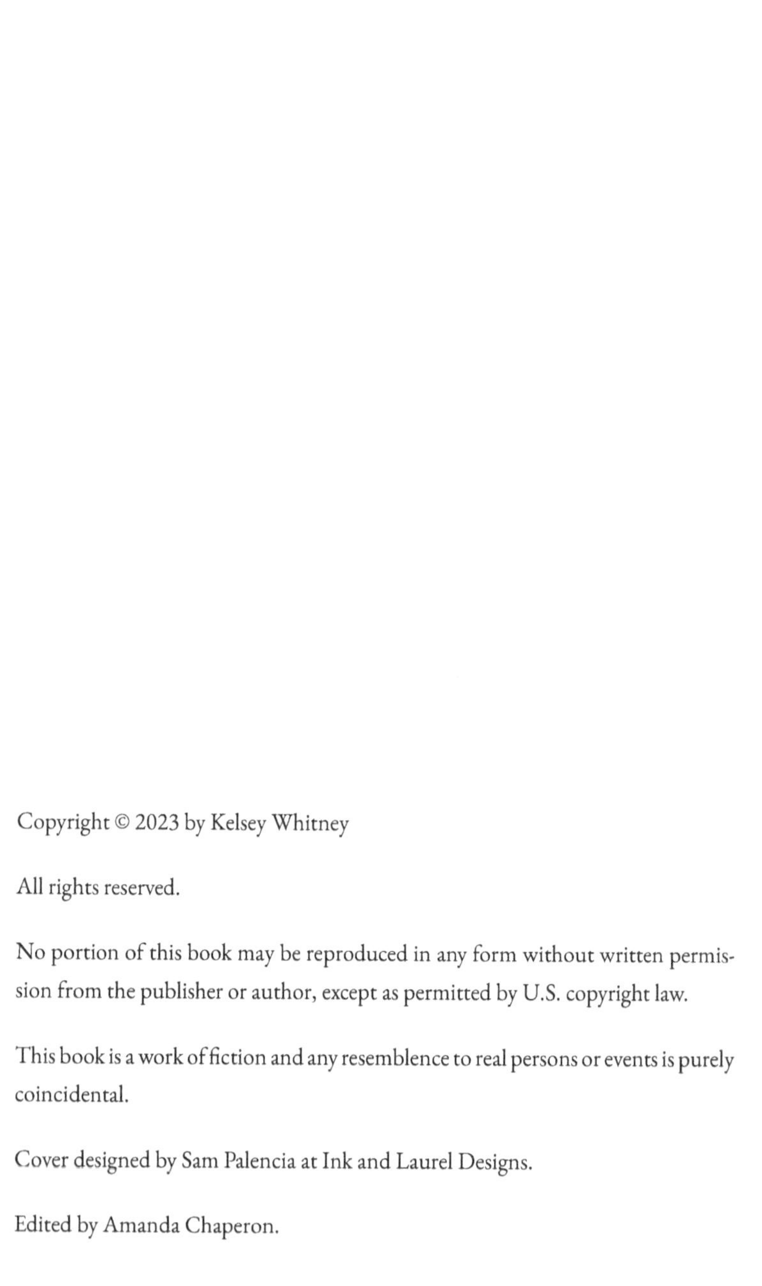

PRAISE FOR *DEAR ADAM*

"Full of southern summer vibes and the sweetest love story, Dear Adam is a must-read rom-com!" -**Amanda Chaperon,** author of *Every Rule Worth Breaking*

"Rom-com and dog lovers rejoice, this gives sugary sweet spoonfuls of both that will satisfy any palate!" -**Sydney Filkins**

"Dear Adam has everything you could want in a romantic comedy: laugh out loud moments, a swoony setting, and a love story for the ages." -**Juliana Smith,** author of *Per My Last Email*

"Laugh-out-loud funny and achingly sweet, *Dear Adam* is utterly unputdownable!" -**Madison Wright,** author of *Just Between Us*

For Mom,

I love you more.

CHAPTER ONE

ALY

Taylor Swift's *Midnights* album blares from my speakers as I drive past the iconic, pastel houses of Rainbow Row. The window boxes are packed with flowers of every variety, and Spanish moss drips from the trees lining the street. I follow the natural curve of the road and glance left toward the harbor, never getting tired of the way the sun glistens off the water or the way the whole city is basked in a golden hue during this hour before sunset.

I roll up to my parent's house and type in the code. The wrought iron gates silently swing open as if on a breeze, revealing the long, ornately landscape-lined driveway and the breathtaking, historical colonial mansion beyond it. The crunch of cobblestones beneath my tires is an all too familiar sound as I shift into park beside Adam's truck.

Immediately, the idyllic scene is interrupted by my engine backfiring, the loud pop still echoing as my dad comes running out the front door, brandishing a golf club.

"Hi, Dad," I attempt weakly.

Dad looks around frantically before realizing it's only me. "Alyson Jane, I swear if you don't get a new vehicle—"

"Dad, what are you doing with your golf club?" my twin brother, Adam, asks, coming out the same door, saving me from whatever threat our father was about to make. Adam's eyes dart between me, Dad, and the golf club, and he stifles a laugh behind his balled fist.

"I thought I heard shots, but it was just your sister's piece of junk," Dad answers through pursed lips, staring at me disapprovingly. He pushes his hand through his hair, and there's no mistaking the disappointment in his glare.

"Dad, it's a 1966 Ford Bronco. People pay a lot of money for these," I say defensively.

"People pay a lot of money for them when they are *restored*, Alyson. Not when you buy them from an auction as is. *That* is anything but restored."

Truthfully, when my flower shop was only a start-up and I was running it out of my apartment kitchen, this Bronco was the only thing I could afford. I found it on an online auction, saw the next to nothing starting bid, made sure the description said it ran, and typed in my bid with crossed fingers. Apparently, no one else wanted a rusty yellow Bronco with a single purple door, but Betsy and I have been through a lot together, and I'm not sure I'd trade her for anything else.

I hop out of the driver's seat, and the hinges squeak as I slam the door shut. As if on cue, a little pile of rust dust catches in the breeze and floats to the ground. I barely hold back a cringe.

Adam gives me a quick hug, then pulls back to search my face. Staring at my twin is like looking in the mirror and seeing the male version of myself: the same sandy-brown hair, deep blue eyes the color of the Charleston harbor, and a golden tan that never seems to fade.

Nervously, he bites his lower lip, then whispers, "Mom and Dad invited Hudson."

"What? Why didn't you warn me?" My heart sinks, and I search around frantically for any sign of him.

"I tried, but you didn't answer my call!"

I pull my phone from my crossbody and see that there is indeed a missed call from Adam.

"You must've called while I was working on my sink," I groan.

"You know you could hire people for that," Adam says.

I scoff. I *could*...if I could afford to.

My old, rusty, leaky faucet must've been original to my cottage, and I'd only recently got around to replacing it. Lucky for me, there's a YouTube video for everything. Thanks to the bushy-mustache man behind MrFixIt64, I successfully installed a new faucet, accompanied by too much muttering, some head scratching, several wedgie adjustments, and a few curse words thrown in for good measure.

As if on cue, the gates swing open a second time, and a sleek black Jaguar pulls up next to my Bronco. Hudson casually gets out and points the fob in its direction, the car giving a little *beep beep* as he locks it. I struggle not to roll my eyes, but am unable to stifle a groan. We were in a gated driveway for heaven's sake.

It shouldn't surprise me that my dad invited Hudson. To my parents, Hudson is the solution to all of their woes in regards to their children.

Honestly, I've never seen parents so disappointed about their kids being self-sufficient. Adam lives in a loft in the city, and while my house may be a fixer-upper I bought at a foreclosure auction, we both have steady jobs and are happy and healthy. But we're both twenty-seven and single, which annoys our parents to no end.

At least Adam has a leg up on me, because he chose to work for the family business while I did not.

Adam hates working for our family's boat and yacht service company, but he's incredible at his job and lands deals with the biggest of clients. Recently, he sold a yacht to Taylor Swift, and I definitely did *not* ask Adam to include a line in the purchase agreement entitling me to BFF rights with her.

I had to shoot my shot, you know?

But apparently, Adam's sales numbers are down this month, and I know my dad invited Hudson over to help get him back on track.

And then there's me.

My parents would love it if I married Hudson, and take every opportunity to throw us together to make that happen.

Adam recently told me a story about how Hudson had gone to dinner downtown and had to send his meal back four times before they drizzled the sauce on it correctly.

"'It's a simple thing to do,'" Adam had imitated Hudson's voice perfectly. "'But they just couldn't get it right. I guess that's why they make minimum wage and I don't.' And then he winked at me, Aly. He *winked*."

"That sounds about right," I'd said with a snort.

The memory pulls another groan from me.

Hudson is nearly fifteen years older than I am and incredibly entitled with his old, southern family money, but he *is* undeniably attractive. He's got the perfect chiseled jaw and smooth skin, not a pore in sight. I've even questioned what products he uses because I would kill for skin like his.

Today, Hudson is wearing a button up with a little whale on the pocket, slacks, and loafers sans socks. I grew up in the south and have lived here all my life, but I still couldn't get past the leather loafers without socks. In what world was it ever okay to do that? *Especially* in the south? It gets *hot* here. Now all I can think about is if his pinky toes are chafing and how bad his shoes must stink.

I look down at my own attire and run my hands along my wrinkled sundress I tie-dyed with my best friend, Emma, a few summers ago. I don't own anything that lives up to Mom and Dad's standards of pearls and shirts with collars, so I picked out the one clean thing from the mound of laundry piled in the corner of my bedroom I thought would suffice.

But that's part of the problem. Hudson probably spends a good portion of his salary on skincare and nice suits. My entire paycheck goes to renovations on my cottage. Whatever is left goes into a little piggy bank. Like, a legitimate piggy bank. It's pink, it oinks when you slide anything in it, *and* you have to bust it to get the money out. I'm not proud of it, but I was short on cash a few weeks ago and so desperate for an iced vanilla latte that I managed to turn the pig upside down and shake out a few quarters with the help of a nail file I shimmied up in there.

"Hey, boss man," Hudson says, sticking out his hand for Dad to shake.

"Hudson!" Dad cries, pumping his hand enthusiastically. "It's good to see you."

"Didn't you two just see each other Friday?" I mutter. I catch Adam's eye and we both roll our eyes at the same time. I stifle a laugh but stop cold when Hudson slips an arm around my shoulders. Adam's jaw flexes and he cocks an eyebrow. I wiggle out from underneath Hudson's arm, and awkwardly shake his hand instead.

"Hello, beautiful," he says, and tucks my hair behind both my ears. Like…all of my hair behind my ears. Not just a piece. My ears are completely exposed and that, my friends, is one of the worst feelings in the world. I shudder and quickly shake the strands loose.

Ever since the day Hudson walked into Dad's office for a job and charmed him with his excessively useless knowledge of every pro golfer since the nineteen eighties, it's been a constant battle between my parents, Adam, and me.

"Adam, if you paid a little more attention to Hudson, you might be able to make a few more sales. Really take note of the way he's so personable with the clients." Or, "Alyson, Hudson would make a fantastic husband. You'd never have to worry about money and you could get out of that nasty little cottage and live somewhere proper." Or my personal favorite which we hear at least twenty times a week, "Hudson is just the best, isn't he?"

Sorry, Mom and Dad, that we are such utter disappointments.

I don't even know if it's Hudson himself that turns me off so badly or the fact that we hear about him and his greatness nonstop. He might actually be a good guy and we're just not giving him a chance. But, if I hear one more thing about how wonderful he is...I think we both might snap.

"Hi Hudson," I say through a forced smile.

"Aly, let's get Pretzel's things switched over into your car while we're out here."

Pretzel is Adam's one-year-old wiener dog. A couple days ago, Adam told me he was going out of town for work and asked me to watch her. I wasn't keen on the idea, considering the last time I watched her, when she was only a few months old, she managed to find the bag of my new panties I had picked up at the seven for twenty seven sale and chewed the crotch out of every single pair. I found her with a pair draped casually over one ear, the other ear turned inside out.

Then she puked the panty pieces all over my shoe.

Even thinking about it now makes me shudder.

"How long do you need me to watch her?" I asked Adam.

"Ten days or so," Adam had coughed out.

"Ten days?" I'd screeched. Money signs had blurred my vision as I thought about all the new underwear I'd have to replace. "Where are you going?"

"I have a client that wants to wine and dine me before I sell him a boat," Adam had joked. "He's in Santa Monica, and I figured while I was there, I could see Levi for a few days."

"I guess I can watch her," I'd conceded. "But remind me to make sure all my underwear are somewhere safe. Pretzel has a real taste for bikini cut."

In the background, Pretzel had yipped, almost as if she was agreeing with me. Weirdo.

We'd agreed to trade off today, since Adam was leaving in the morning.

Adam heads toward his truck and I practically skip behind him, happy for any chance to get away from the awkward situation from moments before. I channel all the twin vibes I can possibly muster to send him a silent thank you.

"Where is Pretzel anyway?" I ask, and then I hear the unmistakable sound of dishes clattering to the floor from inside the house.

"*Pretzel!*" Mom's angry voice floats out to us. For a split second, I feel sorry for Pretzel. I've been on the receiving end of one of mom's scolding too many times to count, and they are anything but pleasant. But then I remember the underwear incident and don't feel as bad.

Mom's yell rings out again, and I look around to see who's going to get eyes on the situation inside. Adam is wrestling with my rusty tailgate, muttering something unintelligible under his breath, and Dad and Hudson are practically making googly eyes at each other, talking about their most recent yacht sale, leaving only me to heroically dash inside to try and save Pretzel.

In a hurry, I kick off my white sneakers by the front door, then listen for any more signs of Pretzel wreaking havoc. Another dish clatters to the floor, and my mismatched socks slide on the shiny hardwoods as I dash around the corner into the dining room to find the natural disaster herself, Pretzel, destroying everything in her wake. She's standing on top of the dining room table, frayed rope dangling from her collar, her face completely submerged into a bowl of buttery mashed potatoes. Fine china is scattered around like hurricane debris, because my parents think it's a sin to eat off paper plates. Each dish that's managed to stay on the table has at least one bite taken out of it, leaving nothing salvageable. I hear something gurgling, and tilt my head in confusion when I realize it's coming from Pretzel, who is blowing bubbles into the gravy bowl with her nose.

And this is why I'm apprehensive to watch Pretzel. I own a flower shop, and I'm terrified of the trouble she could get into during the long hours each day I'm gone.

I'd asked Adam if she'd matured enough to be left alone, and he said yes, but I knew he was lying.

Turns out, based on the scene in front of me, I knew I was right.

"Get that *rat* off the dining room table," my mom snarls, pointing a perfectly manicured nail toward Pretzel.

Adam catches up beside me and we both stare at each other in horror. My mom wails, literally *wails*, when Pretzel scoots the bowl of green beans off the edge of the table with her nose, and pretends to faint with the back of her hand pressed against her forehead. My dad lets her gracelessly slide to the floor instead of catching her and instead chases Pretzel with the golf club he's still holding.

They're having a stare down now. Pretzel has bits of mashed potatoes in the fur around her face, a piece of ham stuck to the side of her snout, and gravy dripping from her nose. Dad has the golf club in his hand, thwacking it into his palm. I feel like I'm watching Monday night football with the scene that unfolds. Pretzel jukes left, Dad jukes left. Pretzel shifts right, Dad does too. This goes on for a solid minute before I realize a five pound dog is faking out my dad, and Adam and I fall over, laughing.

Incredulously, Dad turns to look at us and Pretzel makes her move. She soars off the dining room table...and lands straight on Hudson's face, who has been staring silently, mouth agape at the whole ordeal. Hudson blindly runs around the dining room, waving his hands in the air, Pretzel holding on for dear life, before running into the wall. He lands with a grunt, and Pretzel hops off, happily trotting down the hallway.

"I should probably go get my dog," Adam mutters at the same time a choked sob escapes from our mother.

The silence is so thick you could cut it with a blade as we sit around the kitchen table, Italian takeout containers spread in front of us. Dad is holding his plastic silverware with disdain, ineffectively cutting at a piece of chicken parmesan. Mom's lips are so pursed, they've begun to turn white. We're effectively avoiding eye contact with one another, the scrapes of plastic forks and knives against the plates replacing any kind of conversation. In the dining room down the hall, housekeepers, armed with trash bags and vacuums, are making quick work of the disaster Pretzel created.

Finally, unable to stand the silence any longer, Dad clears his throat and says, "Hudson, I don't even know how to properly apologize. Had we any idea that dog was such an untrained rodent, we never would've allowed Adam to bring her." He practically spits out the words *untrained rodent,* and I do my best not to giggle. She's a five pound wiener dog for heaven's sake.

A strangled whine comes from the floor below, and I feel a little sorry for Pretzel, who is locked in the downstairs laundry room like a prisoner with no chance of getting out on bail.

"Did you apologize, Adam?" Dad asks. "Maybe Hudson can teach you a thing or two about tying a proper knot in a rope too." He stares at Adam, disappointment laced with embarrassment etched into every crevice of his face. It feels like we are in high school all over again.

Adam clears his throat. "Yeah sorry about that, Hudson. Pretzel is always a little hyper but has never done anything like that." The corner of his mouth twitches, and my twin senses tell me he's secretly pleased with the events of this evening.

Hudson lays a hand on Adam's shoulder and squeezes it. "It's okay, *buddy*," he says. "Things happen. It's not a big deal at all." Adam's shoulders tense under Hudson's touch, and his jaw clenches as he fights to keep his mouth in a tight smile.

"Buddy?" I mouth with disgust when Adam briefly meets my eye.

"Adam, why were you putting all of that little rat's things into the back of Alyson's sorry excuse for a vehicle?" Dad asks. "Did you finally realize an apartment is no place for a dog?"

"Dad, Adam lives in a *loft*. And his loft is bigger than my cottage. Just because it's in a building where other people live doesn't mean it's smaller than a house," I correct.

The noise dad makes in the back of his throat grates my nerves like an eyelash I can't seem to get out of my eye. Beside him, Mom's tugging at the collar of her shirt and fanning away at the nonexistent beads of perspiration she wants us to believe have gathered there. The dramatics of this woman. "But no," I continue. "I'm just watching Pretzel for a few days while Adam goes out of town."

"Oh yeah?" Dad asks. "Did you request time off?" He leans back in his chair and puts both hands behind his head. His incredibly strong cologne, a blend of musky spice and hundred dollar bills, floats across the table, and I choke back a grimace. He cocks an eyebrow in Adam's direction, no doubt already thinking he knows his answer.

"No dad, this is for work. I'm selling a fishing yacht to Harry Styles, remember?" Adam's annoyance is understandable but I can't help but stare at him, mouth agape.

"Harry Styles?" I squeak out. He didn't tell me *that*.

"Harry who?" Mom asks.

"That's right. I forgot you mentioned going to California to dilly dally with a pop star before you try and sell him a yacht," Dad scoffs.

Adam throws his hands up. "A sale is a sale, isn't it, dad? Regardless of who it is? Didn't you just talk about the importance of closing deals by any means necessary in our last business meeting? You told everyone there that my sales were the worst of any employee this month, and this is going to be a *huge* deal."

"Maybe you should ask Hudson for some pointers. He did just make a sale with Tiger Woods last month after all."

Of course my dad would think the ultimate celebrity is a pro golfer. Meanwhile, I'm still a guppy out of water with the way my mouth opens and closes, completely shook that Adam is about to meet *Harry Styles*. Hudson looks like he's been watching a tennis tournament, his head bouncing back and forth between each of us.

"Hudson?" Dad asks. "Would you care to give Adam some extra training?"

"Yeah sure, buddy. I can give you some pointers." The veins in Adam's neck bulge at the use of *buddy* again, and I know it's probably time to pull out an emergency card to save Adam from this one.

"Wow," I say, taking pointers from Mom and fanning myself wildly. "Is it hot in here or is this takeout about to do unspeakable things to my stomach? You know all that cheese can't contribute to keeping you regular."

"Oh for Christ's sake, Alyson," Mom groans, and Dad's face is beet red, either from embarrassment or anger. Before he can reprimand me, I scoot my chair back from the table.

"I need to get out of here. Sorry to cut out before dessert but I think all that sugar on top of all the cheese I ate will be no bueno if you know what I mean. Adam, would you mind helping me load up Pretzel?" Before I'm able to finish my sentence, Adam's chair scrapes against the hardwoods as he stands.

"Thanks for dinner," we say in unison, hightailing it downstairs leaving behind Mom, Dad, and Hudson to stare after us, bewildered.

Chapter Two

Aly

By the time I park in the crushed-shell driveway of my little sun-bleached yellow cottage, I am utterly exhausted. My Bronco's air conditioning doesn't work and the whole ride home, Pretzel attempted to jump out of the open window; I've never hated my hand cranked windows more.

With a world-weary sigh, I get out, thinking this is even worse than the time it took an extra twenty seconds to roll down my window in the coffee shop drive-thru, and the grandma in a pearly white Cadillac behind me flipped me off.

I would've been more offended if she didn't remind me of myself in fifty years.

Pretzel takes advantage of the second I've got my back turned to open my door and at last, soars out the opposite window. A curse slips from my lips as I chase after her and

I groan as she rockets herself into the harbor, sending a spray of water droplets across my skin. Although it's shallow in this area, frustration still claws at me. It's been too long of a day and a wet, disobedient dog is the last thing I want to deal with tonight.

"Pretzel, please," I beg and clap my hands together. Pretzel has found a duck to torment and is happily doggy paddling around behind it.

"Pretzel," I hiss through clenched teeth. My voice wavers, the exhaustion and impatience seeping through. She doesn't even give me a side eye at the mention of her name, and I'm beginning to wonder if she even *knows* her name. Is she just this disobedient, *still*?

My chest heaves with a sigh as I slide off my flip flops and tear my wrinkled dress over my head. The cool water is surprisingly soothing after a long, eventful day as I wade in after her. A piece of driftwood floats by and I grab it, finally stealing Pretzel's attention away from the duck. Relieved, the duck paddles off and out of sight.

"Good dog," I say soothingly when she starts paddling towards me. "Come here, good girl." She gets close enough that I'm able to grab ahold of her harness. I hoist her into my arms and she grunts, realizing her play time is up. As I carry a wriggling, soaking wet dog back to the house, my shoulders slump like someone who's done manual labor their whole life with the weight of my frustration. As I'm bending over to let Pretzel down through the front door, someone coughs, causing me to snap up and look around.

Mr. Barnes, my eighty-three-year-old neighbor, is standing in his front yard, watering his already perfectly emerald green lawn, mouth ajar. It doesn't matter what day it is, what the temperature is, or how green his grass is, Mr. Barnes is *always* watering his lawn and always eavesdropping into my life. My frustration and impatience must be at an all-time high because instead of being the nice neighbor who typically offers a wave and smile, I throw one hand up and mouth, *what?*

He clears his throat, blinks rapidly, and goes back to watering his lawn. I look down, and that's when it hits me. The panties I grabbed from the clean laundry pile before dinner this evening in a hurry to make it on time are lime green and have "Cutie Patootie" across the butt. My bra isn't any better, with its sheer lace cups and purple bows under each boob. *And* I'm sort of chilly now after getting out of the water, so little is left to the imagination. My cheeks flame from embarrassment, and I feel like that Italian take out from dinner is about to do unspeakable things to my stomach. With a grimace and a little wave, I scamper through the front door and Pretzel wriggles out of my arms.

She's still soaking wet and standing dangerously close to the sofa I recently purchased from Facebook Marketplace. It's got embroidered yellow daisies all over its pale pink velvet and looks like it's straight from the seventies. I've never seen a more perfect couch. I narrow my eyes and I swear she does the same, almost as if she's testing my limits. At this point, I'm ready to get on my hands and knees for a five-pound wiener dog. My hands are clasped together in front of my chest and I inch toward the bedroom. Pretzel cocks her head to the side, clearly interested.

She blinks up at me through dark, round eyes and, for a second, I think I've finally broken through to her. She's finally understood that I'm the boss around here. A smug smile turns the corners of my lips upward and immediately her little wiener dog eyes fill with malice. Within seconds, water droplets spray from one wall of the tiny living room to the other, including all over my perfectly new couch.

A sigh of frustration seeps out from behind pursed lips and I clamp the bridge of my nose between two fingers. "It's going to be a long ten days," I mutter and head to find the blow dryer.

The following morning, I open my eyes to the pale yellow rays of sun peeking through my windows. Grudgingly, I throw the covers off and roll over, ready to get up. Right as I'm about to set my feet onto the floor, Pretzel flies off the bed to paw at the door. She's whining and doing her own version of the potty dance, shifting from side to side, her nails click-clacking on my floor.

"Hold on," I grumble and shuffle out to the front door. I slip on her harness and check three times to make sure the leash is attached. I wag a finger at her and say, "Don't try anything." My voice is still raspy with sleep, and Pretzel either understands or really has to pee because she gingerly crawls down the front porch steps and does her business in the flower bed. I would prefer she not pee on the hydrangea bushes I'm trying to coax back to life, but I'm still too groggy with sleep to scold her.

While I get ready for the busy day ahead, Pretzel follows me around like a...well like a lost puppy. The entire time I shower, she's got her nose pressed to the glass, fogging it up. When I use the bathroom, her head peeks around the corner like a little creeper. It's almost laughable until I realize she probably doesn't have much else to do. I put every chewable or breakable item up before I even left for dinner Sunday. There's not a pair of tauntingly lacy bikini cut panties in sight.

I throw on a yellow sundress with little roses embroidered on it from the clean clothes mound and pile my wavy hair into a loose ponytail. Any other day, I would take my Vespa to work since it's only a short drive from my cottage in Mount Pleasant to my floral studio on King Street. Today though, with Pretzel,

I decide on the Bronco...with the windows only cracked this time.

We arrive at Bloomie's in less than ten minutes, and I say a silent prayer of thanks when I find a parking spot near the front entrance. I'm trying to unlock the door and juggle my laptop in one hand while trying to hold Pretzel—who is apparently *very* nosy and wants to lick, smell, and touch everything she can—with the other when my phone goes off in my crossbody. Adam's face fills the screen, with his goofy smile and hair sticking up in all directions. I manage to wedge the laptop between my chin and my boobs, creating a very sexy double chin and stab at the green button on the screen to answer.

Although...it's not Adam who answers. It's very grown up, very beautiful...*Levi.*

Growing up, I had always had a tiny crush on him, and I'd be lying if I said I hadn't occasionally tried to look up his social media profiles. He didn't have any that I could find, leaving me to only guess at what he could possibly look like after ten years of no contact with him. I stare blankly at the screen for a few seconds, trying to figure out if this is the same guy who used to relentlessly tease me for my eccentric taste in clothing and well...everything else. This handsome stranger with large blue eyes, hair as dark as the midnight sky, and beard speckled across his chiseled jaw couldn't possibly be the same guy who wore headgear at one point.

"Aly!" Levi's voice booms through the speakers. "How are ya? Long time no see." I catch sight of my double chin in my reflection on the bottom right corner of the screen and immediately straighten my neck to fix my posture, causing my laptop to fall flat on my feet.

"Ouch!" I yell, bouncing and flailing around, Pretzel standing on her hind legs to join in on the commotion with me.

"Aly?" Adam's familiar voice comes through the speakers, concern weaved through every word. "Aly, are you okay?"

"One second," I grumble as I hang up and stick the key into the lock to open the door. Pretzel goes zooming in, and I scoop my laptop off the ground and follow. Immediately, I run to the bathroom and take a look in the mirror. The lack of air conditioning on the way over has done no favors to my hair so I quickly redo my pony tail and pinch my cheeks for some color, a trick Nana taught me back in the day but never actually used until now. I take one last final glance, and oh my gosh, is that a booger? Did Levi see this little flapper hanging out in my left nostril during all that commotion? I blow my nose, and stare at myself in the mirror. *Get it together, Bloomington.*

Finally, everything looks decent enough that if Levi happens to answer again, I won't be too upset about it...until I notice the boob sweat forming.

Not a problem, I think. *I'll just have to keep my face and nothing else on the screen. That won't be weird at all.*

Except it will be super weird because who FaceTimes with nothing but a close up of your face unless you are seventy two and should be using a Jitterbug flip phone and have no business FaceTiming to begin with? With no other options, I sigh and hit Adam's name on my phone. When he answers instead of Levi, I try not to sound too disappointed.

"Aly, what happened?" he asks, his brow furrowed.

"I dropped my laptop and it landed on my feet," I answer sheepishly, leaving out the reason *why* I dropped my laptop in the first place. I change the subject and ask the question I've been dying to ask since Adam arrived in California. "Have you met with Harry yet?"

"Yes and before you ask, no. I did not have him sign your ratty old t-shirt."

"That wasn't any old ratty t-shirt, Adam. That was my 2011 One Direction concert t-shirt. It's a collector's item."

Or, probably would be if the pits didn't have sweat stains and there wasn't a hole around the collar. I don't know how that got there because I rarely ever wear it....during the day.

Only at night....on the days that end in Y.

Adam rolls his eyes. Behind him, palms tower and a pier extends far out into the ocean.

"Are you on the beach?" I ask. A seagull caws loudly in answer. He flips the camera around and shows me the beach. It's a jagged cliff that drops off to a huge expanse of sand that meets towering waves and I spot a group of surfers in the distance sitting on boards past the breaking waves. Right before he flips the camera back to himself, I catch a glimpse of Levi exiting the water. He does a little shake of his head and water droplets fly from his dark brown waves and roll down his hard, tight, chest. There's a tattoo on his right peck I can't quite make out. I'm momentarily mesmerized, mouth agape, when I realize Adam has already flipped the camera back around to face him.

"Aly?" Adam asks. "I asked what you thought of the place?"

"Hot," I answer, snapping my mouth shut. "I mean the place looks really hot. But really fun. Are you having fun?" I pull the phone from my face to pinch the bridge of my nose, realizing I'm rambling.

"Yeah, we're having a blast. Hey, how's Pretzel? Are you two getting along?" It's my turn to flip the camera around. Pretzel, sensing her human on the phone, has been the most polite and well-mannered puppy you could ask for. Thinking maybe we've finally rounded a corner, I decide not to tell Adam about Pretzel's recent antics. "Where's my sweet girl?" Adam asks in a ridiculously over the top baby voice. Pretzel sniffs the phone and gives it a huge, slobbery lick. My whole body shudders before I wipe it off on my dress.

"Is that the old Hardware Store on King Street?" Levi asks, and I instantly get a little clammy and my mouth goes dry. Why is this happening? I see half naked, perfectly handsome men on the beach all the time. I tell myself to snap out of it, but not before trying to catch a glimpse of that mysteriously delicious tattoo. It's hidden out of the screen which is so disappointing and reluctantly flip the camera around to begin the tour of Bloomie's.

"It is," Adam and I answer at the same time.

My heart swells with the pride in Adam's voice. He helped me with every single renovation in this old building and together, we did a pretty great job.

Turning a hardware store into a floral studio was no easy feat. Scuffed hardwoods, mismatched paint, and the generically stale scent of a hardware store became refinished flooring, white shiplapped walls, open shelving, and a huge floral showpiece hanging above the register. Two large coolers sit in the back, and in front of that is a workbench Adam and I had made from reclaimed wood from a barn right outside of Charleston. Fresh flowers sit in buckets all around the store, mixed in with trinkets and candles and come together in a way that makes Bloomie's so unique. We've acquired quite the business over the past two years, and our spot on King Street guarantees steady business from locals and tourists alike, which is something we need to keep up with the hefty rent. Last year, we were even featured in *Southern Living* as a top ten destination for Charleston. Since then, business has only grown.

"Wow, that looks great, Aly!" Levi says.

"Thanks," I answered shyly right when the bell above the front door jingles.

"Wow, it's hotter than Charlie Hunam outside. I never thought I would say that, because he's smoking."

Emma's loud and boisterous voice fills the studio as she bustles through the front door. Today, she's wearing a tie dyed Bloomie's tee, a pair of camouflage cargo pants, and a pair of hot pink Converse. She lays her stuff on the counter and fans herself wildly, tiny giraffes swinging from her ears. Her blonde pixie cut is starting to frizz and I smile to myself, knowing Emma thinks her outfit today is pure gold.

When I say I have eccentric taste, I mean I err on the side of 60s and 70s outfits from the thrift store. If I can find a vintage Lily Pulitzer for under twenty dollars, it's been a good day. On the other hand, Emma's style is one hundred percent Emma. Nothing about it makes sense other than she likes it, and I think that's one of the major reasons we have been best friends since high school. Emma is her own person, and she's changing for no one.

She rambles about a few online orders we received last night, clearly unaware that I'm FaceTiming with my childhood crush who's grown into an impossibly hotter version of my wildest dreams, when she notices Pretzel laying behind the counter.

Pretzel trots over and gives her a lazy lick on the hand, clearly happy to see her.

I frown, wondering why she only hates *me* and return my attention to my phone. "I'll let you all go. Send me pics of the good stuff, Adam!"

I hang up, wondering why I'm imagining another shirtless picture of Levi coming through my phone. When I said *the good stuff,* I meant the beaches, the scenery, the food. Definitely *not* shirtless Levi.

I shake my head to clear my mind and turn to Emma. She's already grabbed a vase from the shelf and is making five large arrangements, all with daisies, poppies, and sunflowers spilling out.

"Did you say we had some orders come through the website last night?" I ask.

"If by some, you mean thirty-two, then yes," she replies, a smile playing at her lips. She tosses me an apron. "You have a little bit of...drool, right at the corner of your lip." She narrows her eyes and wipes at her own mouth to direct me where to go. I wipe furiously until she busts out laughing. "Did Alyson Bloomingdale's crush on her brother's best friend never go away?"

"What? No!" I say, turning from her so she can't see the blush spread across my cheeks. I tie the apron on and get to work on the wildflower arrangements beside her.

"Remember all those nights we'd lie in bed and you'd practice your wedding vows to me? 'I'll love you forever and ever until the day I die, Lev-,'" Emma cuts off when I elbow her in the side.

"Sorry, I slipped," I say when she side-eyes me.

Emma doesn't say anything else, only smiles to herself. A moment later, though, she says, "Wow Aly. Are you nervous or something? What did you *eat?*"

I whirl around to find Pretzel, happily snoozing under the front table. One eye cracks open and an ear twitches. "Pretzel?" I ask, tone dripping with accusation.

The very tip of her tail wags in guilty confession.

That night, I'm lying in bed reading, Pretzel unfortunately right beside me, when my phone lights up and begins buzzing on my nightstand, alerting me of an incoming FaceTime call. It's an unknown number, so I hit decline and settle back into the bed, not in the mood to chat about my car's extended warranty. I crack open my novel again when it begins buzzing a second time. Annoyed, I swipe it open, ready to let whoever's on the other end know my 1960s Bronco can't exactly be warrantied.

"Aly!" Levi's voice booms through the speaker and his face fills the screen. He's holding the phone entirely too close and his cheeks are flushed.

"Levi?" I ask, pushing my glasses up into my hair. "What are you doing? Is Adam okay?"

Adam's face fills the screen now and it looks equally as flushed. "I'm fine. I wanted to see Pretzel, and I forgot my phone," he confides with sad eyes. "And for you to see how amazing this place is." He switches the camera around to show a sandy beach bar with twinkling lights strung along the ceiling. It's so beautiful I can't help but be a little jealous. Levi shifts the camera to point at the water, and the view of the glowing sun dipping lower into the turquoise waves is breathtaking.

"That's beautiful," I breathe. "It looks like y'all are having fun."

Suddenly, the camera jerks and the screen goes dark. A few seconds later, Levi picks it up and uses the corner of his shirt to wipe the sand from the camera. I'm treated to the shortest, most decadent peek at his toned torso. I'm about to wipe the drool from the corner of my mouth when his face appears. "How have you been, Aly?"

Before I can answer, Adam comes into view with two very blonde, very *pretty* girls. "Levi, meet Olivia!" he says, taking the phone from him. An unrecognizable expression crosses Levi's face before Adam whisper-screams into the speaker, "Bye *sis*!" as if trying to be as clear as possible that they are incredibly, one hundred percent single. As if the fact that we look exactly alike wasn't a clear enough giveaway.

He ends the call, but not before I get one more glimpse of *Olivia* with her perfectly perfect blonde waves and juicy, pink, pouty lips, wrapping her perfectly painted red fingers around Levi's bicep. He didn't even get to see Pretzel.

I roll my eyes and pick up my book but give up three seconds later. How am I supposed to focus now? I look over at Pretzel and honestly, she looks annoyed that her man's out with another woman. "Disgusting, right?" I ask and scratch behind her ears. She winks, which obviously means she's agreeing with me.

I pick my phone up and toy with the idea of texting Levi, only to see if he'll answer while he's with her. I can't think of anything witty enough, though, and I don't want to look desperate. Plus, we haven't talked in years. I have nothing to say to him other than, "When did you grow up to look like *that*? And can you please tell me what your tattoo is because I've only thought about it all night." I know I'm just sleepy enough that anything could pop out of my mouth, which is exactly what I do not need.

Growing up, Adam never actually told me to stay away from his best friend, but he always made it pretty clear that he'd kill me if I so much as looked at Levi for more than two seconds.

For instance, one time we went out to celebrate after Adam and Levi's soccer team won a championship. The ice cream shop was packed after the big win, and Adam went to the bathroom as soon as we got inside. There were only two spots open at the bar, so Levi and I awkwardly wedged our way in. We were forced to sit so close that my right knee brushed up against his left. I was secretly dying inside from being so close to the hottest guy at our high school, the guy that I only doodled about in my notebook during every single class.

The waitress, busy from the rush, had forgotten my milkshake. "Do you want to share mine?" Levi had asked, pushing it toward me.

I blushed at the thought of sharing the same straw. Did this mean he had a crush on me? I took a sip, letting the strawberry ice cream and whip cream dance around my tongue before swallowing. When I looked up, Levi's eyes were trained on my bottom lip.

"You have a little bit of...here let me get it," he murmured, gently brushing his thumb over a stray gob of whipped cream on my lip. When he pulled away, I bit the spot he had touched nervously.

"Congrats on your hat trick." My breath hitched in my throat when he lazily dragged his eyes from my bottom lip to meet my gaze. Heat spread across my cheeks like a wildfire when he leaned in, resting a hand on my knee. Heat seared through my jeans, his touch electrifying.

His mouth was inches from mine, and all it would take was one little tilt of my head and we'd be—

"Did you guys order yet?"

Adam wedged himself between us, oblivious that he had interrupted what I'm pretty sure was about to be an amazing kiss with the boy of my dreams.

Once the seat next to me emptied, he literally pushed me off my stool and sat in my place, forcing me to move even farther from Levi. Now two seats down, Levi offered a half smile that only made my heart flip uncontrollably in my chest. I questioned whether he was really into me, or simply on an emotional high from winning the game.

From that day forward, Adam had an annoying habit of making sure Levi and I were never alone again.

Pretzel rolls over in her sleep and lets out a soft snore. She almost looks, dare I say, cute. I softly scratch her belly and pick up my phone again to text Emma.

Beach Sunday?

Almost immediately, a text pops up.

I thought you'd never ask.

I set my phone on the nightstand and snuggle deep into the covers. Pretzel curls up next to me. I'm beginning to think we're bonding until she opens her sleepy eyes, gives me the most disgusted look as if she's forgotten I'm not Adam in her sleep induced haze, and moves to the opposite end of the bed.

"I didn't want to cuddle with you anyway," I mutter.

Chapter Three

Levi

The music is already blaring and the tiki torches lining the beach have already been lit at my favorite beach bar, though the sun is still a few hours from setting.

I say *favorite* like I actually go out a lot.

Spoiler, I don't.

It's not that I don't *want* to go out. I'd love to unwind and maybe have a pretty girl hit on me every now and then. But by the time I'm done working, sometimes twelve-hour days, the last thing I want to do is go somewhere and look like a creeper sitting at the bar all by myself.

No Scrubs is playing, and I want more than anything to sing along with every word, but I clamp my mouth shut.

In high school, this was Aly's favorite song so I was left with no choice but to memorize every word in hopes of one day impressing her. We just got off FaceTime with her, and I can't stop myself from remembering how grown up she is. I've always thought she was pretty, but the ten years since we saw each other last have been *very* kind to her.

"I've got to move here," Adam says, eyes wide, the dumbest smile plastered on his face.

He's frothing at the mouth over the girls in California when I'd give anything to be back in southern belle territory. The girls here just don't seem to have enough syllables in their words and balk at the idea of sweet tea.

"You mean you purposefully add calories into a drink?" Eliza, a girl I dated *very* briefly, asked when I ordered sweet tea one evening with dinner.

"We have unsweet tea but I'd be happy to bring you some sugar packets," the waiter had offered.

"Maybe bring him some Stevia," Eliza had suggested. "Less calories."

"Stevia? Are you kidding me?" She thought I was joking and tilted her head back to laugh. It was like a little tinkle, and I knew it was fake because she was afraid to contort her face too much and risk screwing up her Botox results.

I was, in fact, not joking, and ended up telling our waiter to forget the tea and bring me a Coke instead. Everyone knows the proper way to make sweet tea is by adding the sugar in while it's hot so it melts anyway. Otherwise, it's just a sad excuse for sweet tea and frankly, disgusting.

Needless to say, Eliza and I did not last long.

While Adam is busy charming the two girls he just met, I sidle up to the bar and order a round of the local draft beer for me and Adam.

It must be a Hawaiian-themed night, because everyone either has a lei around their neck or—if they're already really drunk—on their head.

A moment later, Adam joins me, and as if on cue, the bartender slides us our beers and throws us each a lei.

"Aly would love this place," Adam says, taking in the disco ball hanging from the ceiling of the tiki hut, the open-air bar, and the waves crashing in the distance. "She loves themed parties."

I try to keep my face neutral at the mention of Aly. All I can think about is her eyes, which are the perfect shade of blue. They're not too blue like the fake contacts the girls here wear. They're the exact color of the water in the Charleston Harbor that I miss so much, tinged with a little gray like the mist that hangs over it each morning. Her cheeks were pink, and her full, pouty lips formed an O of shock at finding me—not her brother—on the phone. It was enough to send me into a tailspin of thoughts that Adam would certainly kill me for having.

"Oh yeah?" I say, thinking of the crush I had on her back in high school. She was cute then, with her thick glasses, long ponytail, and tan legs for days. But now? Now, she's drop dead gorgeous. How had I let Adam weasel his way into every attempt I had of being smooth with her that he could? "How is she?" I ask, finishing off my beer. Before I can even ask, the bartender, bless her heart, is already pouring me another.

I didn't really get the chance to actually talk to her either of the times we called her today, so I'm hoping Adam takes my curiosity as more friendly than desperate for any tidbit of information about her I can get.

"She's good," he answers skeptically.

"That's great," I say. "She looks fantastic. Who is she seeing these days?"

I know I'm pushing my limits, but one beer has me thinking that doors that have always been shut are suddenly wide open.

Adam doesn't answer right away, and instantly I panic. *He knows.* He knows I have inappropriate thoughts about his sister.

"She's really hit her stride with the flower shop," he says, and I can tell how proud he is of her. I wait for him to say more but when he doesn't, I point to a couple seats that just opened up at the bar. We move over to them and the bartender slides us two more glasses. I ignore this one and instead push it to the guy next to me. He happily takes it and moves off toward the dance floor.

Adam and I stay at the bar catching up until Adam's eyes glaze over and his words start to slur. He's telling me a story about Pretzel when he stops abruptly and says, "Oh my gosh. Could you imagine if your German Shepherd had puppies with my Weiner Dog? We'd have… Weiner Shepherds." Adam's already red face deepens even more crimson as his laughter fills the small space between us.

"Right. Weiner Shepherds," I echo dryly, aware that maybe we should be getting home sooner rather than later. Adam's still chuckling, so amused at his joke that would make middle school boys everywhere laugh too.

Then, the girls from earlier find us at the bar, and I groan. I just *know* Aly got the complete wrong idea earlier when whatever-her-name-is had her hand wrapped possessively around my bicep.

Adam's already headed to the makeshift dance floor in the sand, which is illuminated by hundreds of Edison lights. This girl is tugging on my arm, and I have no choice but to follow. She wraps her arms around my neck and presses herself against me.

You know how when you're holding someone, and they fit perfectly against you? Like how I can tuck my mom perfectly under my chin, or a baby fits perfectly in the cradle of its mother's arms?

That doesn't happen here. Amelia's body just doesn't conform to mine.

"Do you want to get out of here?" she whispers in my ear.

"More than you know," I mutter, thinking of my bed, empty with the exception of my dog, Hank, who takes up enough room for two people. I glance at Adam to check on him, and he's wearing that same dopey grin from earlier.

This girl—Amelia, is it?—must have misunderstood me, because her eyes have shifted into a weird expression. I think she's trying to look sexy, but mostly she looks like she has a grain of sand stuck in one.

"Are you okay?" I ask, but not really willing to help if something is really stuck in her eye. Eyes freak me out.

"Never better!" she squeals, and tosses a long blonde curl over her shoulder. I catch a whiff of something burnt and scan the room for any downed tiki torches or someone having set their lei on fire.

When Amelia tosses another perfect curl over her shoulder, I realize it's the smell of her hair. Is her hair even real? She's doing that funky thing with her eyes again, and now I really am kind of scared.

"I'm going to run to the bathroom," I say, breaking free from Amelia.

Adam follows me and yells, "Are we the luckiest guys in California right now or what?"

I ignore him, and a few minutes later as I'm washing my hands, I wonder why in the world I'm turning down a pretty girl on a Friday night. Adam is still in line for the next open stall, so I walk back out to the bar. Amelia and her friend are there, waiting for us and her eyes light up when she sees me. Frantically, I rack my brain for a way out of this. Suddenly, it comes to me, and I wait for the guilt to hit. When it doesn't, I soldier on.

"Adam's not really feeling well," I say with a grimace. "He's a bit of a... you know. *Lightweight*," I whisper. Consider it retribution for all those times he pushed me away from Aly in high school. "Why don't you write down your numbers on this napkin and we'll give you a call?"

I pull a napkin from the holder on the bar and the girls both pout but write down their numbers anyway. I tuck the napkin into my pocket with a gentle pat. *See ladies? We won't forget about you.* "You don't want to stay around for this," I say, gently guiding them to the door, knowing Adam could come out at any minute and ruin my plan.

Amelia's eyes are doing that thing again and her head tilts to the left. She closes her eyes and brings her face toward mine and...*oh boy.*

"Y'all be safe, okay? Sorry your eyes have been bothering you all night, Amelia."

"*Amelia*?" she screeches. "I'm *Olivia*, you dirtbag."

She kicks sand at my feet, and okay, I'll give her that one. I absolutely deserved that. Bestie in tow, she teeters away on her heels, in search of an Uber. She shoots me one more dirty look along with her middle finger before she slides into the backseat. I sigh and pull out the phone numbers, knowing there's no way I can give these to Adam after that little whoopsie. When he finds me, I quickly wad it up and toss it into the nearest trash can.

"Where'd they go?" Eagerly, he searches the parking lot and finally lands on the Uber pulling away from the curb. A pair of round butt cheeks are plastered against the back window and he eyes me suspiciously.

"Something was in Amelia's eye. They had to go." I say, shrugging my shoulders.

"Seriously?" Adam whines. "They were so pretty."

"Mhm," I hum noncommittally, checking my phone. "So pretty."

Adam pouts and kicks at a stray piece of gravel. "Her eyes did look kinda weird, didn't they?"

I nod in agreement. "You'll be okay," I say, patting his shoulder.

"Did you at least get their numbers?"

"Look! Our Uber." A luxury black sedan slides up to the curb, and I practically throw myself inside to avoid answering. He buckles up next to me and rubs the leather interior with his palms.

"Wow," he muses, eyeing the fancy buttons and sleek interior of the foreign car. "This is swanky. You know you don't have to go all out just for me though, right? Don't worry about upgrading our Ubers on my account."

"I do what I can," I say, peeking out the windows. A white, older model Corolla slips into our spot and I watch in horror as a couple meanders from the bar in search of what I can only presume is the luxury, black sedan Uber they ordered. Sorry about the Corolla, folks.

"What now?" Adam asks, already mentally preparing for our next stop.

"Bed, my friend," I say, buckling myself in. Disappointment briefly crosses Adam's face but he gets over it quickly by muttering he doesn't feel well and leaning his head against the window. As his soft snores fill the space around us, I can't help but to reminisce on memories of Adam and I in high school. Between soccer, surfing at the beach on weekends, and hanging out at each other's houses every minute in between, we were practically inseparable. Along with that came plenty of time with his sister, too. It would've been hard for me *not* to develop a crush on the tan, leggy beauty back then, but now? I was a goner. I could only wonder if the glimpse we shared of each other tonight had the same kind of effect on her that it did on me.

CHAPTER FOUR

ALY

Pretzel's hot, turkey and rice kibble breath, wakes me from an admittedly strange yet glorious dream.

Levi had just saved me from a twelve-hour day at Bloomie's. He was shirtless, and somewhere in the mix was an endless supply of ice cream. Dreaming about food is normal for me, considering ice cream makes its way into every conscious *and* subconscious thought, but dreaming about Levi...what in the world? Was that man really so gorgeous he managed to sneak into my dreams too? I should not be having dreams about someone who lives across the country...unless they're Harry Styles.

The fact that I dream about food so much is actually kind of concerning, but considering all my free time is spent working at Bloomie's and remodeling my cottage, I'm usually left heating up a subpar Lean Cuisine in the evenings. And okay, yes, it's the kid's version because the adult ones don't come with those decadent ooey-gooey brownies.

I blink furiously to erase the sleep from my eyes and come face to face with Pretzel, who's little head is dangerously close to my very open, very dry mouth. I snap it shut and throw my arm over my eyes, groaning. Pretzel, ever persistent, knocks it off with her cold, wet nose and whines. I mimic her, and she tilts her head to the side, ears perked up. It's almost adorable until I remember it's Sunday, mine and Emma's one day off from Bloomie's. From the looks of the sun barely peeking through my windows, it's only around six thirty in the morning.

I throw the covers off and trail behind Pretzel to the front door. "No funny business," I say as sternly as I can but my morning voice comes out a little raspy.

While Pretzel is doing her business, Mr. Barnes clears his throat, the noise floating across the road from his porch to mine. And while I do realize I'm wearing the pajama set Emma gifted me with a million Harry Styles faces plastered all over the matching tank and shorts, I also know Mr. Barnes can mind his own. I throw a pointed look his way as Pretzel and I go back inside.

I check my phone for any missed texts or calls from Adam. There's one from 11:24 p.m. It must have come in when I was fast asleep, and when I open it, the most gorgeous sunset photo fills my screen. Levi must've captured it because in the bottom left corner, Adam is smiling at the camera. He's standing on a cliff, and the sky behind him is a mixture of dark purples, oranges, and reds. Palm trees sway in the distance and there's even a seagull flying behind him.

What really catches my attention though, is how *happy* Adam looks. The photo must've been taken as Adam was laughing, because he's looking at the camera, and his mouth is still slightly ajar. His wide smile meets his sparkling eyes, which crinkle at the corners. I don't normally get to see this side of Adam now that he works for our dad. Time away from the boat business and family must be good for him. I type out, *Cali looks good on you,* and hit send, knowing with the three-hour time difference he's more than likely still asleep.

Emma and I have plans to go to Folly Beach today, but I know she won't be up until at least eleven-thirty. The books I unpacked and stacked neatly on the built-ins in the living room are calling my name, but so are the boxes of tile piled in the corner of the kitchen for the backsplash. The bowl of sea glass I've found throughout the years of living on the coast is sitting on the counter by the tile and I'll admit, I am a little excited to see how I can mix the two to make the backsplash unique. I saw something similar on Grant Dawes's Instagram—who is an amazing contractor from Georgia—a few weeks ago and I saved it to my highlights. I make a cup of coffee, pull the picture up, turn on my favorite Swiftie playlist, and get to work.

Five hours later, I'm covered in mortar but my backsplash is complete. Different shades of blues and whites mix together in an abstract pattern, and now I'm itching to take the doors off the oak cabinets and paint them a seafoam green to match. I've got the last door halfway off when my phone rings and Emma's face fills the screen.

"Good afternoon, sleeping beauty," I answer. I peek around the living room to check on Pretzel. She's been gnawing on a bone I bought her from the grocery store yesterday. She's still happily chewing and wagging her tail.

Emma yawns into the phone. "Yeah, yeah. Are you ready?"

"Considering I've been up since six-thirty this morning and have already managed to tile the backsplash in the kitchen and take the doors off the cabinets to sand and paint, yeah. I'm ready." I manage to sound like I've been laboring away all morning, which don't get me wrong, I have. But really, the kitchen isn't that big. There's only eight cabinets and a few feet worth of backsplash that needed to be done.

"Remind me to buy the coffee you drink next time I go shopping," Emma rasps, yawning again.

"Pretzel actually woke me up," I admit. At the sound of her name, her tail thumps against the hardwood floor. "I'll pick you up in twenty minutes?"

"See you then," Emma says and hangs up.

I look at Pretzel, who is sitting pretty at my feet. "You ready to go to the beach?"

I swear she smiles in response.

Pretzel has her head out the back window and Emma's in the passenger seat. Sunglasses are pushed atop her hair, which is dip-dyed purple at the ends, and she's wearing her favorite unicorn bikini and denim cut offs. She's staring down at her phone and squealing.

"What?" I cry, pulling into a parking spot.

We've driven to the far end of the island where the beach is a little less crowded. Don't get me wrong, I love the beach right by the pier and the ability to walk across the street and eat as much Taco Boy as my heart desires, but having Pretzel makes me a little nervous to be around so many people.

"Have you seen Adam's Snapchat stories?! Levi is *fine*. Where has he been for the past ten years, and how did he grow up to look like that?"

"What? No," I mumble, fighting her for the phone. I could easily pull up Snapchat on my own phone, but it's in my beach bag in the back seat that Pretzel is currently using as a cushion to sit on.

"You're friends with my brother on Snapchat?" I ask, finally winning the phone from her grasp and replaying his stories. They're littered with photos of the past few days in California. I hold my finger down on one with Levi for admittedly too long. I know Adam meant to capture the scenery but Levi's headed into the ocean and his backside is a glorious sight. Broad, muscular shoulders taper down into a firm, tight...

"Aly? Where do you keep your napkins?"

"My napkins?" I repeat, my voice unusually high.

"Yeah, the ones you get from drive-thrus. Where do you cram your extra ones?"

I open the glovebox and blindly feel around, unable to peel my eyes from the heavenly scene on the screen in front of me. "Here you go," I answer absently. I drop the crumpled wad onto her lap, missing her upturned palm. She picks them up and begins dabbing at the corners of my mouth. Reluctantly, I tear my eyes away from her phone. "What are you doing?"

"Wiping the drool from your face." Emma continues to dab, a smirk resting on her lips, while I swat ineffectively at her hand.

Why do I feel like this? I don't even *know* Levi, not anymore at least. I drop Emma's phone into her lap and reach for the handle to get out of the car. Pretzel thumps her tail impatiently, waiting to be let out too.

"Why would you think I'm drooling over Levi?" I ask, playing dumb.

"Listen, Aly. All I'm saying is he's more your type than Hudson. You should talk to him." Emma says, slinging her sequined beach bag over her shoulder.

"No," I say vehemently. "He lives in California and I live here. It would never work. Plus, I have zero idea what he's even like now. He could be a major weirdo and I'd have no idea."

Even to my own ears, these excuses are lame. But there is one big, legitimate reason why nothing could ever happen between me and Levi.

"He's obviously not or Adam wouldn't be having so much fun with him," Emma says.

And there it is: Adam. My brother would *never* allow it.

I shoot her a glare and she throws her hands up in the air in mock surrender. I turn all my focus to Pretzel, who is straining her leash for the nearest seagull, requiring two hands on her leash and all my strength to hold her back.

"Remember how weird Adam used to get when we'd so much as glance in the other's direction?" I remind Emma. Pretzel lurches for a bird, misses, instead pouncing on a man wearing a Speedo, waking him up. Dazed, he looks around for the culprit who's now digging for a crab, kicking sand on nearby sunbathers. "Sorry!" I say timidly with a little wave.

"All I'm hearing from you are lame excuses as to why you shouldn't give it a shot." A victim of Pretzel's digging sits up and tears off her sunglasses, like she's about to come have a word.

"You'll be fine," Emma tells the girl, flashing her palm. The girl, either too stunned to speak or genuinely scared of Emma, only lets out a huff and stays where she is.

"You're such a baddie," I say to Emma, picking up a wriggling Pretzel and tucking her under my arm. Emma reaches over and takes Pretzel from me, putting her back on the ground. Pretzel gives her an affectionate lick and settles immediately. "Why is she only bad for me?" I whine.

"Don't avoid the question."

I stare at her, purposefully. "Fine, whatever. I know the truth. You *do* still have a crush on him after all these years."

I think of ways to circumvent her statement and settle on mocking her by sticking my tongue out in my best attempt at being a five-year-old.

"Real mature, Aly."

"Real mature, Aly," I parrot.

We find a spot in the sand far away from anyone else, and I set up Pretzel's long leash, allowing her to enjoy a ten foot radius for chasing seagulls. Only, she surprises me by curling up beside Emma's beach chair and promptly falling asleep. I roll my eyes, settle into my own chair, and pull a fun rom-com novel out of my bag.

Emma is slathering SPF 70 all over her body when she looks over and says, "I bet I can tell you how that ends."

"No you can't," I scoff.

"They fall in love and live happily ever after. They all end the same way. Doesn't that ever get boring to you?" Her tone isn't patronizing. She's asking because she seriously doesn't understand how someone can waste hours reading a book knowing it'll probably end exactly as she said. She just doesn't understand; it's a book lover thing.

"Happily ever afters never get boring to me, thank you very much," I say, and ignore her as I fly through the next half of the book uninterrupted, happy as can be.

Cracking my eyes open, I blink a few times before looking around and noticing several beach goers have already packed up and left for the day. My novel is splayed out across my torso and when I move it, I find a weird tan line forming underneath. Emma and Pretzel are gone, so I can only assume they went for a walk. The sun has moved across the sky and the tide is coming in again, and I wonder how long I was asleep.

I pull back our chairs and bags to avoid a rogue wave and catch sight of my phone lit up in my bag. I pull it out and notice the time. It's late in the afternoon. I rub my eyes, wondering how I could've slept that long, and unlock my phone. There are several missed calls from an unknown number and almost the same amount from my parents.

I click on one of the voicemails, hold it up to my ear, and immediately wish I hadn't.

A woman's shrill voice filters out. She's very factual, to the point, and I only catch bits and pieces of what she's saying before the world around me shifts, the sand beneath my feet feeling like quicksand. It sounds like she's speaking another language. I must be dreaming. No, this is a nightmare. My *worst* nightmare. I look around for anything to help wake me up, but come up with nothing. This is real life. My head spins uncontrollably. I can't gather my thoughts, can't swallow properly, can't move, can't do anything.

My mouth dries and my heart threatens to beat out my chest as I fall to my knees. I hear a wail and realize it's coming from my own lips. It sounds strange to my own ears, like it's coming from miles away. Unable to bear anymore, to know the outcome of this phone call that seems to be never ending, I drop the phone before I finish the rest of the message. Bits and pieces of what I did manage to hear swirl in my head.

San Diego Hospital…Adam Bloomington…bad wreck…coma.

Emma and Pretzel come into view, and when she realizes something's wrong, runs toward me.

"Aly!" She screams. "What happened? Are you okay?"

My head feels like it's stuffed with gauze and I can't think straight. I drop my face into my hands and choke back a sob. "It's Adam," I manage.

Her face drains of color and she spots my phone in the sand, picking it up and hitting play. As the nurse relays her message again, I let out another strangled sob. Eventually, she tucks my phone safely into her pocket and wraps her arms around me.

"He's okay," she says reassuringly, although the concern and worry etched into every detail of her face tell me otherwise. Her brow is furrowed, her eyes wide with fear. She takes my hand in her own and gives it a gentle squeeze, but the tremor she's trying to suppress works its way through anyway. "Did you listen to the entire message?"

I shake my head, tears streaming down my face. "I don't want to know," I whisper.

"He's alive and he's at the hospital getting the best care possible right now," she tells me anyway. Pretzel sticks her cold, wet nose against my hand and lets out a whine, as if she can sense something is wrong. Emma picks me up and brushes the sand from my shins and knees. "Let's get you home."

When I wake, the sun has settled lower in the horizon, deepening the sky to a burnt orange. I reach for my phone to check the time. It's not there, but Emma is. For a split second, I'm confused, until the events of the day come rushing back, forceful enough to make my head start pounding again. Immediately, my chest heaves, and I throw my arm over my eyes in a weak attempt to block out the world around me. Gently, Emma pries it off and tucks a salty, tear-matted piece of hair behind my ear.

"How did you get me home?" I ask faintly. Every moment from listening to that voicemail to now is a blur.

"I drove you home."

"You can't drive a stick shift."

"It wasn't the smoothest ride, and I did get flipped off more than once when I stalled out at an intersection," she confesses. "But I did it. You were needing a new transmission anyway."

A small laugh escapes me, but it feels wrong. I shouldn't be laughing with Adam, my best friend, my twin, my other half, a million miles away from me...*in a coma.*

"Have you heard any updates?" I ask tentatively, afraid of the answer.

"He's pretty banged up, Aly, but he's still stable." I can tell she's trying to protect me from the entire truth of exactly how bad it is. She takes a raggedy breath, mustering the courage to continue. "Your parents called from the airport. They were getting ready to board a flight to San Diego to go be with him."

"They went without me?" I cry, sitting up so fast that Pretzel, who was curled up next to me, lets out a yelp of protest and moves to the other side of the bed. A mixture of rage and guilt instantly courses through my veins.

I should be the one sitting beside Adam right now, not mom and dad. *I* understand everything about Adam, not them. Selfishness over falling asleep when my twin needs me crashes into me. I throw back my covers, ready to stand, to leave, to do *something*, but Emma gently forces me to sit back down.

"Aly, wait," she says, placing a hand on each of my shoulders. "They called you a little while ago and I answered it. They made it to the hospital in California and talked to his doctors. They're saying he's stable enough to transfer to South Carolina. I think your mom demanded to meet the CEO of the hospital or something and got the job done." She attempts a halfhearted smile. That sounds like Mom. She's a royal pain ninety-nine percent of the time, but occasionally it's useful. She hands me my phone, and I place it on the side table.

"Did they say when he'll be here?"

"In the morning," she says. I sit on the edge of the mattress and Emma joins me.

Suddenly, I remember Levi was probably in the car too. "How's Levi?" I ask, panic seizing my chest again.

"Levi is actually doing okay from what I understand. Most of the impact was on your brother's side. Levi was driving when a teenager ran a stoplight and t-boned them," Emma gently explains. She's trying her best to stay strong for me, but I can still see the worry and fear in her eyes.

Panic begins to loosen its grip on my chest and my heartbeat slows, returning to its normal rhythm. I close my eyes and whisper a silent prayer of thanks.

"I'm going to turn on a Meg Ryan movie marathon and let Pretzel out. Don't move, okay?" I settle back into the mattress and she tucks the covers around me before hitting play on the TV. Under Emma's tough exterior is a heart of gold for the people she loves, and I know how lucky I am to have her.

"Okay," I whisper, too exhausted to manage much else.

Emma quietly shuffles into the kitchen and returns a few moments later with two cups of steaming lavender and honey tea. She slides in beside me and asks, "Did I miss anything?" even though she knows this movie by heart and could recite any line from it at any given time. Pretzel jumps up into the bed, too, and wedges herself between us. She does the same thing she did the night I first brought here and digs her nose under the covers only to pop out again, fully covered, completely cozy. I take a sip of my tea and my shoulders loosen, if only a little bit.

"Are we sure Pretzel is really a dog?" she whispers.

CHAPTER FIVE

ALY

After I pinky swore to Emma that Pretzel and I were okay, she headed back to her apartment, but not before calling in one last pizza delivery and leaving a fresh kettle of tea on the stove. Pretzel and I make a fort on the living room floor and watch more romantic comedies solely for the background noise, my mind still too foggy to think straight.

I went to bed with my phone under my pillow so I wouldn't miss the phone call from Mom and Dad about Adam's arrival back in Charleston. I called them earlier and begged them to let me know the second he landed safe and sound. Sure enough, right around five this morning, the buzzing under my pillow was my mom confirming his arrival. Her call was short and to the point with her barking out orders to the hospital staff in between her words to me.

I was awake when the call came in, staring at my ceiling fan going around and around, Pretzel snoring softly beside me. I'd finished painting the kitchen cabinets and organizing all my mismatched china, unable to sleep with worry over my brother being flown across the country in a coma. She tells me I can come see him whenever, and I'm out of bed before she finishes the thought. I give Pretzel a goodbye pat on the head, and throw on some clothes.

Once I'm dressed, I call Emma, my fingers wobbly as I press her name on my phone. She answers groggily on the next to last ring. "He's home," I breathe, my shoulders relaxing the tiniest bit.

I head out the door of my cottage and hop into my Bronco, putting Emma on speaker and dropping the phone onto the seat next to me. I shift into gear and peel out of the driveway.

"He is? That's great, Al!" she says, more alert now. I can hear the smallest bit of tension leave her voice.

"I'm sorry, Em. I didn't realize how early it was," I say. "Go back to sleep."

"I'm glad you called me. I need to get up and run to the flower market this morning for some more orders that came through yesterday. You know how greedy those people at Fourth Street Flowers can be, so I want to get there early," she grumbles.

I'm going over the Ravenel Bridge, and the sunrise is breathtaking, painting the sky in those special shades of orange and pink that you're only privy to in the low country. Any other day, I'd probably enjoy it a little more.

"Thank you for taking care of Bloomie's for a few days, Em. I don't know what I'd do without you."

"Yeah, yeah. Don't get all sappy on me. Just give me a raise around Christmas and we'll call it good. Call me later, okay?"

Emma deserves a raise and then some at this point. When I say I don't know what I'd do without Emma, I truly mean it. "Will do. Thanks again."

I'm pulling into the hospital as I hang up, and I find a parking spot near the entrance and rush inside. When the elevator doors don't magically open in half a second after the four thousandth time I've jabbed the button with my finger, I anxiously climb the stairs two at a time. I'm out of breath when I make it to Adam's door and try to compose myself with a couple deep breaths before entering.

My white knuckles rap gently against the door, and I push it open. My heart drops when I see Adam laying in the bed, his eyes closed and what seems like a million monitors beeping around him. His right leg is in a cast and stitches crisscross over a deep gash above his left eyebrow. Deep purple bruises paint the skin that's visible outside his papery hospital gown, and an oxygen tube rests in his nose. His eyes are swollen shut, leaving him barely recognizable as the twin that left me for California only days ago.

In the corner, Mom is dabbing at her eyes with a Kleenex and Dad is pacing, mumbling under his breath into his phone, no doubt trying to figure out who he can sue for this happening. It occurs to me then that I've never seen my mom cry, and I want to reach out and comfort her with a hug, but I don't think we've ever done that before. Not that I can remember anyway. Hugs or any form of affection were few and far between in the Bloomington house when Adam and I were growing up.

"Hi Mom. Hi Dad," I say, my voice barely above a whisper. I gingerly sit on the edge of Adam's bed and brush his sandy brown hair off his forehead. "Hi Adam," I say even quieter.

This whole time, I've embarrassingly thought all it would take is for me, his twin sister, to speak to him and comfort him and he would immediately open his eyes and start talking. I'm holding my breath now, the harsh realization that this won't be the case dawning. The monitors continue to beep steadily, but nothing else changes. My heart sinks.

I look over at Mom, who is still biting her lower lip and dabbing furiously at the corners of her eyes. Dad's ignoring her and still pacing. Suddenly, I realize this isn't what Adam needs at all. Instead of sadness and fear and worry, he needs positivity and happiness.

"I'll be right back," I say, bending down to give my brother a quick kiss on the cheek then slipping quietly out the door.

Twenty minutes later, I return with a giant teddy bear, some rainbow wall stickers, and every balloon available for purchase down in the gift shop.

I'm busy placing them all around the room when Dad clears his throat, his phone safely tucked away in his pocket now. "Alyson?"

"Yes?" I ask. I position the teddy bear by the bed with a "Welcome Home Baby Boy!" balloon in its hand, right under the "Congratulations, you did it!" banner.

"What do you think you're doing?" His arms are folded over his chest, clearly annoyed.

I ignore the slight tapping of his shoe and walk over to the drawn curtains and open them wide, letting the bright southern sunlight filter into the room. The sun does nothing to lighten the mood. When I face my parents again, I'm met with even more displeased expressions.

"I'm making things cheery," I say matter-of-factly.

"This is ridiculous," Dad says, his voice so low I'm taken aback. He stares at a balloon with "Hello World" written across it in gold letters like he would love nothing more than to pop it.

"No it's not," I argue. "He's sitting in this dark room with nothing but the sound of his ventilator and heart monitor to keep him company. Of course he's not going to wake up to that."

My dad narrows his eyes, opens his mouth to speak, then shuts it and instead walks over to my mom, who stands to join him. She won't meet my eyes as they make their way to the door. I want to ask where they're going, but stop myself because, do I really care? The door shuts behind them with a click, and I'm left alone with Adam. I look around at the ridiculous balloons and teddy bear, afraid I overdid it.

No, I think to myself. *This is* exactly *what Adam would've done for me if the roles were reversed right now.* He'd come up with some impractical and ridiculously over the top way to make sure I smiled.

Settling into a chair at his bedside, I flip on the TV and Meg Ryan's voice fills the room.

I sit there with him until my stomach grumbles so viciously I can't ignore it any longer. As I'm dragging my chair back against the wall, the door opens and my mom walks in. Her eyes are puffy and I can tell she's tried to cover up her ruined makeup with the Chanel compact she always carries in her handbag. My mother has never so much as stepped foot out of her bedroom door let alone the house without her perfectly coiffed bob and full face of makeup.

Meanwhile, I've been up all night painting my kitchen cabinets, something she'd never dream of doing. If she wanted different color kitchen cabinets, she'd simply order them and pay someone to install them for her. To her, there's no problem big enough that can't be fixed by throwing a little money at it. As if reading my mind, her gaze lands on the paint in my hair, and distaste rolls off her in waves.

I've always struggled to connect with my mom. While she is clean and orderly in her head to toe designer brands, I'm disheveled chaos in last week's thrifted sundress, which I found crumpled in the corner of my closet and threw on before I came here.

"Where's dad?" I ask, needing to break the tense silence.

She motions for me to take a seat. "He's having a hard time with this, Alyson," she says. "I'm not sure if you know this or not, but he's not very good at expressing his emotions." I work to suppress a snort. That might just be the understatement of the century. "He headed back to the office. He needs to get his mind off Adam for a little while."

Anger rises in my chest, searing hot. "He needed to get his mind off his son?" I ask, my voice dripping with acid. Her blue eyes search mine, looking for any sign of understanding. But she's not going to find it. "I've got to go, Mom. I'll be back tomorrow." I give Adam a kiss on the cheek and push open the door. A nurse is standing on the other side, her hand on the door handle, ready to come in.

"Excuse me," she says. "I was just about to get some vitals." I slip out from the door jamb into the hallway and quietly close the door behind me.

"I'm Adam's sister, Aly," I explain quietly. The last thing I want is for Mom to come out and take control of this conversation. "Can you tell me how he's doing? Like how he is *really* doing? I need to know."

The nurse lets out a little sigh. She pulls his chart out from under her arm and scans it before her gaze meets mine. "Can I show you something?" she asks. I nod, too afraid to speak. She pulls the results of a CT scan out of the stack of papers and sets them on top. "This is your brother's brain. The bright white area is blood and this area over here has some swelling." I squint my eyes as if I'm concentrating extra hard but really, I just don't want to cry right now. I need to stay strong so she will tell me exactly what she knows.

"The doctors were also able to reset his broken arm. His vitals are stable and they have been for over twenty-four hours now, so that's a really good sign. Once that swelling goes down, we'll have a better idea of next steps." She takes her glasses off and slides them into the front pocket of her scrubs.

"When do you think he will wake up?"

"It could be tomorrow, it could be..." her voice trails off. "Rest assured, he's in the best of hands right now, Aly. We'll let you know if anything changes."

"Thank you," I whisper. She gives my shoulder a gentle squeeze and moves toward the door again. I'm walking toward the elevator when I hear her call my name. I look over my shoulder and she's grinning from the open doorway.

"Good call with the balloons."

When I arrive home, I can tell Emma's been over. For starters, there's takeout from my favorite Thai restaurant in the fridge that wasn't there when I left, and Pretzel is happily chewing on a new stuffed unicorn in the middle of my bed. I flop down next to her and play tug with the new stuffed toy until we both tire out.

When she snuggles up next to me and lays her head on my shoulder, she lets out a small, sad sigh that lets me know she misses Adam. I'm Googling ways to smuggle her into the hospital when my phone beeps. It's a text from Emma asking if Pretzel likes her new unicorn. I tell her she loves it and snap her a selfie of the three of us, even though the unicorn is now missing an eye and half its horn.

Adam would love this picture. He's so obsessed with Pretzel that anything that makes her happy, makes him happy, too. He's the perfect dog dad. A mixture of emotions stir inside me when I realize the one person I want to talk to about what's going on is the one person who can't reply back. He's always been the one I've relied on, the one that's always there, even if it's three a.m. when I can't sleep and need to talk to someone about the latest Netflix series I've binged. He's more than my twin brother; he's my very best friend.

Then, an idea comes to me. Scrolling through my phone, I find my text thread with Adam and open it up.

Dear Adam, I type then delete it thinking that might be too formal. He's my twin, not someone I'm trying to impress. But then I realize my formality would probably make him laugh, so I type it out again, and keep typing until I feel like I've caught him up on everything he's missed the last few days.

After attaching the picture of me and Pretzel, I hit send.

Chapter Six

Levi

"Make sure you take it easy, okay?" The doctor says as I finish signing the last of my discharge papers. I nod and scrawl my name one last time with a shaky hand. The past forty eight hours have been unexpected to say the least.

An older nurse with graying hair pulled back into a low ponytail brings me a bag full of my belongings and pats me on the shoulder. "They flew your friend back to South Carolina early this morning," she says quietly.

"Did he make it okay? Have you heard anything?" Anxiety grips my chest and the familiar guilt settles low in my belly. I had begged the nurses to take me to Adam's room yesterday, and although they had warned me what I would see, nothing had prepared me for the way seeing my best friend in that hospital bed would make me feel.

"I'm not supposed to share information with anyone outside of his family," she says, lowering her voice. "But I called a little while ago for an update. I knew you'd ask and I didn't think it was fair to keep it from you." She gives me a shy, nervous smile and looks around for any eavesdroppers before continuing. "He arrived in stable condition. He still hasn't woken up but so far, so good." I nod, unable to speak.

She walks me to the door and I manage a feeble, "Thank you."

As I'm walking to my Uber, flashbacks of that night hit me hard enough to make my knees buckle. I stop, leaning against the railing for support.

We had been heading back to the house after lunch one afternoon when it happened. I was driving and although I thought I hadn't seen anyone coming at an intersection, a teenager had run a redlight and T-boned us. Adam was in the passenger seat, and absorbed most of the impact while I was left with only a concussion, dislocated shoulder, and a totaled truck. Seeing Adam lying in those stark white hospital sheets with bandages wrapping so much of his body and the sound of machines whooshing to keep him alive...guilt settled on my chest, making it hard to breathe.

If Adam hadn't gone to the bathroom before we left, if I hadn't stopped to tie my shoe on the way back to the car...*if...if...if.* I regain some of my composure and feebly continue toward the car parked at the curb.

The accident had made me introspective, and I couldn't help but miss all the time I'd wasted. Now, when Adam and I finally reconnect, he winds up in a coma.

How had I let ten years slip between graduation—the last time I'd seen him—and now? Moving to California after graduation seemed like the right thing to do at the time, but now I'm wondering if I made a mistake.

"I'm going to expand your company, Dad," I had proudly told him one night at dinner. I was newly eighteen with nothing on my mind but graduating. And possibly the girl who had stolen my heart the first time I laid eyes on her. But she was my best friend's sister, meaning she was off limits, and I knew it had been time I faced that.

Dad had eyed me skeptically. "Things are going so well here that I really think we can do the same thing on the West Coast," I said, eager to prove my point. That night, I had shown him all the research I had done and numbers I had crunched in an attempt to sway him in letting me open a branch of his construction business in San Diego.

The day after graduation, I had loaded up my beat up old Ford with everything I could fit into it and set out for a reasonably priced office in San Diego that I had found on Craigslist.

Two days later, I arrived, exhausted and a little stale, but eager nonetheless to prove myself and make my parents proud.

Thoughts of Aly had filled my mind the entire drive. The way she loved to watch romantic comedies, how her glasses were always precariously close to falling off the tip of her nose, the way she surfed better than any of the boys our age, and the way she could sing *No Scrubs* line for line; those were only a few of the thoughts dancing around in my mind. Early in the trip, I had popped in my TLC CD and almost turned around right then and there, the thought of leaving her almost unbearable. But I shoved the memories as far down as I could, reminding myself it would never happen.

The night I arrived in California, I had blown up an air mattress in the loft of the office and dreamed about the day I would have enough saved for a little cottage on the outskirts of town.

Before long, word of mouth spread news of my business, and I began picking up enough jobs to break even. It's been the same ever since. Now, ten years later, I'm still living in the loft of the office and still only making enough to cover the necessities.

The Uber pulls up to the office, breaking me from my reminiscing, greeted by Hank, my German Shepherd, with his nose pressed to the front window, fogging it up. I make a mental note to thank Glenda, my secretary, for taking care of him while I was in the hospital. I push open the door and Hank comes bounding up to me. He gives me a lick across the face while I'm bent over untying my shoes, undoubtedly sensing my somber attitude, then nudges his favorite tennis ball toward me with his nose in an attempt to cheer me up.

"I'm sorry, buddy, I can't play right now," I say, my shoulder throbbing dully.

Hank cocks his head to the side, clearly confused.

I give him an ear scratch, promising to take him for a long walk later, then set off toward the bathroom, eager to shower the last few days off.

Later, I'm settled into the couch with a frozen pizza, about to turn on a movie, when something chimes. I flip over my phone to find a black screen and chalk it up to exhaustion from the past couple of days making me crazy. Two minutes later, I hear it again. I sit forward, listening intently, waiting for the sound. Finally, I pinpoint it to the white bag of my belongings from the hospital and rifle through it until I find a phone that's definitely not mine.

I tap the screen alight and find a picture of Pretzel when she was a puppy.

Somehow, Adam's phone must've gotten mixed up with mine in all the chaos after the accident. The phone pings again in my hand, and I see Aly's name pop up.

Unable to stop myself, I attempt to unlock the screen, mentally running through ideas for Adam's passcode. But, I'm surprised when it opens without resistance. I chuckle because *of course* Adam doesn't have any security on his phone.

I click into the text thread with his sister and read.

Dear Adam,

I know you can't actually read this right now, but when you wake up, I want you to have an easy way to catch up on what you've missed. I know how bad you get FOMO. Your dog is weird and has terrible gas but we are starting to get along now. Emma and I took her to the beach and she wanted to chase every seagull she saw. She had fun though. I've only caught her chewing on one pair of my underwear since she's been here, but it was definitely still the crotch she chewed out so idk, maybe you need to have a talk with her about that? That's kind of weird. I swear it's like she's fighting me for female dominance or something. Anyway, I love you and I'll see you soon.

Attached is a picture of Aly snuggled up with Pretzel, who is chewing on a stuffed unicorn. Aly's eyes are red rimmed and puffy and her long, sandy brown waves are piled haphazardly onto her head with a pink scrunchy. Gone are the braces and the thick rimmed glasses I remember from high school. Instead, two rows of pearly whites and the most gorgeous pale-blue eyes I've ever seen stare back at me. I catch myself smiling when I notice the stack of worn paperbacks on her nightstand. Aly always did have her nose stuck in a book, and I'm comforted by the fact that it seems like that hasn't changed.

My nostalgia is quickly replaced by guilt when I remember this text and this picture were never meant for my eyes, and it's my fault she can't actually share this with her brother right now. I set the phone on the counter, and run my hands through my hair. Tomorrow, I'll take Adam's phone to the post office and everything will be fine.

Satisfied with my decision, I return to the couch. Hank joins me, and I press play again on *Sleepless in Seattle*, which was Aly's favorite back in high school. I wonder if it still is.

Say what you will, but I'll take 1993 Meg Ryan over just about anyone famous in today's day and age...except maybe Taylor Swift.

I stretch out across the couch and Hank curls up at my feet. When I reach the part where Annie hears Sam over the radio and falls for him, my eyelids grow heavy.

How do you fall for someone you don't even know? I wonder in my sleep induced haze.

My last thought before finally dozing off is Aly, all grown up and more beautiful than I could imagine.

I wake to a whine and a cold, wet nose pressed against my temple. I crack open one eye and squint, realizing Hank's nose is probably the only thing keeping me on the couch at this point. His mouth is open and he's panting heavily into my face. My gag reflex threatens to kick in, but before I can get up, he drags his sandpapery tongue along the length of my cheek.

"Have you been in the trash this morning?" I ask, narrowing my eyes. Hank instantly lowers his head and looks up at me through his eyelashes. I swear he watches romance movies when he's not on the job site with me and learns little things like this to get him out of trouble. I give him a little scratch under the chin.

The rich aroma of fresh-brewed coffee fills my nose as I pour it into a to-go cup and slip on my tennis shoes. I'm attaching Hank's leash to his collar when I remember Adam's phone and the entire reason for going out this morning. The whole fifteen second walk from the door to the kitchen counter, I'm wrestling with the thought of checking it again. I decide I will because no one will know, then immediately change to no, because it's none of my business. But when I flip the phone over from its face down position on the counter, it instantly lights up, and I'm able to see there are no new texts from Aly. Guilt washes over me again as I slip it into my back pocket.

I decide on a longer route into town that follows the water's edge along the cliffs in hopes of clearing my mind and sorting through my thoughts about Aly. The temperature is in the low seventies and it's slightly overcast, which I normally wouldn't mind. Today though, the weather only adds to my pensive mood.

FaceTiming Aly a few nights ago did nothing to keep the memories and feelings that I always keep locked down from resurfacing. Instead, seeing her was like one of those magic tricks where you pull on the end of a scarf and instead of only the one you saw the magician shove up into his sleeve, a million more tumble free, and you're left wondering how that many things could fit in such a tiny spot and where exactly they all came from. Seeing Aly for the first time in ten years didn't simply stir up a tiny bit of interest. It brought back all the feelings I had for her and then some.

To make matters worse, I see what kind of message she sends to her comatose brother. I mean, who does that? Who, other than Aly, would think to keep someone updated on everything they're missing like that? She's still got the biggest heart and all the love in the world to give to the people she cares about. The realization also does nothing to help the way I've tried to suppress all my feelings for her.

My walk does nothing to clear my mind and only leaves me more confused. When we finally make it to the post office, I tug on the door and it doesn't budge. It's then I realize it's

Memorial Day. Today was the day Adam was supposed to go back to Charleston.

As if on cue, his phone buzzes in my pocket. I look at Hank. "What do I do?" I ask him. "Should I look at it?" Hank winks, something he does fairly often because he's a dog, but I take it as a yes. When I pull the phone out, there's a text from Aly. I read it once, then again, before I slip the phone back into my pocket, promising myself I'll return it tomorrow. Or the next day. *No*, definitely tomorrow.

"You're a terrible influence," I growl at Hank, kneeling to give him a scratch under the chin. He wags his tail and stares at me, unaware of the inner turmoil I'm facing right now.

Another text comes through and I sigh as I pull the phone back out. This time it's a picture of Pretzel, the stuffed unicorn clamped between her teeth, its head sticking out one side of her mouth, butt the other. I'm still kneeling beside Hank when I lock the phone and look over at him. "We're in trouble aren't we, buddy?"

CHAPTER SEVEN

LEVI

The next day, with the weight of all I've refused to acknowledge settled on my shoulders, I'm wrapping up the last job I have scheduled for a while.

I don't have any more big jobs lined up after this one.

I've been working on building a modest, two story home in the suburbs and when the payout hits the bank account, it'll be enough to live off of for a little while, but what if...

I don't even let myself finish that thought. Another job will come. It always does. This is simply the name of the game for a small construction company like mine; this is what happens trying to roll with the big dogs. I shake it off and pack up all my gear in the truck, where Hank already waits in the passenger seat.

"Burgers?" I ask, already knowing his answer. In response, he lets out a small howl of confirmation. A moment later, we pull into Buck's Burgers, and Aly's name lights up on Adam's phone in the cupholder. I meant to return it this morning, I really did, but when I went to the post office on my lunch break, they were on lunch, too. What a coincidence.

Hank looks at the phone and then at me. "It won't hurt to take a peek, will it?" I ask him. Drool slides from the corner of his mouth, and I take that as my sign from the universe to pick up the phone and read her latest text.

Hudson is dropping by the store more and more and it's almost hilarious how little he knows me. Yesterday, he brought me lactose-free ice cream and said he knew of other women who had sensitive stomachs and just wanted to be safe. I mean seriously, what do our parents see in him? I appreciate the ice cream, I really do, but I'd like all the lactose, please.

I'm grinning when three little dots appear again. Instantly, my grin is replaced by pure, unadulterated, hate for this Hudson guy.

He is kind of hot though, just saying.

Aly thinks Hudson is *hot*? The tool that Adam said works for his dad and has feet so small he wears women's loafers? That might not actually be true, but Adam swore it's a possibility. Against my better judgment, I channel my inner scorned woman, do a quick google search of his name and, wow, who cares if he has small feet with a chiseled face like that? There's no way Aly's going to stay away from him forever. She'll fall in love, they'll get married, have chiseled-jaw, small-footed babies, and live happily ever after. How many times a day do you actually look at someone's feet, anyway?

My finger hovers over the search bar, and Hank nudges my arm with a warm, wet nose. I know he's ready to order our burgers, but I take that as another sign to type in Aly's name. Instantly, pictures of her in front of Bloomie's, her flower shop, pop up. There's an article from the *Post and Courier* about the new flower shop on King Street, so I click on it.

A picture of her holding scissors cutting a ribbon is at the top of the article. Adam is standing beside her, pride radiating from his wide smile. Emma is on the other side, equally as excited. Like Aly, she looks like she hasn't changed a bit since high school. She's still got the funkiest style in clothing I've ever seen, and her hair is still a shade of neon that I'm sure she changed only the night before from some other color of the rainbow.

The realization that Aly and Adam's parents aren't in the shot irks me. They were always a bit pretentious—their noses were so far in the air, they'd drown in a heavy rainfall—but the fact they weren't there to celebrate their daughter's major accomplishment doesn't sit well with me. I shake it off and continue scrolling.

Underneath that picture is another with her holding a bouquet of wildflowers up to her nose, eyes closed in pure bliss, standing in front of the shiplapped walls holding shelf after shelf of vases. Her wavy, sun-bleached hair cascades over one shoulder, the other side tucked behind her ear. Underneath her Bloomie's apron, she's barefoot in a golden yellow sundress. If it weren't for the pair of tortoiseshell glasses perched on her cute little nose, it would look like she just stepped out of the ocean after a day full of surfing. My heart thumps hard enough in my chest at the breathtaking sight of her that I count to three to calm my ragged breathing.

"Should I message her?" I ask Hank. "I mean, it's only fair to check in on her, and see how her brother's doing, right?"

I had been staying updated thanks to her texts to Adam, but no one else knows that. Now that I'm thinking about it, I bet I seem like a terrible friend. Hank nudges my arm again, so with wobbly fingers, I find her number from when Adam used my phone to FaceTime her and type out a quick message.

Hey Ali, it's Levi. I just wanted to check and see how Adam was and if you were doing okay. I look forward to hearing from you.

I hurry and delete the last sentence. *I look forward to hearing from you* sounds more like a business email. Yuck. I hit send and finally attach the leash to Hank's collar so we can get some burgers.

A while later, I'm home on the couch in a burger-induced coma, wearing ketchup stains and engrossed in another rom com when my phone buzzes.

Aly: *Hey Levi! Adam is back in South Carolina now and is staying stable. He's still in a coma but his doctors are staying optimistic and hopeful. How are you? I actually called the hospital to check on you a few days ago and they said you had been released and were doing okay. I had to pretend to be your little sister to get any kind of info from them...hope you don't mind lol*

She called to check on me? Grin on my face, I type back, *I am doing pretty good, all things considered. I'm really sorry about Adam. I hope you know I would trade places with him in a heartbeat if I could.*

Instantly, those three dots appear followed by another message. *Don't say that. It was a freak accident that no one deserved to be a part of.*

Me: *Still...How are you though? Are you doing okay?*

The dots pop up and then disappear a few times before a new text comes through. *Yeah...I'm doing okay. It's weird not being able to talk to your best friend like you have every day for the past twenty-seven years though.*

Me: *I can only imagine. I'm here if you need anything.*

Aly: *Thank you, Levi.*

While I'm struggling to think of a response, another message pops up from her.

Aly: *Hey, can I ask you for some construction advice? Our toilet in the back isn't working right and I'm wondering how to fix it or if it's even fixable. I checked with my landlord and apparently it's my responsibility to get it looked at which kinda stinks. No pun intended.*

Me: *It could be a leaky wax ring or a bad seal. I'd have it checked out sooner rather than later.*

Aly: *That's what I was afraid of. Is your dad still in business? Maybe I can give him a call.*

My thumbs take on a mind of their own as I type the next sentence.

Me: *Actually, no need. I'm flying in tomorrow so I can come take a look at it.*

I frown at the screen for a second, anxiety gripping my chest. I jab at the text repeatedly, looking for any way to unsend it. What had I done? I had no plans of going back to Charleston anytime soon, let alone *tomorrow*. She might not even want to see me. Those infernal dots appear a moment later, and I hold my breath waiting for her reply.

Get a grip, Middleton. You are calm, you are cool, you are collected. Some might even say you're a nice, handsome, tall drink of water. Or...maybe that's just Mom. Whatever you are, you are not *the middle school girl you're acting like.*

As I'm giving myself my pep talk, Aly's text comes through.

Aly: *You are? That's great! I have plans around seven tomorrow evening but if you get in before that, maybe you could swing by? Or anytime you're free!*

Relief floods my chest and I send a thumbs up emoji in an attempt to not sound so eager. Then, I open Google and scrounge around for a last minute flight to Charleston.

CHAPTER EIGHT

LEVI

"How exactly did it happen?" my mom asks. Her reading glasses are perched precariously on the tip of her nose and she's frowning at the piece of pink paper she's holding.

"We were almost out," I say, releasing a huff of air. "I could *see* the exit doors. But a toddler at baggage claim screamed he had to potty, and that word is Hank's kryptonite. He went nuts."

"Potty?" Dad asks, his face wrinkled in confusion. He leans against the counter and takes the slip of paper from Mom, scanning it over.

"It's how I trained him to go outside to do his business," I explain.

"So you're telling me, he busted out of his crate, and then just...did it?" Mom and Dad both share a look then do their best to stifle their giggles.

I groan, reliving the memory. "I still don't understand how. One second he was firmly in his crate, and the next he was free and headed toward a garden of faux plants roped off in the middle of the airport. I tried to stop him but, by the time I caught up with him, he had already hurdled the ropes and hunkered down."

Dad grimaces then hands the ticket to me before wandering outside. I scan it before wadding it up and shoving it in my pocket, then let out a low whistle. "Two hundred fifty dollars, all thanks to a nervous stomach."

Hank, relieved to be out of the airport, is laying under the kitchen table, happily snoozing. I glance toward him and notice a couple of the legs on the chairs scattered around the table are a little wobbly.

"Mom, do you want me to fix your kitchen chairs?" I ask, already bending down to examine them.

"Your dad was supposed to fix them months ago. It's just so hard on his knees to squat." She joins me and rubs my back. "Don't worry about it right now. First, you need to eat." She sets a sandwich piled high with bacon, lettuce, and tomato in front of me. My mouth waters. Nothing compares to my mom's BLTs on her homemade sourdough bread. She's added my favorite barbeque kettle cooked potato chips to the plate, and my stomach grumbles louder when she sets down a home-made glass of sweet tea.

I pull out one of the few good kitchen chairs, the scrape finally waking Hank from his slumber. He mopes over and rests his head on my knee while I enjoy one of my favorite meals in the kitchen where I grew up. I glance around the kitchen, unsure of how things have stayed exactly the same, yet feel completely different in the ten years I've been gone.

Looking around, I find all my school pictures still lined up in the hallway leading to the bathroom, where lines and dates mark the doorframe, showing my height at different ages. The windows are open and the salty breeze from the inlet outside and sweet scent of roses from mom's flower garden greet my nose. I've missed this place more than I realized. I take a deep breath and swallow the last bite of my sandwich, lost in the memories of growing up here. I'm so deep in nostalgia, I almost miss the buzzing in my pocket.

Hesitating only a moment when I realize it's Adam's, I quickly pull it out, eager to see what Aly sent this time. When I open the text, I find a picture of Aly eating an ice cream cone, clad only in a bikini top, and my cheeks heat at the sight of all that golden skin.

Don't worry, I'm keeping your seat warm at Dolce Banana Cafe.

Her hair looks a little wet and wavy, like she's just come from the ocean. Another text comes through while I'm still staring slack-jawed at her picture.

The waves were so good today. You would've loved it.

Feeling extra guilty now, I hastily shove the phone back into my pocket, before pulling out my own and typing a message to her.

Hey Aly! I made it back to Charleston. Let me know a good time to come take a look at your shop and I'll be there.

Immediately, dots appear.

I'm loading up the car right now on Folly. I can meet you there in twenty?

Not wanting to seem too eager, I wait a full two minutes and thirty seconds before responding with, *See you then.*

"What's got your cheeks all red like that?" Dad asks, startling me. "You need to go lay down after the trip or something?" A smirk plays at the corner of his mouth.

"Maybe," I mutter. "Can I borrow your truck?"

"Nope," Dad says. He's changed into a pair of khaki shorts and a polo, which I know is his idea of a *fancy* outfit. I raise an eyebrow. "It's poker night," he explains. "You can come if you want."

"I'm going to go take a look at some work that needs done at Bloomie's on King Street for Aly, Adam's sister."

"I know who Aly is," Dad says, his smirk growing. "You can't take the truck but you're welcome to take the Teenie Mobile."

My mom pops her head out of the laundry room and says, "Be careful when you park her, though. Sometimes her eyelashes stick out farther than you think and you might bump them into the car in front of you."

A groan escapes me. The Teenie Mobile is my mom's turquoise Mini Cooper with eyelashes on the headlights, affectionately named after her. "Can you maybe take mom's car just this once? We can trade?" I ask, afraid of the impression I'll make on Aly if I show up in what is basically a clown car.

"Nope," Dad says, fighting a full on laugh now. I barely resist the urge to roll my eyes. This must be *so* much fun for him. "The keys are in it. I'll be back around eleven," he says without turning as he walks down the steps to his truck. His large, manly, blacked out, not-at-all-embarrassing truck.

Did I mention it's also very manly?

"You sure?" I call after him. "I really don't mind trading with you." Maybe if I make it seem like an offer...

"No can do." The truck door slams and the engine roars to life. Seconds later, Hank and I are left standing in his dust.

"I just put a new air freshener in there," Mom says. "It's strawberries and cream in the shape of a centaur. You'll love it!"

"Great, thanks." I muster a smile to mom and whistle for Hank. He comes bounding over and together, we make our way to the garage.

Even though there are a few parking spots in front of Bloomie's, I find one a block away. Pulling up to Bloomie's in such a ridiculous car isn't exactly how I planned to kick this reunion with Aly off. I pull off the centaur air freshener from the rear view mirror and shove it under my seat, then unfold myself from the car and reach into the back to grab the tool bag I stuffed in beside Hank.

"You think I can do this, don't you Hank? I'm success-ful-ish, I have decently sized feet unlike *some* men, and I can grow a full beard. Chicks dig beards, right?" Hank only side-eyes me, drool hanging from one corner of his mouth.

Bloomie's is already closed for the day, but through the windows, I can see someone moving around. Her back is to me, but when she pulls the elastic free from her hair, and her sandy waves float perfectly around her bare shoulders, I know without a doubt it's Aly. When she pulls off her apron and turns, she reveals a polka dotted sundress.

"Levi?" she says when she spots me through the window. "Is that really you?" She opens the door and Hank noses his way through.

"Long time no see," I laugh. Awkwardly, we stand there, and I'm not sure if I should give her a quick hug or not. Hank decides for me by jumping onto his hind legs to lick her in the face. A weenie dog comes flying from the back room at the sound of new voices, and I swear Hank drools a little more when he sees her.

"Sorry about that. Hank's a bit of a ladies' man." Aly wipes the slobber from her cheek and bends down to scratch his belly, which he's happily made available by rolling over at her feet. The little hoe. "I hope it's okay that I brought him. He was a little too anxious from our flight to leave him alone at the house with my mom."

"He's precious," she coos with a smile. "Pretzel sure seems to be smitten."

Pretzel is using Hank's tail as a chew toy, clearly desperate for attention from him. In that moment, I almost slip and mention the pictures she's been sending to Adam, which makes me think of his phone. I had it in the front pocket of my carry on...which is now in the house. How could I have forgotten to bring it? Do I tell her I have it but forgot it, or is it too awkward now?

"How are you doing?" she asks, noticing the way I'm absentmindedly rubbing my shoulder.

"I can't complain," I respond, dropping my hand. "I went to see Adam earlier." Her shoulders slump the slightest, but she meets my gaze with a practiced smile.

"Thank you for checking on him."

"The nurse came in while I was there. She wouldn't say much but made it seem like he might be doing a little better," I say in my best attempt to comfort her.

"Yeah, he's stable, which is a good sign." Unshed tears well in her eyes. She quickly turns her back to me, adjusting a vase on the shelf behind her, but I don't miss the way she swipes at her eyes before turning to me again. "Let me show you that toilet."

She leads me to the back of the store, toward the sound of running water. When we reach the bathroom, I move around her, trying to ignore the way my heart practically leaps out of my chest when our hands barely brush. Once I pull off the lid on the tank, I adjust the chain to the flapper, and the water immediately stops running.

"How did you do that?" she asks, astonished.

"Must've just needed my touch." I grin and wipe my hands off on a towel by the sink.

Aly's shoulders slump and her brow furrows. "Usually I'm pretty good at fixing stuff like this. I've basically YouTubed my whole way through my cottage renovation so far. I can't believe I couldn't figure this one out. Thank God you didn't come all the way from the West Coast for that."

If you only knew. "Ah, it's alright. You know what they say." She cocks an eyebrow, urging me to continue. "Don't pet the sweaty stuff." Aly stares at me blankly. "You know...like don't sweat the petty stuff? But pet the sweaty stuff." She pushes her glasses back up her nose, staring intently, and waiting for more. Only...there isn't more.

"You know what I'm trying to say, right? Like this isn't a big deal at all. It's totally fine." Why can't I stop talking? Mentally, I'm gagging from shoving my foot so far in my mouth. Desperate for a subject change, I ask, "So you bought a cottage?"

Excitedly, she nods, her eyes taking on a whole new sparkle. "It's right on the harbor. I bought it for next to nothing at a foreclosure auction. My neighbor is nosey, and it needs a lot of work but I'll get there...one day." Her nose crinkles. "We've just been so busy here—which is great—but it doesn't leave time for much else."

"So business is good?" I ask, sweeping my gaze across the room once more. "I can't believe this used to be an old hardware store. You'd never know it with what you've done to the place."

"Thank you, Levi. We've worked really hard on it for the past year, and it's just now starting to pay off." She smiles and looks around before her eyes meet mine again. "How are things going out in San Diego?"

"They're going gre—" I start to say but stop myself. Aly's built this store up with her bare hands and for some reason, lying to her doesn't seem like the right thing to do. "Honestly, business isn't great right now. Nor has it ever been, really. I've been out there for ten years now, and we're still barely breaking even. It sucks, but it's the truth." My cheeks redden with embarrassment for unloading all this on her.

"How long will you be in town?" she asks suddenly.

"I'm not sure. Maybe a week or so?"

"What if..." She stops and places a finger on her chin, considering her next words. Once again, her eyes sparkle, and I know I'll say yes to whatever it is she wants. "What if I help you with advertising your business on social media? You don't have any, right?"

I shake my head side to side, secretly thrilled that she's tried to look me up online.

"In return, you can help me at the cottage with all the stuff that YouTube can't teach me."

"Like what, exactly?" I ask. *Please don't say any more plumbing. I really hate plumbing.*

"Plumbing, mostly," she answers. And dang it, she looks so cute with her hands clasped in front of her chest and a smile as big as the Montana sky that I can't help what comes out of my mouth next.

"It sounds like we've got ourselves a deal." I hold out my hand for her to shake, fully aware I hadn't planned on staying in Charleston long enough to get any sort of meaningful work done on her cottage but unwilling to back out now. When she slides her hand into mine, an electric current pulses up my arm and straight to my chest. Did she feel that, too?

She breaks the contact and glances down at her watch. "I'm really sorry to leave, but I'm meeting Emma for dinner, and she'll get cranky if I cancel."

It could be wishful thinking on my part, but she seems a little reluctant to go.

"Yeah no worries at all," I say, trying to hide my disappointment. I refuse to let myself read too much into the way she's chewing on her bottom lip.

"I'd reschedule if I could, but I know if I don't go, it's all I'll hear about for the next year and half from her. It's our weekly taco dinner, too." She scrunches her nose again, and a million butterflies take flight in my chest. "Thank you for doing this though," she adds quickly. "I really appreciate it. When do you want to come over and take a look at the cottage? I'll get a game plan ready for your social media too."

Play it cool, man, I tell myself and scroll through my very empty calendar before answering.

"Anytime is fine. I'd like to catch a few waves sooner rather than later, too," I say, feigning nonchalance. Really, my mind is on the picture she had sent to Adam in her bikini. I hope Dad kept one of my boards at the house, or I'm going to have to spend money I don't have on a new one in order to see this girl again.

Her eyes light up. "I'd love that! If you wanted, we could go tomorrow morning. Maybe around sunrise? Bloomie's is closed on Sundays."

A sunrise surf with the most gorgeous girl I've ever laid eyes on? Someone pinch me.

Before I can daydream too long, Pretzel runs by, Hank right behind her. His big tail catches a vase on the counter and I watch in horror, as it teeters. Aly and I reach for it at the same time, my rough, callused hands wrapping around her smooth, slender ones to secure it. Her hands are so small and delicate next to mine. Unwillingly, I pull away and brush my palms along my jeans.

"That was a close one," she jokes and sets it back on the counter.

"Very close," I say, every nerve ending where she touched me on fire. "Sorry about Hank. Sometimes he forgets how big he is."

"Honestly, Pretzel is very much the same. Which is probably why I've had a constant cramp in my lower back since I've been dog sitting. Somehow, she takes up the bulk of the bed, leaving me to hang onto the edge for dear life." She checks her watch again and blows out a puff of air. "I really do need to go before Emma shows up wondering where I am…"

Before she can finish, the bell above the door tinkles, and a man wearing an expensive-looking outfit and tiny Italian loafers strides through the door.

Hudson.

CHAPTER NINE

ALY

"You should see this Mini Cooper parked down the street," Hudson says, walking to where I'm standing, straight past Levi as if he doesn't exist.

He's wearing a chambray shirt with cufflinks and khaki shorts that look like they could fit Pretzel. If he moved an inch in the wrong direction, I'm pretty sure they'd split apart at the seams. He hands me a bouquet of flowers, which I think is a little strange given that I run my own floral shop. Then, to make matters worse, he gives me a quick kiss, *on the lips,* and I'm stunned speechless for a second.

Where did that come from?

Immediately, my eyes shoot to Levi. His jaw is clenched, and the smile plastered to his face is so fake and forced, it almost looks painful. His eyes flash with something unrecognizable—anger maybe—and I'm secretly thrilled at the thought.

I politely smile at the bouquet Hudson gave me. "Can you believe someone bought that hideous excuse for a vehicle for their teenage daughter? Honestly I should call CPS. Hopefully it's still out there when we leave so you can see it. It's so bad."

Levi clears his throat like he's about to say something, but Hudson pretends not to notice, instead asking how Adam is. After I give him a quick update, he turns and acts as though he's just now seeing Levi for the first time.

"Hey, buddy. Thanks for taking care of my girl's problem. It's hard to find a good plumber these days."

The shudder that racks my body when he calls me his *girl* is enough to shake my mouth open as if it's on a hinge. *What was he doing*?

"He's actually a contractor," I say, finally finding my words. Levi shoots me a grateful look.

"Plumber, contractor. Same thing." He brushes Levi off and turns to face me completely. "Hey, I came by to see if you wanted to grab dinner with me tomorrow evening. I'll pick you up at six." He doesn't give me a chance to decline before he's rattling off the menu options at some fancy restaurant down by the marina.

"Hudson," I say gently. Now he's talking about the proper way to slurp oysters down, sounds and all. Why must his face be so pretty but the rest of him so...not? "Hudson," I say again, louder this time. "I'm not available tomorrow."

"You're not?" he asks, bewildered. "Just cancel whatever plans you have. Problem solved. You won't regret it." He winks, and I taste the sandwich I had for lunch as it crawls back up my throat.

"No. I'm meeting with my contractor," I say firmly, pointing to Levi.

Levi gives a little wave, wearing the smuggest, most satisfactory smirk I've ever seen.

Hudson fake smiles at me then stage-whispers out of the corner of his mouth, "Are you sure you want to trust someone who's not exactly reputable to work on the house you live in? I can give you some names of contractors. You've worked hard for this, Al."

"Levi and I went to high school together, Hudson. And he's Adam's best friend. I can definitely trust him."

With raised eyebrows, Hudson hesitantly says, "Okay, but don't say I didn't warn you..."

"My family runs one of the oldest contracting companies in Charleston," Levi says, finally speaking up. "Even if it weren't for the fact that I've known Aly since we were kids, I think you can rest assured that I wouldn't jeopardize my family's company by doing shoddy work."

Levi's jaw muscles flex again, and I have to say…it's kind of hot. Like the Mr. Darcy hand flex of the jaw, if you will. I've already taken a mental snapshot of the way he looks, but I let my eyes roam over his faded blue jeans and snug black tee once more before forcing myself to look away so I don't get caught. It should be a sin to look that good in something as simple as a black tee and jeans. The way the tee hugs his biceps makes me a little jealous, and I wonder if it's normal to be jealous of a shirt. It makes me want to rip it off him and…

"Aly?" Hudson asks. "Did you hear me?"

"Of course I did," I say even though I most definitely did not.

"Then let's go tonight?" Hudson says, annoyed. "I'll call and see if I can pay extra or something for a good table since we didn't make reservations."

I grab the vase that had almost fallen to the floor earlier and fill it with water from the sink, pretending Hudson doesn't exist. Instead, I think of the way Levi's calloused hands cradled mine when we both reached to save this vase, and how they fit so perfectly together.

I plop the flowers Hudson brought me into it and do a poor job of hiding the look on my face when I notice they're from Fourth Street Flowers. I have no problem with women supporting women. I'm actually all about it. But, they are our biggest competition and haven't exactly been the friendliest since we opened. Hudson must notice me staring at the sticker on the outside of the bouquet.

"I've always bought my flowers from there. They do such a good job, don't they? Probably one of the best in town." I blink once, then twice, trying to formulate a response to that.

"Hudson, you do know *I* own a flower shop, right?" I ask, incredulously gesturing at the store around us.

"So, dinner tonight?" he says, completely ignoring me. I'm so bewildered, I'm convinced he didn't hear me.

Before responding, I attach Pretzel's leash to her collar, then move to the light switch by the front door and flip it off. The soft glow disappears, and I turn the open sign over.

"I can't tonight either, Hudson. It's taco night with Emma." Hudson looks utterly defeated, and my heart sinks the tiniest bit. I can't stand to disappoint anyone so when I say, "Maybe another time though?" Instantly, I want to inhale the words right back in.

"How about next week then?" he asks, his expression far too eager for me to say no outright.

I sigh and try not to glance at Levi, to see what he thinks of all this. "That works," I tell Hudson.

"Great. Oh, and Levi?" he asks, turning toward him. "It was great to meet you."

"Likewise," Levi answers dryly. We make our way outside, and I'm locking the door when Levi speaks up again, loud enough for Hudson to hear. "Aly?" When I look at him, he's biting back a smirk. He glances towards Hudson and says, "I'll see you tomorrow morning, okay?"

I bite the inside of my cheek, trying not to laugh. I would give anything to have the look on Hudson's face right now framed.

"What's tomorrow morning?" Hudson asks, brow furrowing.

I ignore Hudson's question and let my lips curl into a tiny smile. "See you then," I say to Levi. With a huff, Hudson climbs into his fancy car and speeds off, and Levi takes off down the block.

I get in my own car with Pretzel and, a few minutes later, drive past Levi in time to witness him shoving Hank's butt into the tiny backseat of a turquoise Mini Cooper. I roll down my window and wait for him to turn around, enjoying the view in the meantime. When he faces me, he instantly pales.

"It's not mine," he stammers.

"I think it's cute." I stifle a chuckle with my fist and roll up my window, wondering exactly what I'm getting myself into, making plans with my childhood crush.

"Well, was it any good at least?" Emma asks, referring to Hudson's kiss. She spoons another dollop of sour cream onto her taco.

"It was…a kiss?" I say with a shrug. We're sitting outside at our favorite Mexican restaurant, trying to enjoy our margaritas and tacos. Unfortunately, Pretzel has nearly knocked over the table twice by wrapping her leash around the legs and then bolting for anything that catches her eye.

"Come on. Give me some details. Tongue, no tongue? Chin caressing? I want to know it all."

"I mean…his lips are soft? I don't know what you want, Emma. It lasted half a second. I didn't feel the Earth move beneath my feet, if that's what you're asking." I take another chip from the bowl sitting between us and dip it into the guacamole.

She takes another bite and nods her head, clearly thinking while she chews. "So did Levi look like every dream you've had of him since you were a kid?"

"I don't dream about him," I say in a voice that's about two octaves too high.

She narrows her eyes. "Why can't you just admit you like his butt?"

"Emma!" I scold, and great, now I *am* thinking about his butt in those perfectly worn and faded Wranglers…again.

"Fine, whatever," she says and holds a chip under the table for Pretzel.

"You know you're not sneaky if I can hear her crunching on it, right? Besides, she's going to expect people food at every meal now."

"Have you ever considered that maybe Pretzel hates you because you're no fun?" Emma teases, tossing a chip at me. Pretzel shoots out from under the table, nearly knocking it over again, and immediately gobbles it up. The umbrella above the table wobbles precariously, and I reach out to steady it before shooting Emma the dirtiest look I can muster.

"Okay, ouch? And I don't think she hates me anymore. I think we're starting to bond. I think she's just missing Adam," I say, giving her a scratch under her chin. Her back leg thumps in appreciation, but her nose nudges my palm for a chip that isn't there.

"How's he doing?" she asks, her voice softening.

I let out a small sigh and trace the water droplets beading on my glass with my finger. "I went and saw him this morning. He's still doing okay, I guess. His labs are all good and his vitals are stable. We're just waiting for him to wake up."

Emma leans back in her chair with folded arms. "And how are *you* doing?"

"I miss him," I whisper. In a second she's beside me, her arms wrapped around my neck.

"It's going to be okay," she tells me. "He's missing you right now just as much as you're missing him."

"I didn't realize how much I relied on him until he wasn't there to talk to," I say quietly. "I think our relationship with our parents really forced us to rely on each other. No one but him understood the pressure of growing up in a household where everything had to be perfect and nothing was ever good enough, you know?'"

Emma nods, aware of what life was like growing up in the Bloomington household.

She hugs me for a second longer before she pulls away. "Want to go surfing tomorrow morning? Maybe get your mind off things?"

I bite my lip and busy myself with fixing up another taco. "I can't."

"Why?"

"I'm...already going," I say.

"With who?" she presses.

Maybe if I ignore her, she'll go away.

"With *who*?" she asks, again.

"Levi," I murmur.

"LIKE A DATE?" she screeches so loud that Pretzel whines from under the table.

"No! Definitely not a date. We're just working together. I'm going to help him with the social media for his business and he's going to help me with cottage renovations."

"And you're going to do that in the ocean on a surfboard. Okay. Got it." She gives me an over exaggerated wink.

"He lives in California, Emma. Things would never work. And besides, Adam always made it very clear that he wanted his best friend and his sister to stay far away from each other," I say.

"Do you hear that?" she asks, suddenly.

We both turn our heads and find Pretzel, who somehow managed to jump onto the table while we were in deep conversation. She's got both front paws in the bowl of salsa, lapping it up enthusiastically.

"Pretzel, NO!" I yell. As soon as I reach for the bowl, she lifts her head only enough to make eye contact with me as she nudges it straight onto the floor.

Open-mouthed, I stare down at the mess. My feet and ankles are completely covered in salsa.

Breaking the silence, Emma says, "I can definitely see where you'd think you two are bonding."

Dear Adam,

Hudson brought me flowers to Bloomie's today...from Fourth Street Flowers. It was super annoying, and he now wants to go to dinner. Do you think he knows what I do for a living? Also, I just realized I haven't updated you on Levi. He's doing really well and is in town right now. He said he stopped by to see you. He stopped by Bloomie's, too, and fixed the leaky toilet in the back of the shop. I almost didn't recognize him. I can't believe it's been ten years.

Chapter Ten

Levi

"Hey, do you know where the paper clips are?" Glenda, my assistant back in California, asks. I set my phone on Aly's counter and hit the speaker button so I can use both hands to hang a light fixture in the hallway.

"Glenda, I don't even use paper clips. Why don't you know where they are?" I say, annoyed.

I hired Glenda based on her highly impressive resume, which I'm now suspecting she printed off Google and swapped the name. In fact, she does *not* have incredible organizational or problem solving skills, nor do I believe she's ever even opened QuickBooks, let alone knows how to use it proficiently. She does, however, have the same pair of pants in five different colors that she likes to rotate throughout the week. She always wears them clear up to her chin with a different printed button up shirt each day. She's in her early-sixties, never married as far as I know, and incredibly bad at her job. Somehow though, she's weaseled her way into my life, and though I'm reluctant to admit, I don't know what I'd do without her.

"Well do you know where the stapler is, then?" she asks.

"Why do you even need a stapler, Glenda?" As my office manager, she should really know where all of this is. I take a deep breath to calm my rising impatience.

"Teenie emailed me a recipe this morning, and I want to keep the pages together," she answers matter-of-factly.

"There might be one in my left desk drawer," I tell her, eager to get off the phone. "Wait...you talked to my mom? Why?"

"I tried to call you four times this morning and you wouldn't answer. I looked through some of your discharge papers from the hospital and found your mom's number as your emergency contact. I thought maybe she might be able to get a hold of you," she says, like it's the most normal thing in the world to look through your boss's private documents.

"Glenda..." I say through gritted teeth. "Those papers were on my dresser in my bedroom. Why were you in there?"

"I already told you! I needed to get a hold of you and you weren't answering!" I hear some clanking, and she utters a curse word under her breath. "Your stapler is jammed."

"What was so important that you called me four times this morning, Glenda?" I ask, my voice rising ever so slightly, on the verge of losing my mind.

"Oh, right!" she says. "You received a letter in the mail that you are past due on your rent for the building here."

"How much?" I ask. She tells me the number, and I sigh as I run my hands through my hair. "Okay. I'll figure something out. Who was that addressed to?"

"You, duh," she says.

"Glenda, it's a federal offense to open someone else's—" I start.

She pretends to not hear me and says, "Your mom said you went on a date this morning! She said the girl is just the cutest little thing. She's going to email me a picture of her later if she can pull her on the FaceButt app. Why didn't you tell me your mom was so nice?"

I dash toward my phone on the counter and fumble around, trying to take it off speaker. The second Glenda's voice cuts off, Aly pokes her head around the corner. She's got paint in her hair, and she's holding a wriggling Pretzel. Hank trails behind, tongue lolling out the side of his mouth, stars in his eyes as he stares at Pretzel.

"I'm going to take them out," she whispers and goes out the back door.

"I've got to go," I say to Glenda with a sigh. "Call me only if you *really* need me, okay?"

Around midday, we take a break from working to sit on Aly's back deck and eat. It's a gorgeous early summer day, with cotton candy clouds overhead and cargo ships pulling in and out of the harbor. She made peanut butter and jelly sandwiches, and I don't have the heart to ask how she managed to make the simplest food in the world taste so terrible.

One look around her kitchen earlier might explain things, though. She had exactly one pot, one pan, and a salt and pepper shaker which tells me she either doesn't love to cook or just doesn't know how. Her fridge even rivaled that of the most eligible bachelor I know, *me*, holding only a case of strawberries, a half-gallon of almond milk, and a jar of grape jelly which I'm beginning to think is expired.

She looks over at me. "Do you not like grape jelly?" she asks, her brows drawn in concern at the barely-eaten sandwich in my hand.

"I *love* grape jelly," I tell her and quickly shove another bite in my mouth.

Right as I'm wondering how I'm going to stomach the rest of my sandwich, Hank comes up from behind me and snatches it from my hand.

Problem solved.

"How's the bathroom painting going?" I ask quickly, before she can notice.

"I should be finished in the next hour or so. I know you've only been helping me for a day, but I feel like we've accomplished a lot," she says, tucking her hair behind her ear. My mood instantly shifts. I don't want to think about our time together ending. "Thanks for putting the cabinet doors back up in the kitchen. Once I order a new stove, I think we can check that room off the list."

I nod, and reach for another chip. "Everything okay?" she asks. "You seem a little quiet."

I want to ask her how much of my conversation with Glenda she overheard. If Aly heard Glenda refer to surfing this morning as a *date*, I might never forgive her. While surfing had been nothing short of incredible, I don't think either of us would classify it as a date.

The water was cold enough to make goosebumps dot across my flesh and the waves were perfect height, curling over at just the right time. I was enthralled by how effortless Aly made catching each one seem. Her confidence and grace were mesmerizing, and it was hard to peel my eyes off her for more than a second. The distraction had me flailing in the water, looking like I'd never surfed a day in my life.

Really, though, I was a goner the moment Aly had jumped out of that Bronco in nothing more than an itty-bitty orange bikini and a pair of unbuttoned denim shorts rolled at the waist.

And the way the water droplets ran from her long, wavy hair down her spine as she straddled her board when the sun was just beginning to rise in the background? That was an image I hoped I never forgot.

"My assistant, if you even want to call her that, called this morning to let me know some bad news. We just really need to drum up some business before too long or I'm not sure what might happen."

Aly puts a finger to lips, considering me for a moment.

"Let me take some pictures of you today!" she squeals suddenly. "Maybe we can put the ladder back under the light fixture in the hallway, and you can pretend like you're hanging it again! Your biceps looked huge when you were doing that earlier. I bet if we made you an Instagram account and posted it, people everywhere would be lining up outside your door to make an appointment with you." Her eyes sparkle with excitement.

"You think my biceps are big?" I say and give her a little nudge with one arm while I unabashedly flex the other.

She swallows hard, as if finally realizing what she said. "That's not what I said." Her cheeks are the color of ripe little strawberries, and she's trying and failing to look anywhere but my flexed arm. "I *basically* just said anyone who needs a light fixture installed or anything of that sort may give you a call."

"You *basically* said I was a hot contractor," I tease.

My eyes are drawn to her lower lip as she sucks it in and chews nervously. As she fidgets, she quickly turns her attention to the harbor. "Fine, don't pose for a picture," she says. "I'm just saying what I think might work. It's part of our deal anyway. You help me, I help you. I don't tell you the best way to hang light fixtures, and you don't tell me the best way to market your company." She crosses her arms and looks at me again, face set in determination.

A chuckle escapes me. "Fine. A deal is a deal, and I'm a man of my word."

I dust the crumbs from my fingers off on my pants then get up to go inside, Aly following me. Eagerly, she scoots past me and grabs the ladder, positioning it under the light fixture. After several adjustments, she motions for me to climb on.

"Move your left arm up just a little more...perfect! Flex it a little maybe? Yes!" she says, and snaps a picture. She looks at it for a second and frowns. "Okay, maybe take your right arm and move it forward just a little." I try to do what she says and she shakes her head. "No, more forward." I try again and she huffs. "Hold on," she mutters and steps on the bottom step behind me.

Any other time, I would be thinking how incredibly unsafe this is, but right now, all I can think about is Aly's closeness. When she grabs my elbow softly and positions it how she wants, I realize I'm holding my breath. A shiver runs down my spine when her body brushes against mine. Then, in an instant, she's gone, back across the room and snapping more photos.

"Every new picture you take, my self-esteem drops a little more," I say, pretending to be irritated. "Is it really necessary to take that many?"

She giggles and finally, after a few more pictures, puts her phone down. "I think one of these will do."

Moving next to her, I watch over her shoulder as she opens up her Instagram app and pictures of flowers, Bloomie's, and random shots of Charleston fill the screen. Each little square looks so bright and happy. I want to look through each of them and catch up on the past ten years of Aly's life before she clicks away.

She quickly creates a new profile for me and asks, "Which filter? This one or this one?" She shows me the different options but I know nothing about filters, and they both look the same to me.

"I don't know," I groan. "I don't even know what a filter is. Can't we just post a picture of the light fixture and call it good?"

"Levi," she says, her face set in a determination again. "If I were scrolling through Instagram and I saw a picture of the light fixture in my hallway, I would absolutely not like that photo. That's so boring."

"But, you'd like it if a hot contractor was in it?" I ask, grinning.

Her cheeks turn pink again and she looks away. "Fine. I'm picking this filter whether you like it or not." She types a few more things and then exclaims, "Done!"

She hands the phone over to me, and I read the caption.

Need an extra hand with renovations? Call Middleton Construction!

She also posted my phone number below and only about a million little pound signs with words that don't make sense to me. Immediately, her phone pings with a notification.

"Look," she says, pointing to her screen. "You've already got your first like."

She clicks on the name, and a brunette's profile fills the screen, featuring pictures that leave little to the imagination. "Maybe I went a little overboard on the hashtags," she mutters, and I wish I knew what she was talking about.

"Maybe we can post every other day. I think that should gain a lot of attraction to the page and I bet your phone will be ringing off the hook in no time. Do you want to know your handle and password so you can login and look around?"

"My handle?" I ask, cocking an eyebrow.

"Maybe not. We'll take baby steps for now."

She grins and walks into the living room, where Pretzel and Hank have been playing with Pretzel's stuffed unicorn. "Umm...Levi?" she says. "Why is your sandwich on the floor? And covered in..."

I stop in my tracks right behind her. A half-eaten sandwich covered in slobber sits next to Hank's nervously thumping tail, and I choke back a laugh. The sandwich must've been worse than I thought if he didn't want to eat it. She whirls around and gives me a quizzical look.

"Do you want to maybe go out for lunch next time?" I ask.

Chapter Eleven

Aly

Monday mornings typically are my favorite. A new week, a new palette of colors and flowers to choose from at the market, and an all-around fresh start.

Unfortunately, this morning couldn't be any more different.

For starters, I woke up to find Pretzel had once again found the hamper and chewed through every single pair of underwear I own, right when I thought we were finally getting along. Last night, she fell asleep with her head on my shoulder, little snores and all, and it was so adorable that her little traitorous move this morning was the last thing I expected. Now, I'm wearing a pair that I found in the depths of my closet, turned inside out for good measure just in case, and they're about two sizes too small. Nothing makes you feel like a less powerful woman than uncomfortable panties.

Then, Betsy wouldn't start, which has happened before and normally isn't a big deal because I have the Vespa. But today is market day, and I needed a big trunk to fit at least twenty variously-sized and shaped boxes of flowers and vases.

Reluctantly, I dial Emma's number, fully expecting an ear full for calling so early. She answers on the first ring. "Hello?"

"Emma? Why are you awake this early? You never wake up until fifteen minutes before you leave for work." I hear voices in the background and an elevator dinging.

"I had to run to the doctor's office," she says.

"Everything okay?" I ask, concern beginning to seep into every corner of my body. I'm barely managing Adam being in the hospital right now. I don't think I could handle it if Emma was sick, too.

"Everything is fine!" she chirps in a voice that's an octave or two higher than normal. She's acting weird. "Just a...regular visit."

"*Oh*. It was one of *those* appointments," I say, realizing she's been to the lady doctor.

A car door slams on her end and everything quiets until her engine turns over. "Would you be able to run to the market? Betsy won't start again. I can meet you back at the shop and help you unload in a half an hour?"

"Yeah, I can do that," she says through a yawn.

Thirty minutes later, I'm pulling up to Bloomie's on the Vespa, backpack strapped to my chest with Pretzel—who is wearing a pair of children's swim goggles I picked up from the gas station on the way—poking her head out the front. She gives a little yip when we stop, and I scratch her behind the ears for not jumping out.

Emma pulls up a few seconds later and backs up to the door. "Fourth Street Flowers beat us there," she says when she jumps out. "So I got what I could, but I think we can make it work. Also, you do realize you just became the new meme that's going to be plastered all over the internet, right?"

Up until now, she'd been valiantly stifling a laugh with her fist, but finally gives up to double over in a full on fit of giggles.

"What else was I supposed to do?" I unstrap my backpack and peel off Pretzel's goggles. She shakes and runs inside when I open the door for her. I reach for a box of vases in Emma's trunk and wince.

"What's wrong?" Emma asks.

"I'm a little sore. Levi helped me at the house all day yesterday and we got a lot accomplished, but it came with a price." I massage my right shoulder and catch Emma wiggling her eyebrows out of the corner of my eye.

"So what did you accomplish?" she asks in a sing-song voice. I roll my eyes and reach for the box again, ignoring her suggestive tone. "I saw his new Instagram account. Has he said if his phone is blowing up yet?"

"No, why?" I ask as I haul the box inside.

"Did you not see how many likes his picture got?" Emma asks, following with a box of her own.

"No, I honestly forgot to check it. This morning has been a little crazy." I set the box down inside, and pull my phone from the front pocket of my overalls. In seconds, Levi's profile fills the screen, and I'm floored at the amount of likes, comments, and DMs that are waiting to be looked at.

I click one of the messages and begin reading. It's from a girl in San Diego who does *not* need help with any renovations, but *would* like to know if he's available for dinner one evening soon. She also looks like she's straight from a Victoria Secret catalog with platinum-blonde hair, full pink lips, and wide, doe eyes. I frown, wondering if her genetics are that good or if her appearance is the result of a fantastic West Coast doctor.

Before I can think better of it, I delete the message. What Levi doesn't know won't hurt him, right? I delete a few more for good measure before I'm fully engulfed by jealousy and slam the phone face down on the counter.

Emma comes back in with a couple more boxes. She's smirking, mouth open to speak, but I hold up my hand to stop her. "Don't."

"Oh girl. You've got it bad," she says anyway and pats me on the arm. I brush her off and grab a ranunculus from a bucket for the arrangement I'm working on. Its delicate stem snaps, so I grab another and when it does the same, Emma slides the box over to her side of the table with a grimace, clearly not trusting me to try a third time.

A few minutes later, the bell above the door tinkles. "Sorry, we don't open until nine," I say, and look up to find Hudson walking through the door, carrying a box of macarons and a coffee from my favorite bakery downtown.

"Good morning, gorgeous," he says and hands me the treats while giving me air kisses on each cheek. I eagerly take a slurp of the coffee and almost whimper at how good it tastes. It's a cinnamon latte, one of my favorites.

"Thanks, Hudson," I say between sips. "You don't know how much I needed this today."

"I had a feeling," he beams. Right as he's closing in for a hug, Emma comes out of the back, eyebrows raised in surprise.

"Aly, can you come help me with this arrangement?" she asks.

"Gotta go," I say and swerve around him. "Thanks for the coffee and the macarons."

"Wait. I wanted to see if you were free tonight. You owe me a date, remember?" He catches my hand, and I do my best to wiggle out of his hold without seeming rude.

"Tonight?" I repeat. I don't know why it's so hard for me to say yes. He's handsome, has a great job, and my parents love him. Saying yes would solve a lot of problems.

"Yes. I can pick you up around six?" he asks hopefully with a shy smile, eyes shining eagerly.

"That should work," I say before giving it too much consideration. "I've got to go now, though. Thank you again." I raise my coffee cup in a mock salute, and he smiles over his shoulder before walking back outside.

Emma's standing at the work table in the back of the room, arms folded. "Did you just agree to a date with *Hudson*?" She grimaces and practically spits out his name. "What about Levi?"

"What about him?" I ask, annoyed. She raises an eyebrow and then shakes her head. "He lives across the country, Emma. And even if things weren't possible, he's still my brother's best friend. Something about that doesn't feel right, especially with Adam in a coma."

Emma doesn't say anything; she simply keeps shoving sunflowers into the vase and taking them out again to rearrange.

"I do like Levi," I confess. "I've always liked him. From the moment Adam brought him home after a soccer game and he told me the color I had picked for the bands on my braces was cool. It was burnt orange, by the way. But I don't think it could work."

"I think you're thinking too much, Aly. One date doesn't mean you have to marry him. You're also ten years older now. Do you really think your brother will be that upset if you go out with him?" I shoot her a menacing look and she backs away, hands in the air. "Or you can just go on a date with Hudson and be miserable. It's your life. Not mine."

"Hudson's cute and you know it," I say defensively.

Emma shrugs and says, "I can see where some people might find the just-stepped-out-of-GQ look attractive, but it's not for me."

"Tonight will be fine. Maybe even fun. You'll see."

Dear Adam,

I'm going on a date tonight with Hudson. I know you'd be so annoyed with me right now and I'M SORRY. But he showed up to work this morning with coffee and macarons after Betsy decided to die on market day and you know what macarons do to me. I'm only human. Plus, would it be such a bad thing to go out on a date with him if it makes mom and dad so happy?

P.S. Your dog ate all my underwear again.

P.P.S. When you wake up…If you see a meme going around of a woman driving a Vespa with a wiener dog strapped to her chest wearing swim goggles, IT'S NOT ME AND PRETZEL.

P.P.P.S. It's totally me and Pretzel.

"Excuse me, waitress? Waitress?" Hudson picks up his wine glass and taps the side with his knife, which is completely unnecessary given it's a Monday night and we have most of the dining room to ourselves. The two women seated in the corner shoot us annoyed looks, and I squirm a little in my seat. The waitress comes around the corner, *again,* and eyes Hudson warily.

"This one is dirty, too." He picks up his wine glass and holds it in front of the waitress's face. "See? Right here." He points to a nonexistent smudge, and the waitress squints.

"I apologize," she says, struggling to keep her smile in place. "I'll be right back with a new one." When she leaves I hear her mutter, "Again," and I can't blame her.

Hudson has been a handful since the moment we stepped inside the restaurant. When they found our reservation on Friday instead of tonight, I thought he was going to lose his mind. His face turned tomato red, a vein bulged in his neck, and he tried to slide the hostess a hundred dollar bill before she politely explained that it's Monday night and reservations weren't even needed, which only made him more belligerent.

Then, he ordered for me, and okay, I see how someone could think that might be cute. But he ordered me *spaghetti squash.* At one of the nicest restaurants on the harbor. Not the sea bass, not the filet. *The spaghetti squash.* I didn't even get to pick my salad dressing. Meanwhile, he ordered himself the ribeye. The description alone had me wanting to lick the menu.

I'm shoving an olive around my plate of salad with oil and vinegar dressing, fighting an eye roll when the waitress returns with another glass of wine.

"I've had my boss double check this one just in case. I truly apologize," she says so sweetly that I instantly assume they've both taken turns shining it with their own spit before bringing it out.

Hudson sighs and takes the glass reluctantly, then inspects it thoroughly before sitting it down. The waitress backs away slowly then all but runs back to the kitchen when she realizes he has nothing to say.

"So...how's business?" I ask, but my phone lights up in my bag, pulling my focus. I reach down, hoping it's news on Adam, and see one new message from Levi.

Watching a Meg Ryan movie. Wanna join? It can be just like old times.

I stifle a giggle and type back, *Can't right now. At dinner.*

Levi: *I'll let you watch the elevator scene twice. I know that part always got you back in the day.*

Me: *That part gets anyone with a heart and you know it.*

Levi: *I'm so glad you introduced me to Meg Ryan.*

Me: *Me? If I remember correctly, I walked in on you and Adam watching it in the basement with a box of tissues between you. That was the first time I'd ever even heard of this movie.*

Levi: *It sounds better if I say I walked in on you watching it though, doesn't it?*

Me: *Ha ha. I'm at dinner though. I've gotta go.*

"Funny you should ask. I was just named Sales Associate of the Month again." He wiggles his eyebrows and raises his glass for a toast. "Aly? Did you hear me?"

"What? Oh, yes!" I politely tap my glass against his and mentally calculate how many sales associates Dad has under him. I only come up with five, including Adam. Hudson seems really happy, though, so I decide not to mention it isn't exactly a big pool to choose from.

"That's great," I say, feigning enthusiasm. The waitress sets our entrees on the table, and I immediately reach for the garlic toast. Hudson grimaces and I pull back. "What's wrong?"

"It's just that...do you know how many carbs are in that piece of bread?" I fake a laugh, knowing there's no way someone in their right mind actually said that without joking, and reach for it again, looking at him. Suddenly, I realize he's being completely serious. His expression is pure, unadulterated horror.

"Do you not eat carbs?" I ask. I peel off the tiniest bit from the corner and pop it into my mouth. The butter and garlic melt on my taste buds, and it's so delicious, I could cry.

He visibly shudders. "Do you think I could have the body of a god if I ate carbs like that?"

"I don't know," I answer, unsure of what to say.

"You don't chance ruining perfectly chiseled pecs like these with too many carbs. I mean, have you seen these things?"

"Umm...no I haven't," I answer, distracted by the way he's bouncing his pecs under his perfectly starched white shirt. Is that supposed to be turning me on?

"Don't worry. You will tonight." He shoots me a wink and I feel the red wine I've been drinking begin its ascent up my throat.

"I'll be right back," I say and grab my purse from the floor. "Lady issues," I whisper and point to my purse. He grimaces and turns back to his steak.

The second my back is turned to him, I text Levi.

On second thought, that sounds great. Pick me up in front of the steak house on the harbor. Not trying to rush you but ASAP would be nice.

Chapter Twelve

LEVI

I'm on cloud nine right now, literally skipping down the front porch steps and humming "Thunderstruck." I'm unstoppable. Somebody call nine-one-one, because I'm on fire. When Aly texted me to come get her, I've never moved so fast in my life. I'm talking Usain Bolt fast. That is until I realize this Knight in Shining Armor's chariot is nothing less than the Teenie Mobile. When I start the engine and the purple under glow shines to life, I just know my man card has been revoked. It's dusk, so you can *really* see it, too.

You've got to be kidding me.

I hit every button on the dash at least twice and nothing turns it off, so reluctantly, I give up. My phone lights up with a slew of incoming messages right as I'm about to turn out of my driveway.

I give it maybe five more minutes before my date comes looking for me. SOS. HELP.

I'm going to start walking.

I don't know directions very well so I'm turning left outside the restaurant.

I'm wearing a red dress. Unless someone has stolen your phone in the ten minutes we've been texting. Then it's a pink dress and I'm turning right.

I chuckle and type out a quick, *OMW.*

OMW? Obscene madwoman where? Are you trying to ask for my location discreetly? Is this a ploy? Levi, if this is really you, tell me what your favorite color is.

I turn down Meeting Street and sure enough, I see a girl wearing a red dress typing furiously into her phone. I pull up beside her and roll down my window.

"Do you even know what my favorite color is?"

She jumps, but relief washes over her face as she walks towards the car. "No. But if you said something more complex than blue, I would've absolutely known your phone had been stolen." She slides into the passenger seat gracefully and takes a look around. "I didn't peg you for a turquoise man, though. Or one to have motivational quotes on their car freshener."

""'She believed she could, so she did' really just sets my mood for the day, you know?" She giggles and shoves her phone into her handbag. "This," I say, gesturing to the dashboard that's all of three feet wide, "is the Teenie Mobile, my mom's most prized possession."

"That's what I'd say too," she says with a wink and an elbow in the arm.

"Careful. These puppies are huge, remember? I don't want you to hurt yourself." I flex my right arm, and her cheeks flush to the colors of raspberries as she tries to hide a smile.

"Is it alright if we watch *Sleepless in Seattle* at your place? Mom and Dad are both home right now, and I'm not really in the mood to feel like I'm in high school again," I say, then realize how that must've sounded. "Not that, you know, there would be anything for them to walk in on. I just...I...Did you even really want to watch *Sleepless in Seattle*? I can just take you home if you want," I ramble and immediately want to kick myself in the face.

"Oh, we're definitely watching *Sleepless in Seattle*," she says. "You can't ruin a perfectly good date by texting someone with that kind of temptation only to let a girl down."

Perfectly good date? "So, you were on a date?" I ask, trying and failing to sound nonchalant.

"Yeah, with Hudson, the guy who works for my dad and with Adam. He's...something else," she says.

"Oh yeah? Like what?" I press. I hope I'm not being too forward, but I *need* to know how this date went.

She sighs and says, "For starters, he found a smudge on every wine glass they brought him. Then he ordered me spaghetti squash and himself a ribeye. Oh, and here's the kicker: when I looked at my garlic toast, he freaked out about the number of carbs in that one piece."

"Yikes," I say, mentally preparing my attack on Hudson. I'm envisioning a full on Old West quick draw, complete with tumbleweeds.

"Levi?" she says, interrupting my fantasy.

"Hmm?"

"Are you hungry? Have you eaten?"

I'd actually just eaten dinner with my mom and dad, but I would *never* tell her that and risk losing out on spending time with her. "Starving," I fib.

"Me too. I left before I actually got to eat anything. Can we swing through a drive-thru?"

"I wonder when Hudson realized I left," Aly says, curled up on the corner of her couch, a chicken tender box cradled in her hands. She's changed into an oversized sweatshirt and a pair of cotton shorts, and her wavy hair is pulled back with a thick scrunchy. Even her greasy fingers and the way she talks with her mouth a little full don't stop me from finding her absolutely beautiful right now.

I'm sitting on the opposite side of the couch with my chicken sandwich in one hand and Pretzel curled in my lap. I shrug my shoulders and say, "Who knows. I bet he finished his ribeye though."

"Probably," she laughs.

I hit play on *Sleepless in Seattle* and she settles deeper into the couch.

"I can't believe Pretzel is curled up on your lap right now," she says, and I detect a hint of jealousy.

"She probably just wants me for my chicken sandwich," I say and give Pretzel a scratch under her chin.

"I thought we were getting along so well and then this morning, I found out she chewed a hole through every single pair of underwear I have. A not just a little tear here or a little rip there. I won't go into details, but let's just say a specific part of every pair is missing." Aly chews on a fry, her expression sullen. "I think she really misses Adam. It feels kind of weird to be watching this movie without him, doesn't it?" Tears well in her eyes and threaten to spill over.

"Hey," I say, picking Pretzel up from my lap and scooting us closer to Aly. "You okay?"

"Yeah," she says, one tear finally spilling over and running down her cheek. "I just miss him." I wipe at the tear with the pad of my thumb. "I really wish I could get Pretzel in there somehow."

"Why can't you?" I ask.

"I can't take a dog into a hospital," she laughs. "Especially not that little troublemaker."

"Sure you can. She's tiny. Just stick her in one of your bags." I point to her handbag on the counter. "That would probably work."

She frowns, seeming to consider it, then asks, "What if it doesn't work and they kick me out and I can never go visit him again?"

"You should probably go incognito. Trench coat, ball cap, sunglasses *inside* the building. The works."

"You're right," she muses, eyes sparkling with mischief. "That could work."

"And if it doesn't," I say, "this wasn't my idea at all."

She giggles and swats my arm. I try to ignore the searing heat rippling along my skin from the lightest of her touches, but I find myself wishing she'd do it again.

"How's my picture doing?" I ask, settling back into the couch. It hasn't escaped my notice that the only thing separating us now is a very small wiener dog. "Has the CEO of a multimillion dollar company that wants to build in San Diego and hire me for the job liked my photo yet? Send a message perhaps?"

She grins and cocks an eyebrow. "You are on the verge of being internet famous. I bet if we posted a shirtless picture of you holding a hammer, it would do the trick."

I sit up straight and turn to face her again. Concern etches my brow when I ask, "Alyson Bloomington, are you suggesting I solicit business using my body?"

Her face instantly drains of color. "N-no. Your last post just did so well and I think it was because..." She fidgets with the blanket strewn across her lap and chews on that bottom lip again.

"Because?" I press.

"I mean...the filter and the hashtags might've helped. It was also still kind of early when we posted that pic so that probably helped too. I think engagement is always better in the morning...and I mean no one hates seeing an attractive contractor in their element." She's rambling now, and her cheeks are that same shade of tomato red as earlier. I find it more than adorable.

Get it together, Levi.

"Aly," I interrupt her and try my best to stifle a laugh. "I'm just kidding."

Her mouth instantly flattens to a hard, straight line. She's squinting at me now and..."I thought you were really mad!"

she whines, swatting at my bicep again, the heat of her touch returning to the spot.

"How could I be mad when you just admitted I'm... how did you say it? An 'attractive contractor'?" I waggle my eyebrows and shoot her a cocky grin.

Her eyes widen. "Shut up," she says, and tosses me half of her blanket, an invite to scoot closer. "You're going to miss the elevator scene. Don't think I didn't notice how you used to conveniently always need a drink after this scene. I saw those misty eyes head to the bathroom for a tissue instead."

I roll my eyes, and snuggle deeper into the couch, wondering if she notices the way our knees touch under the blanket, and if it's affecting her the same as it is me. Pretzel pops her head up from under the blanket then each front arm, one at a time. I shoot Aly a quizzical look and she chuckles and shakes her head. "It's a thing she does. I don't think she knows she's a dog."

"*Weird,*" I mouth, eyeing Pretzel suspiciously. Aly nods in agreement. She's propped her head on her hand, staring at the TV. Something about this just feels so *right.*

It reminds me of when we were in high school, of lazy weekends filled with romantic comedies in my basement with Adam and Aly, snacks strewn across the coffee table. Now, things feel much the same yet completely different. The air between Aly and me is charged with something that was missing when Adam was here to act as a buffer.

Then I remember, he can't be here because of *me*. Guilt washes over me like a heavy spring shower. Still, I can't help but imagine that this is what life could look like every night if I stayed in Charleston, and Aly and I were together. Evenings with boxes of chicken tenders and waffle fries scattered across the coffee table, Aly in her worn pajamas that are honestly the sexiest thing I've ever laid eyes on. We've fallen so effortlessly back into our friendship that I can't help but wonder, could it *finally* be more than a friendship this time?

Aly excuses herself to the bathroom and I notice she grabs her phone on the way. Jealousy courses through my veins at the thought of her texting Hudson, and I immediately breathe into the palm of my hand for a quick sniff test. Is it me? Did I do something wrong? Frantically, I replay the last couple of hours in my head.

Suddenly, I feel a buzz in my pocket. It's coming from Adam's phone and I glance around quickly to see if Aly is still in the bathroom. The door is still shut so I pull it out and notice one new text from...*her.*

Dear Adam,

What I thought could go down in history as one of the worst dates of my life turned into one of the best nights of my life. I can't give you all the details now but I promise I will soon. Love and miss you.

CHAPTER THIRTEEN

ALY

"Oh no," I groan and set my phone on the counter at Bloomie's. "No, no, no."

"What's wrong?" Emma asks, coming from the back holding a teetering box of vases in one hand and a bucket of daisies in the other. I take the box from her and set it on the counter. "You don't look so good."

"My dad just left me the voicemail of all voicemails." Suddenly, I'm queasy, and the room around me starts spinning.

"And?" Emma presses.

I hesitate. I know if I tell her what the voicemail is about, I'll also have to tell her about my evening with Levi, and I don't know if I'm ready for that. We spent one harmless evening watching a movie together where *maybe* I ended up snuggling into the crook of his arm, and *maybe* I pretended to fall asleep because I didn't want to move. I'm not ready to talk about how when we woke up this morning, we snuggled under a blanket on my deck with steaming mugs of coffee to watch the sunrise over the harbor. I definitely don't want to let her know that it felt natural and right and like butterflies and rainbows were bursting from a pinata in my belly, because that would mean admitting that I *like* him. And that will not do.

What I definitely don't want to admit to though, is the way he looked at me right before he left, like he wanted to kiss me. So I went in for it, and was rewarded with a kiss on my cheek and a pat on my head.

He *patted my head*. If that doesn't scream *friend zone*, I don't know what does.

"You might want to sit down," she says, pulling two stools from under the counter and gently backing me into one. She settles into the other, her brow creased with worry as she asks, "Is it Adam?"

"No, no," I say quickly. "I went and saw him this morning. He's doing well and his vitals are all back to normal. Everything is healing as it should. He could wake up any day now."

I don't tell her the doctors are baffled as to why he hasn't yet. They say the same thing when I visit every morning.

"It could be today, it could be next week, or it could be never," one brash doctor told me today. Granted, he was only doing his job, and you can't sugarcoat things when you're a doctor. Still, the lack of reassurance set the mood for the entire day. This voicemail from my dad is the icing on the cake.

Her brow softens and her shoulders relax a little, while my body does the opposite. "Tell me what it is, Aly."

"I don't wanna," I whine and try to slip from my stool. She instantly pushes me back down and stares into my eyes, one hand on each shoulder.

"It's about Levi, isn't it?"

"No," I say and cross my arms in the most *mess with me and find out what happens* expression I can muster.

"What then? Are you constipated? You kind of look constipated when you make that face."

"I'm not constipated, you weirdo." I reach over and grab my phone to hit play on the voicemail. My father's barking tone instantly covers the soft Leon Bridges playing through the store's speakers.

"Alyson Jayne! I swear if you don't have a good reason for leaving Hudson at dinner last night, I will make you regret ever stepping foot away from that dinner table. If you don't call me back immediately. Oh I could just…How could you do that to my star employee? I would hate to think I had a selfish, unkind, daughter…"

Emma reaches over and hurriedly turns it off. "Ooookay. That was more than enough. Wow."

I cover my face with my hands and give it two seconds before Emma pries them away.

"Why do you let your parents get to you like this, Aly?" she says, once again looking into my eyes.

"I don't know," I groan. "They're still my parents, you know? I still want them to be proud of me."

Emma gives me a sad smile and nods. "So you left in the middle of your date, huh?" she says, still holding onto my wrists, making me feel even more trapped. I start to squirm when she says, "Why'd you do that?" She's wiggling her eyebrows so hard, I'm afraid one might slide right off her face.

"I got a text from Levi during dinner," I mutter.

"Oh, so it was a booty call!" she squeals and Pretzel, who was being a good girl and napping under the prep table, gives a sharp little yip. She settles down once she realizes everything is okay and is asleep again in seconds, one arm tucked under her stuffed unicorn.

"No, definitely not a booty call," I say, and waves of embarrassment wash over me as I think about how wrongly I read his goodbye this morning.

"So he picked you up from your disastrous date and then what?" She bounces up and down, my wrists still in her hands, causing my arms to flap like wings. My glasses threaten to fall off, so I scrunch my nose in a failed attempt to keep them on.

"Emma, my glasses," I say, hoping she will release me. Instead, she continues peppering me with questions.

"Are his arms as really big as that picture on Instagram made them look? Did you see him shirtless? Is he a good kisser?"

"If you must know, I wouldn't know if he's a good kisser because when he was leaving this morning, I went in for a kiss and he patted my head instead!"

I'm pouting like a full on child, but I don't care. I even stomp my foot for good measure and I'm considering throwing myself on the ground for a full on pity party.

"We're going to revisit the fact that he patted your head in a minute. But first, you said when he was leaving *this morning*?" Her eyebrows are doing that thing again, except this time it's more suggestive.

"We fell asleep on the couch!" I halfway fib because I did fall asleep...eventually. After I finished breathing in all the woodsy, pine scent of him I could while curled under his muscular arm. I mean seriously, who's armpits smell *that* good?

She narrows her eyes. "On opposite ends I'm sure." I bite my lip and look anywhere but her. "Okay fine. I won't make you share all your secrets *yet*. But this head pat...what do you mean you went in for a kiss and he patted your head?"

"It's exactly like it sounds. We were both in the doorway. He looked like he might want to say something. His eyelids started getting all droopy, he was definitely looking at my lips, *and* he had even started tilting his head a little to the right. I closed my eyes and leaned in and instead of kissing me back, he swerved, kissed my cheek, and very awkwardly patted me on the head. It was the most mortifying experience of my life." I shudder thinking about it again.

"Like this?" she asks and pats my head roughly. My glasses slide down my nose again and I shoved them back up. "Or this?" She begins caressing the back of my head and I swat her away.

"Just a little...tap tap," I say, tapping her head with maybe a little more force than necessary. "Whatever. It doesn't matter. He's going back to California anyway, so there's no point in wrapping myself up in something that didn't happen because even if it did, it would never work."

"Oof," Emma says, smoothing out her hair. "That's not good."

Leave it to her to tell me exactly how she feels about the situation. She's always said exactly what's on her mind, so telling me her exact thoughts shouldn't come as a surprise, but it still stings nonetheless.

"It really would've been a lot easier to hear you say, 'Oh Aly, I'm sure it was a misunderstanding and I bet he's beating his head against a wall right now for how embarrassed he is!'"

"Sorry, Aly. That doesn't sound good, though, and you know it," she says as she unpacks the box of vases and arranges them on the nearest empty shelf. I cringe and my stomach churns at the memory. "I think you should probably figure out what you're doing about your dad, though."

"Ignore him?" I say, removing the lid from the trash can and dangling my phone above it. She shoots me a pointed look over her shoulder. I roll my eyes but replace the lid. The bells above the door chime as two girls walk in and make their way around the store. "Can you cover for me while I call him back?"

She nods, and I make my way to the back to call Dad.

"Hello?" he answers on the first ring. His voice is so similar to a bark, I'm expecting Pretzel to chime in at any minute.

"Hey…Dad," my voice wavers. "What a pretty day. How are you and—"

"Cut the crap, Alyson. Why did you leave Hudson in the middle of dinner last night? He was taking you out on his dime, having the decency to give you a chance, and you left him sitting there, all alone. Are you not ashamed of yourself? This isn't the daughter I raised."

Probably because you didn't raise me, a nanny did, I want to say. Instead, I bite my tongue and say, "I'm sorry, Dad. I didn't feel well."

"You didn't feel well? And you couldn't ask him to take you home?"

"I was too…embarrassed," I squeak.

"Rightfully so," Dad says, and blows a puff of air loudly, right into my ear. "Thankfully, he's agreed to come over to the house for dinner tonight. I expect you to be there so you can apologize to him face to face for what you did and come to your senses about him."

"Dad I—" I start before he interrupts me.

"Six o'clock, Alyson. Not a minute past. Do you understand me?"

"Yes," I mutter. Before I can say goodbye, he's already ended the call.

Chapter Fourteen

Aly

I arrive at my parent's house with a minute to spare and park my Vespa next to Hudson's ridiculously fancy car. Pretzel is strapped to my chest again, complete with swim goggles, and I rush to remove them before anyone can see. I know, I know. I'm protecting *Pretzel's* feelings, something I never thought I'd do.

I push open the heavy oak door and follow the chatter into the dining room. My parents and Hudson are already seated around the table, laughing as if they were a happy little family. Rage bubbles deep inside me at the sight of Hudson in Adam's typical seat.

"Put the dog in the basement," Dad commands as soon as I round the corner.

Good to see you too, Dad! "Yes sir," I squeak and quickly run down the stairs.

I pull the stuffed unicorn out of my bag and pour water into a bowl for her. As I'm turning to leave, I see them—a whole pile of fresh laundry, full of mom and dad's undergarments that I *know* Pretzel will love. I kick the basket over. Pretzel looks at me, to the basket, and then at me again with eager eyes.

"Do with that as you please," I tell her. "I saw nothing." I bend to give her a quick scratch under her chin then run back upstairs.

Conveniently, the only seat open at the table is beside Hudson. In an instant, he's up and pulling out my chair for me, but he won't even look at me. He's clearly faking being hurt. I know he is because he keeps doing this annoying forced sigh thing then looking toward the ceiling wistfully.

"Thank you, Hudson," I say as politely as I can muster.

"Well," Dad says, clearing his throat. "Let's take care of the elephant in the room, shall we?"

He's staring so intently at me, I expect laser beams to shoot out of his eyes at any second. Mom's sitting beside him, her lips pursed so tightly, I'm concerned about the circulation of them.

"Hudson. I'm sorry. I shouldn't have left you at dinner last night and not told you what I was doing. That was incredibly selfish of me, and I hope you forgive me," I say in a rush, trying my hand at sighing and looking as wistful as possible. I think I do a pretty good job.

Hudson meets Dad's gaze before speaking up. "I'm not going to lie, Aly. What you did was incredibly hurtful. I sat there for an hour before I had our waitress go check on you, only to realize you weren't even there." His voice cracks with fake grief, and it's enough to make me want to hurl.

"An hour?" I screech. "You were going to let me suffer for an entire hour before you had someone come check on me?"

"You said you were having lady issues!" Hudson retorts, and my mom gasps and covers her mouth with a perfectly manicured hand. I bite my lower lip to keep from chuckling at that. I really had said that, hadn't I? "I drove by your house last night to check on you and..." He drops his gaze to the table for a beat, as if summoning the courage to continue. "Do you know how it felt to see that?" he whispers. He shoots mom and dad a look too, just to make sure they're fully engrained at this point.

Oh no. Oh no, oh no, oh no.

"What? What did you see?" Dad presses.

"A clown car, that's what," Hudson answers smugly, all traces of sadness gone. It's a side of him I've never seen, and that's when it hits me. I'm not sure how I didn't see this coming. Hudson has absolutely no interest in me as a person, only a relationship with me so he can climb the ranks in Dad's company. His voice drips with ice as he continues. "A clown car that belongs to some contractor who thought he could make it in California but apparently can't."

Hudson has declared war.

"His business is doing just fine, for the record. And how dare you creep around my house late at night, you weirdo!" I shoot back.

"Did you have a boy over last night, Alyson?" Mom asks, horrified. I look between Mom and Dad, knowing there's no way out of this one.

"It was late when I drove by, too," Hudson smirks. He knows exactly what to say to make a southern momma madder than a hornet.

Before she can say anything else, I ask, "Why were you driving past my house late at night? Doesn't anyone else think that's weird?"

"I wanted to check on you! I picked up ice cream and chocolate for you because I thought it might help your, you know...lady problems." Hudson's eyes glimmer in a way I've never seen, and I'm honestly a little creeped out.

"He wanted to check on you, Alyson! Where are your manners?" Mom asks.

"My manners?" I ask, incredulously. "He sent back every wine glass they brought him for a smudge that wasn't even there. He ordered the spaghetti squash for me and proceeded to order himself a steak. He tried to make me feel guilty for eating garlic bread!"

"That's enough, Alyson!" Dad booms, his fist slamming into the table so hard, the silverware jumps.

While I would love nothing more to defend myself and tell everyone the rest of the story from my point of view, it would be no use. Even if they listened—which they wouldn't—my words would go in one ear and out the other. Hudson can do no wrong in my parent's eyes. On the other hand, I can do nothing *right*.

Beneath the table, I clench my fists so tightly, I'm sure my nails are biting crescent moons into my palms.

"We are so sorry, Hudson," Mom says. "We're not sure what's gotten into our daughter. I would presume it has something to do with Adam's condition. I hope you can forgive her."

"How dare you blame this on Adam? This is *his* fault!" I point at Hudson.

Hudson turns to me now and his poor, scorned act is back. "I'm sorry you didn't have a good time on our date, Aly. I'll admit, I was too hard on the waitresses. I was so nervous, and I just wanted everything to be perfect. Really, *I* should be apologizing to *you*. I'm so sorry, Aly."

Oh, gag me with a spoon.

He reaches for my hands under the table, and if he notices my fists are clenched, he doesn't say anything. "Please let me make it up to you. Go with me to the end of summer charity gala."

The reminder makes my stomach drop.

Every year, my parents host an over-the-top charity gala. I try not to whine about it too much because they always raise quite a bit of money to donate to the children's hospital. It's the only thing that keeps me from thinking my parents are monsters. It's a black-tie event that the wealthiest of Charleston's residents attend every year. Women wear overpriced, fancy dresses with their hair teased to the heavens, men wear suits with tails, and everyone seems to be in competition for who has the most Benjamins in their wallet.

Adam and I are forced to put on something my parents deem appropriate, sit at a table with them, and look like the happiest little family in Charleston. I've always had Adam to rely on through when the "when are you going to join the family business?" and "when are you getting married and settling down?" questions get to be too much.

Mom and Dad give me eager looks from across the table, and I know if I say no, we'll be right back in the same situation we are in now.

Suddenly, a small, furry torpedo rockets past, a pair of Dad's underwear clenched between her teeth. In a second, Dad is up and out of his seat, chasing Pretzel around with another ever-present golf club, swinging wildly at the floor.

Pretzel turns and locks eyes with me. I swear in that instant, she's finally decided we're a team.

She darts under the table to lose Dad, and I follow, weakly yelling, "Pretzel...noooo...bad dog."

I find her pawing at the front door, clearly ready to leave. When Dad and Hudson catch up, she drops the underwear, and I hand them over, which my father accepts with a look of disgust. He unfolds them, and sure enough, the whole butt is chewed out.

"Sorry about that," I laugh weakly. "I must've forgotten to—"

"If that dog ruins one more family dinner..." Dad warns. My mom finally joins us and is furiously trying to unscrew the cap from a prescription pill bottle.

"Take your blood pressure medication, dear," she says to my dad, shaking two out and trying to force feed them to him.

"You're right," I tell Dad. "I better get her home and put her in time out. Thanks for dinner!" I open the front door, but Hudson grabs my shoulder.

Before he can say anything else about the charity gala, I cut him off. "Hudson, It was a pleasure seeing you as always," I choke out before all but running toward the Vespa.

Dear Adam, I could really use one of your big, smothering hugs right now. I'm really not having a good day.

I'm sitting on a bench by the waterfront, wondering for the millionth time how much longer I'm going to have to keep updating Adam like this. Beside me, Pretzel is happily slurping up a celebratory pup cup for her actions earlier. As a pair of dolphins jump in front of an incoming cargo ship, my phone buzzes with an incoming text.

Chapter Fifteen

Levi

"Glenda, we've gone over this a million times. The code to the front door is one-one-one-one."

"I've tried that and it's not working! I'm just going to Face-Time you, okay?"

"I really don't think that's—"

An incoming FaceTime call jingles my ear, and I mentally kick myself for deciding it was a good idea to buy Glenda an iPhone and add her to the company plan a few months ago. I know she can get in the door just fine, so she must've recently discovered FaceTime and wants to try it out.

I pull the phone away from my ear and peer down at the screen. It's a perfect shot right up Glenda's nose. "Hey Glenda, you might want to turn your camera around so I can see the lock."

"I was getting there," she bristles then adds, "millennials," under her breath. "Watch. I type in one-one-one-one and nothing happens."

"Glenda...you're hitting the seven, not the one."

"Isn't that what you said to do?" I watch as she hits the one four times. Sure enough, the door slides open, exactly as it has every day for the past three years she's worked for me. When she asks to see my face, I'm definitely onto her game.

"Long time, no see!" she beams.

Before I can respond, Adam's phone buzzes in my pocket. Forgetting I'm on FaceTime, I pull it out and read the text, a million things going through my mind. Why is Aly having a bad day? And why do I still have Adam's freaking phone? I set it back on the counter with an all too familiar dullness seeping into every corner of my chest.

"Why do you have two phones? Also, why is your face all red and blotchy? And why are your eyes all googly?" Glenda asks, one eyebrow raised in suspicion.

Shoot. Of all the people to forget I was FaceTiming, it had to be the nosiest person alive. "It's a...um..." I stutter. A flashback of the time I cheated on a test in elementary school and confessed because I felt so guilty comes to mind. I've never been a very good liar.

"Spill the beans," she commands, practically quivering with excitement.

My hand finds my beard and I stroke it absentmindedly, wondering how much to tell her.

"Remember my friend Adam?" I finally ask. When she nods, I continue. "Our things got mixed up at the hospital after the accident, and somehow I wound up with his phone."

"Mhm," she says. "Go on." She's holding the phone under her chin, so I'm once again blessed with the view of the inside of her nostrils.

"What do you mean, 'go on'?" I ask.

"That doesn't explain why you have his phone *now*."

Glenda might be overbearing, a little irritating, and more than I can handle most days, but she *is* trustworthy. And honestly, I'm dying to confess to someone. I'm chewing on my lower lip nervously when suddenly the phone moves so close to her face, all that fits into the screen are her heavily lacquered red lips that are commanding me to *tell her right now*.

"Okay, so...I saw he had a text from his sister. I didn't mean to read it but it popped up on the screen, and I was curious why his sister was texting him when he's, you know...in a coma. Long story short, she's been sending him updates on everything he's been missing so when he wakes up, he has an easy way to catch up."

"That's very sweet. But you're still not telling me why you have his phone."

"I wanted to return it, I really did. But every time I got around to it, something came up." Suddenly, I'm thankful for the nostril shot because there's no way I could look her in the eyes after confessing that. I sound like a complete coward.

"You like her, don't you?"

I nod, and she grins wickedly. "Teenie and I had a feeling you liked her. Actually, I know you really like her because your cheeks are all red and splotchy again."

I pretend not to hear, even though I'm sure she can feel the heat radiating from my face through the screen. "Glenda, I really need to get off here. Call me if you need something *important,* okay?"

"Oh, one more thing!"

My thumb hovers above the end button, and I'm tempted to go ahead and hit it. One little tap and the suffering would be over. "Yes?" I ask instead.

"I'm coming in for the Fourth of July! I'm finally going to meet my best friend, Teenie!" In her excitement, the phone winds up face down on the floor. Muffled clapping comes through the speakers, then seconds later, she picks it up and dusts it off against the side of her pants. Satisfied, she brings it back to her face. "Are you excited to see me?"

"Who invited you?" I ask, rubbing my temple.

"You're mom, silly." She's looking at me as if they've been lifelong best friends and didn't only meet last week over the phone.

"That's…great," I say with feigned enthusiasm. "Listen, I've really got to go."

"Right, okay. Bye!" She ends the call, and I'm left wondering how in the world this crazy woman wove her way not only into my life, but my mom's, too. Then, I remember Aly's text to Adam. On a whim, I pull up her name on my own phone.

Me: *Ice cream?*

Aly: *Tacos?*

Me: *You'd rather have tacos?*

Aly: *What?*

Me: *I was asking if you wanted to get ice cream with me.*

Aly: *Oh. I thought we were guessing each other's favorite foods. Yes, ice cream sounds great.*

Me: *I'll pick you up in twenty.*

Aly: *I'm down at the waterfront. I have Pretzel if you want to bring Hank.*

"You wanna go for a ride, buddy?" Hank's ears perk up, and he's instantly up and trotting to the door. I squish all ninety pounds of him into the back of the Teenie Mobile and head toward the waterfront.

Aly is sitting on a bench, Pretzel in her lap, shoulders hunched, the wind blowing her hair around her face. She's resting her head on her hand, staring out into the harbor, watching people and boats zoom past. She startles when I reach her, then gathers her things to make room for me.

"I didn't see you!" she says. "I must've been zoned out. Here." She pats the seat next to her, then leans down to pat Hank on the head.

"How was your day?" I ask.

"Not the best."

"Anything ice cream can fix?"

She frowns and gazes toward the harbor again. "Mmm, maybe not *fix* but it can definitely help."

Something is definitely wrong. I'm contemplating if it would be overstepping to ask or rude not to when she blurts, "I miss Adam."

My heart sinks at the way her voice breaks. I want to wrap my arms around her, to tell her everything's going to be okay, but something tells me I probably shouldn't. Not after the way I awkwardly left her house the other morning.

Aly had actually gone in for a kiss, and I had no choice but to dodge and kiss her cheek because...I didn't have a toothbrush.

And I *know* my breath is horrendous in the morning. I'm a snorer. We're talking deep sleep, mouth wide open snores. I'm not proud of it, but it is what it is and...okay. Maybe I was also a little embarrassed that she may have heard me snoring. But to make matters worse, *I patted her head.* I should've just yelled, "FRIEND ZONE," and chest bumped her while I was at it.

"How is he?" I ask, returning to the present.

She sniffles and blinks back tears. "His labs are great. His vitals are fantastic. Everything says he should wake up any day now. But I can tell the doctors are getting discouraged. As much as I want to stay positive, I'm starting to worry. It's hard, you know? Talking to someone every single day and then not being able to at the drop of hat, without any warning. I really miss him."

"I went to see him this morning," I say. A tear slides down her cheek and lands on her hand before I gently brush it away with my thumb. Before I overthink it, I thread my hand through hers and instant warmth courses through my body. "I don't know what the future is going to be like, Aly. But I do know that Adam is a fighter and he's got the best support system."

"He doesn't, though!" she cries. "My parents barely acknowledge the fact he's in the hospital. They just go around acting like nothing has changed and everything is fine. Did you know this evening, they made me have dinner with Hudson at their house and forced me to apologize to him? I felt like a toddler again. And to make matters worse, they apologized on my behalf by saying surely my attitude was because of 'Adam's condition.' It's ridiculous." She blows out a puff of air and settles back into the bench. "Hudson even had the audacity to ask if he could take me to the charity gala at the end of summer, when I know he's only acting interested in me to get a promotion at work."

"First thing's first. Adam has *you*," I say, fighting the urge to get straight to talking about Hudson. I'm desperate to know her thoughts about him, to try and change her mind if she's interested in him. "You're an amazing sister, and I know he's missing you, too. Second," I start hesitantly. "Are you upset about Hudson?"

"You're kidding, right? He was going to leave me in the bathroom for an entire hour before he sent someone to come check on me. He can go play in traffic. Can I tell you something?" she asks, quieter now, absentmindedly stroking Hank's fur as he and Pretzel cuddle next to us on the bench. I nod and stroke her hand with my thumb. "I've been texting Adam little updates. I don't want him to wake up and feel like he's missed anything. I want him to have an easy way to catch up. It might sound silly, but it helps to still feel like I can talk to him a little bit, you know?"

Now's the time to tell her! "I think that's sweet," I say. *Tell her now! Tell her you have Adam's phone!* I clear my throat and run a clammy palm along my pants leg. "Aly...I—"

She stands, cradling Pretzel under her arm. "I think I'm done talking about it for today. I'm sorry to spill my guts on you like that, but thank you for listening." She stands on her tip toes and kisses me lightly on the cheek. Smooshed between us, Pretzel lets out a low growl. "Enough sad for tonight though. Let's go get ice cream."

"Yeah, sure," I say through a fake smile.

CHAPTER SIXTEEN

ALY

"Pretend like I'm not even here," I say, pointing my camera toward Levi. Instantly, he freezes, his movements becoming stiff and awkward. He's been tiling my shower all morning, and he has grout smeared in the most adorable places—a little smudge on his cheek, a few streaks on his forearms, *oh those forearms.* Every so often, he stops and runs his hands through his hair and a little gray streak is added. Basically, with his faded blue jeans holding up a tool belt that sits just right on his hips and the black tee—the limits of which are being tested by his chest and biceps—he looks like he stepped out of a Calvin Klein ad. He is every girl's wildest fantasy. Well, maybe not *every* girl, but definitely mine.

"You just said 'pretend like I'm not here,' so now the fact that you're here and pointing a camera at me is all I can think about," he protests. "Can't you just take a picture of the shower when it's done? Maybe like a before and after?"

"I could," I agree. "But I didn't take a before picture. Plus, no one's going to like a picture of a shower. But you know what they will like? A picture of *you* tiling the shower. We've been over this. Remember how the last picture blew up?"

"Glenda said no one called to schedule anything, though, and I thought that was the whole point," he grumbles.

"Patience, young grasshopper. Just turn around and do what you do best."

Levi mumbles something else I can't make out and then turns around, much to my displeasure. *Not.* I'm admiring the view, watching him smear more grout onto the tile and then setting it perfectly on the shower wall, biceps bulging, veins snaking around his arms and down to his large, calloused hands.

I'm considering the pros and cons of pretending to wipe at a smudge on his arm when he says, "What exactly do I do best?"

I snap the photo right as he angles his head and gives me a cocky little grin. A glance at the screen confirms it's a perfect shot.

"Contractor stuff," I say. "Duh."

"My dad does contractor stuff. Do you want to take a few pictures of him, too?"

I think of Levi's dad, with his bushy mustache and belly made round from years of Teenie's southern cooking. "I could certainly take a few father-son pictures if that's what you want."

As he reaches for another piece of tile, he chuckles, low and throaty, and my mouth turns to cotton. "Would you classify him as a *hot contractor,* too?"

Gulping audibly, I'm aware that something has changed in the last couple of hours we've been holed up in this bathroom together. Is it because it's too hot? Or because this bathroom is too small for two people? I need to do something before I embarrass myself, and fast.

Without thinking, I dip my hand into the bucket of grout and sling it at him. As the gray sludge drips from his face, he growls, "You did *not* just do that."

Shrugging, I whisper, "But I did. What are you going to do about it?"

I bite my lower lip and follow his gaze toward the same bucket. I hop from my perch on the sink as he leaps from the step ladder. We both lunge toward the bucket, but he wins by a split second and plunges both hands inside. With a wicked grin, he pulls out two fistfuls of grout and holds them over my head.

"Don't do it," I plead.

"Too late," he replies and opens his fists. Grout pours down my face, covering my glasses.

"You just declared war," I growl. In an instant, Levi bolts from the bathroom. I attempt following him, but run into the wall because I can't see. I rub my forehead and wipe a small window on each lens of my glasses with my shirt hem, then take off after Levi. He's pacing by the couch, keeping an eye on the door, no doubt planning his exit strategy. Slowly, we circle the coffee table, offering up threats.

"You better hope I don't catch you." I like to think I'm spitting the words like venom, akin to a movie heroine. Instead, they sound like a bad impersonation of Moana.

"I think I'm pretty safe considering I heard you run into the wall a minute ago," he replies, a handsome smirk playing at the corners of his mouth.

"You did?" I gasp, letting my guard down. My hand flies to my face, my cheeks turning a rich shade of red to match my forehead. Moana would be so disappointed.

"You might want to put some ice on that," he calls over his shoulder as he flies out of the living room and out the front door. Hank and Pretzel emerge from the bedroom and chase after him, eager to join the fun.

"Pretzel, attack!" I yell with a chuckle. I had absolutely no intention of hurting Levi, I really didn't. Pretzel, on the other hand, must've taken my command seriously. Before I can stop her, a furry missile streaks through the yard and grabs ahold of Levi's pant leg. Furiously, she shakes her head, the fabric of his jeans clamped firmly between her surprisingly strong jaws. Hank, unfazed that his human is being attacked by a wiener dog, wanders over and sits beside me with a grunt.

"Um, Aly?" Levi asks, the panic in his voice unmistakable. I watch as he unbuttons his pants and slides his leg free from the side Pretzel doesn't have in her mouth.

"Sorry! Can't see you. Might bump into the porch railing if I try to help."

His pleading eyes meet my steely gaze, and I can't help but smirk when he reaches up and waves an invisible flag. Pretzel is growling now, really getting into it, and I decide it's probably time to step in. When I reach Levi, Pretzel gives one last furious shake of her head that's enough to send Levi to the ground. He lands with a *thunk*, and Pretzel uses the advantage of his position to fully remove his pants.

Moments later, she's running triumphantly through the yard, Levi's pants trailing after her like a victory flag. Levi, meanwhile, is lying at my feet in the grass, clad in nothing but his black tee and...unicorn boxers. I double over in laughter when Hank clumsily knocks into the backs of my knees. I land ungracefully on top of Levi, still cackling when Hank and Pretzel shoot past, playing tug of war with the jeans.

"Do you...have...unicorns...on your boxers?" I ask between cackles and gulps of air.

"They're old," he clarifies with a defensive tone. "I ran out of clean clothes and found these wadded up in my drawer at Mom and Dad's. They were a gag gift from Christmas a few years back. And in my defense, I've never worn them until now, and I didn't think anyone would see them."

"That's definitely what I would say, too," I say with a giggle and a wink. Levi reaches up and gently sets my glasses back on my face. It's then I realize I'm still lying on top of all gloriously-chiseled six feet of him. Without warning, memories of our movie night flood my mind, most of all how he didn't want to kiss me when he left. Like a bucket of ice water over my head, embarrassment replaces something a little steamier, and I push myself off him to stand. He does the same, and we both awkwardly look anywhere but at each other.

Thankfully, Pretzel diffuses the tension by running up with Levi's jeans. I take them from her and unfold them. The hems are completely shredded from playing tug of war with Hank, and of course, the crotch is ripped wide open.

"Ahem." We both look over to find Mr. Barnes is standing there, watering his front lawn again. I can only imagine what he's thinking after witnessing a wiener dog and a German Shepherd running circles around a man wearing unicorn boxers, hands planted on his hips.

"Sorry, Mr. Barnes! We'll be going inside now."

He clears his throat again, and Levi and I stifle our laughs until we're back inside.

"We could always take a picture of you like *that*," I offer, gesturing to his pants-less body. "People would go crazy over a contractor with a soft side. Who knew underneath all those clothes and that gruff exterior, you'd have unicorns on your boxers?"

"I already told you! They were a gag gift!" he exclaims, then plops on the couch. "Besides, I think posting indecent pictures on the internet is a crime."

"Tell that to the hundreds of women who message you a day," I mutter and sit on the other end of the couch.

"What?" he asks, brows knitting together.

"Nothing," I say with a wave of my hand. "It's not important."

"What are you doing for the Fourth of July?" Levi blurts. He's fidgeting with the hems of his boxers, tugging them down as far as they can stretch.

"Adam and I usually go to the top floor of his building and watch the fireworks from there, but I'm not sure this year..." I trail off.

Levi chews his bottom lip and for a moment, it's enough to distract me from how badly I miss my brother. "What are you doing?" I ask.

"Unlike business in California, business here is actually booming. Dad mentioned having a big cookout with all the employees and our friends and I was going to see if maybe...you'd want to come? I think they're lighting off fireworks at the end of the night, too."

My gaze travels back to his mouth, and scenes from all my favorite romantic comedies of couples kissing under fireworks play in my mind.

"Is that a no? It's fine if you can't...or don't want to," Levi says when I don't answer, shoulders slumping in defeat.

"No! Sorry," I say. "I mean no, that's not what I meant. I would love to go to the Fourth of July cookout with you."

His shoulders perk back up a little, and it would be incredibly adorable if he hadn't turned down my kiss a few days ago. If things hadn't been so awkward, if I hadn't put myself out there, ready and willing for a smooch, I might even have my hopes up right now. But I refuse to put myself in that situation again. He made it clear that we are just friends then and I'm sure this invite is only to cheer me up because of how badly I miss Adam.

"I can pick you up around four if you want?" he asks. "As long as you don't mind the Teenie Mobile." He grimaces, and mental images of the Mini Cooper are enough to make me throw my head back in a cackle.

"It's not that bad," I lie.

"It's *terrible*," he says. "Oh, speaking of Teenie, I guess her and Glenda are friends now and she's coming in for the cook-out too."

"Glenda, as in your assistant from California? How did they become friends?"

"Long story," he says with a shake of his head. "I figured I better warn you. She can be a lot to handle."

"She can't be that bad."

I peer at Levi's boxers, unable to help myself. When he catches me, he reaches for a pillow to cover himself. "What are you staring at, you perv? Haven't you ever seen a man in boxers?"

I giggle and point to one of the unicorns. "Get your mind out of the gutter. They're winking. It's adorable."

His face blushes crimson. "Considering you're pants-less, I totally get it if you want to be done for the day."

"Are you kidding me?" he says. "We've got work to do. I'm not letting this little mishap stop me." He gets up and puts both hands on his hips in his best Captain Underpants impersonation, which is enough to send me into hysterics.

"Why do you keep laughing at me? You're going to give me a complex."

"You don't want to go home and grab some pants?" I ask, still chuckling.

"We have way too much stuff to get done to be taking meaningless pants breaks. I can work just fine in what I'm wearing. But if these unicorns are offending you..."

"No offense here," I giggle. "By all means, let's get back to work."

He shoots me a wink and heads back to the bathroom, leaving me staring after him—and not hating the view. Unicorns and all.

Dear Adam,

Tourists are swarming in from all over for the Fourth of July. I'm hoping you wake up by then but if you don't, I'll video it all for you. I know the Fourth is your favorite. I'm actually going to watch the fireworks with Levi this year at his dad's company cookout. Why didn't you tell me he was such great company? I love having him here, but it's not the same without you. I miss you. I'd love to say Pretzel also misses you...but she's pretty fond of Hank. Love you.

Chapter Seventeen

Levi

*A*m I really tiling Aly's shower in my unicorn boxers right now?

That's the million dollar question that pinballs through my mind. I'd also like to know where exactly this newfound confidence came from. I did not under any circumstances plan on anyone seeing my underwear today, least of all Aly, and especially not *these*. I could only hope she believes they were truly a gag gift.

Spoiler alert: they were not. They're actually my favorite, perfectly soft and supportive in all the right places.

Aly hands me another piece of tile, and it's not lost on me how dangerously close to my butt she is as I stand on this ladder. Why couldn't I have worn my fancy Calvin Klein ones that I keep reserved only for date nights? Date nights that actually never happen. Trying to grow a business in a state completely foreign to you is tough work and most days, after twelve hours on job sites followed by coming home to fix the bookkeeping errors Glenda had made, I was exhausted, and dating was the last thing on my mind.

I can't help but wonder if she's at least enjoying the view, then mentally berate myself. *Keep it together Middleton. This is your best friend's sister! Don't go there.* But oh, how I wanted to go there. I wanted to go there worse than when I was a middle schooler desperate to peek behind the door of Spencer's in the mall only to have my ear jerked by Mom.

Originally, I planned to leave last week, but something about this girl had me pushing back my flights to stay in Charleston a little longer. Maybe even more than that. Ideas of working for my dad have occupied what's left of my brain when I'm not thinking of Aly, and both are more than seductive thoughts. If I stayed in Charleston, I could stop worrying about making ends meet in California. I could help Dad when he so clearly needs any extra hands he can get. *And* I could be with Aly. If she's even still interested after that colossal screw up the morning after our perfect movie night. I try not to dwell on how disappointed she was and instead focus all my attention on making sure she knows how I feel about her at the cookout. Maybe then, I'll have the cojones to man up and tell her how I really feel about her.

Two hours later, she hands me the last piece of tile. After it's positioned perfectly in the top corner, we both take a few steps back and marvel at our handy work. A vibration from the counter pulls Aly's focus, and she picks up her phone to study it.

"That thing has been blowing up ever since we started again." Outwardly, I'm the picture of calm, cool, and collected, but really, I'm wondering who could possibly be trying to reach her so badly, if they are an attractive male, and how I'm going to knock him into yesterday if he's interested in her.

She giggles and swipes open an app on her phone. "It's blowing up because of *you*," she says. "If you thought people loved that pic of you hanging up a light fixture, people are *obsessed* with you tiling a shower in your underwear."

All the color drains from my face, and my stomach instantly plummets to the ground. "Please tell me you didn't actually post me in my underwear," I choke out. I'm not ready for the world to know I love these unicorn boxers.

"If you would just download the app, you could look for yourself." She's still scrolling, and her glasses start sliding down the bridge of her nose. I fight the urge to gently push them up and set them straight. "Not happening. That's one stress I don't need in my life. I need to know though, am I really gracing the social media world with my unicorned butt?"

"No," she replies, the corners of her lips twitching with pleasure at my discomfort. "I'm not *that* heartless. But I did post a picture of you tiling it before you lost your pants, and the people love it." She turns the phone to me and for a moment, I'm awestruck by the number of people who have liked a photo of *me.*

"What are these?" I ask, pointing to the top right hand corner. A ridiculous number of red notifications are glowing there, too.

"Those are nothing," she answers quickly. *Too* quickly. She white-knuckles the phone, and her eyes have grown to the size of golf balls.

"If they're nothing, let me see them."

"Nope." She manages to get one leg around me in an attempt to flee the bathroom, but I wrap both arms around her from behind. With one hand, I reach blindly for the phone. Aly is doing everything in her power to make sure I can't see it, and for a second, the way her body is shimmying and writhing against mine distracts me from my mission.

"Let me read just one!" I spin her around with both hands on her hips. We're close enough now that I can trace constellations in the freckles smattering her sun kissed cheeks and nose. Her breath is warm on my neck, and her chest rises and falls with every breath.

"Why?" she asks in a small voice, grasping the phone in both hands, hanging on for dear life.

"Why are you hiding them from me?" I ask, finally aware this isn't a game to her at all.

"I don't want you to see them," she whispers.

"Are they mean? Are you trying to protect me from some cyber bully? I can handle it, Aly." I don't use social media, but know enough about it to understand that people can be cruel for no reason other than their own sick and twisted pleasure.

"The exact opposite actually." She offers me a tight-lipped smile.

"I won't look at them if you don't want me to." If she doesn't want me to see what's hiding behind those little red notifications, I'm sure she has a good reason, and I trust her.

"Technically though, it *is* your account though," she offers.

"I promise, whatever they are, you can delete them, and I'll never ask about them again."

"Women *love* you," she blurts. "Every day, a hundred new messages come in asking for your number, wanting to know if you'll take them out to dinner, or sometimes... sometimes, they're a little more aggressive than that." She looks away from me, but not fast enough for me to miss the way her cheeks flush crimson.

"And that makes you unhappy?" I ask, tipping her chin up with my index finger.

"It makes me feel a lot of different ways," she admits. Her cheeks blush impossibly deeper and gently, I pry her bottom lip free from her teeth with my thumb.

"You can delete them," I assure her. "I don't want to see them anyway."

"You don't?" she asks, her voice barely above a whisper.

"Nope. We did this to drum up business, remember? That's it."

"You don't even want to see one?" she presses. "Some of these girls are *really* pretty."

"Right now, I don't want to focus on anything but what's in front of me." My voice dips and my eyes trail down to her swollen bottom lip.

This is it. This is the kiss she deserved a few mornings ago. I *did* brush my teeth this morning however, and now nothing can stop me. I close my eyes, lean in, and prepare myself for a soft landing on that perfect mouth. Instead, she dips her head and shimmies out of my grasp. When I open my eyes, she's standing in the doorway with a satisfied smirk, bouncing lightly on her toes.

"Where are you going?" I ask, a little breathless and a whole lot embarrassed.

"I'm hungry," she says simply, all traces of the shyness from moments ago gone. Instead, she looks smug, like she's just won a game I didn't know we were playing.

"You coming or not?" she asks, cocking an eyebrow.

With a frustrated sigh, I nod. "Can we stop by my house for some pants first?"

It's a gorgeous summer evening with a gentle breeze flowing off the water when we pull up to a seafood restaurant, after we've swung by my parents' so I could grab a new pair of jeans. I open the back of Aly's Bronco to find Pretzel and Hank tangled in a snuggle.

"Come on Hank," I say, and pat the tailgate. When he doesn't budge, Pretzel lets out a little growl and Hank reluctantly gets up. "You do know you're about eighty pounds bigger than she is, right?" I whisper in his ear.

"Pretzel can't help that she's a strong-willed woman," Aly coos, clipping on Pretzel's leash. "I would say she's independent, but have you noticed how inseparable they've been lately?"

I nod and follow her to the hostess stand. We're seated on the deck outside, and both dogs settle easily at our feet. In the harbor beyond, boats zip by, and the city is already bustling with tourists preparing for the holiday.

"Is this your first Fourth of July in Charleston since high school?" she asks after our orders have been taken.

"Yeah, it is," I answer, wondering if she's also thinking of the last time.

It was the summer before graduation. Aly had recently gotten her braces taken off and if I thought I couldn't stop staring at her before, it was nothing compared to after. Something between us had changed in the few months prior. Gone were the innocent thoughts of how cute my best friend's sister was. Instead, I had found myself daydreaming about her, wondering where she was, who she was with, and what it would feel like to kiss her.

Adam and I had made plans to surf on Folly all day for the Fourth of July, and he was annoyed when we showed up to find Emma and Aly already out in the water at our favorite spot. Secretly, I was anything but annoyed. Aly had just caught a wave into shore when she looked up, and gave me a small smile. She was wearing a yellow bikini that left me a little breathless and did things to my chest that I hadn't experienced before.

"Don't worry, we're leaving," she had said with a wink. "I think we caught all the good ones. Don't you know the surf is best here first thing in the morning?"

A second later, Emma had dragged her board onto the sand and gave Adam a hard time about something I couldn't quite hear. My mouth was too dry to respond to Aly, so I stupidly nodded.

That night, Adam and I had climbed onto his roof only to have Aly and Emma join us. "What are you doing?" Adam had asked, irritation lacing his voice.

"If you're dying tonight because Mom and Dad find you up here, I am, too. I don't want to live here alone." She had spread out a blanket on the other side of me and laid down, propping her knees up. All I could think about was how we were only inches apart, and all it would take was one small shift for our hands to touch.

"I'm going to grab a soda. Anyone want one?" Adam asked, getting up to climb back through the window.

"I'll take one," Aly had said. "Grape please."

"Me too," Emma added. "Actually, I'll come with you so I can help you carry it all. I think we need snacks too."

Above me, fireworks exploded into the night sky, but all I could think about was tasting grape soda off Aly's lips. Suddenly alone and emboldened by that fact, I rolled over to face her and propped my head up in my hand.

"Grape, huh?"

"It's the best," she said, wrapping her arms around her bare knees.

"Are you cold?" I asked. The air was warm but the goosebumps across her skin were noticeable.

"I got a little bit too much sun today," she said.

"Here," I said, sitting up and wrapping one arm around her shoulders.

"Thanks," she replied. A chill rippled through her body, so I squeezed her closer.

"You looked great out there today, by the way," I said. "You surf better than anyone I know."

Aly dipped her head. "Thank you, but you're pretty great yourself."

"Not as good as you." I turned toward her, and my gaze traveled to her mouth, where she nervously bit her lower lip. "You're something else, Aly."

Her eyes sparkled in a way I had never seen before. Heat spread across my cheeks like a wildfire when she leaned in, resting a hand on my knee. The warmth of her hand, even through my jeans, was electrifying.

Our mouths were inches apart, and all it would take was one little tilt of my head and we'd be—

"We're back!" Adam's voice boomed as he climbed back out onto the roof, Emma right behind him.

Aly shot back from me and eyed her brother nervously. I did, too. If he had noticed anything between me and Aly just now, he'd chosen to ignore it.

The waiter sets our food on the table, breaking me from my reverie. "In some ways, this is the same old city it's always been, but in others, it feels like I came back to a completely different one, too."

"You didn't come home at all?" she asks. "Adam never mentioned you being back in town again, but you never know." I search her face for any sign of judgment but am met only with a creased forehead and eyes sparkling out of sheer curiosity.

"I didn't," I admit, with a shake of my head. "At the time, I thought I was doing the right thing, stepping away from here and focusing all my time and energy onto growing a business out there. I thought if I just spent every waking second putting everything I had into that business, I had no choice but to succeed. Now, I know that's not the case." A sarcastic snort leaves my mouth, surprising me.

"Don't give up hope quite yet," she says softly. "If it's meant to happen, it will. Your next big break could be right around the corner. Just think, Harry Styles could call you at any minute asking for you to build his next home." She smiles in an attempt to lighten the mood.

"That's the thing though," I start. "At the time, I didn't think it would be so crazy to one day work for a celebrity. I just thought if I could find someone who knew someone, someone who could vouch for my work, my ethic, I would get there. So far, that hasn't happened." The back of my neck heats, and I rub at it with my hand. I hadn't planned to unload all of this to Aly, and the confession has me both relieved to finally be getting it off my chest and embarrassed, too. "When I was eighteen, I thought anything was possible."

"It still is, if you want it to be. Don't give up," she says, but her smile is tight, and she quickly glances toward the water after briefly meeting my gaze. "If I could do it all differently, I would. I would've come home for Christmas, and for my parents' birthdays. I would've made sure my dad wasn't getting overrun with work, and I would've absolutely made sure that I didn't lose touch with my best friend."

"You and Adam were so close," she says, her voice faraway. "It made his day when he realized he would be working in the same city as you."

"Honestly, those few days he was in town were some of the best days I'd had since moving out there. We picked right back up where we left off all those years ago."

"Why didn't you even call?" she asks, seeming genuinely curious.

I sigh and toy with the glass of water the waitress sets down. "Truthfully, I knew I would get homesick. I thought if I could erase all my ties to Charleston, it would be easier. I know that's not the case now. If I could do it all differently..."

"Everything happens for a reason," she says. "I'm just glad you're back now."

Her face tells me everything else she wants to ask but won't. *But for how long?*

Chapter Eighteen

Aly

“Don’t stay out too late,” Emma says as we put the last buckets of flowers back in the cooler for the night. Some people in the south would consider it a sin to work on the Fourth of July, but I only consider it a success. With all the tourists in town, we made more money today than we did the entire first month we were open.

“It’s the Fourth of July,” I whine. “You have to stay out late to watch the fireworks.”

“It’s the only piece of advice I could think of to give you,” Emma says. “I was going to say don’t do anything I wouldn’t do, but we know how that would end up.”

“Emma!”

“What? You’ve always been the more reserved of the two of us,” she says with a shrug.

"Speaking of, who are you spending the evening with?" I ask her.

She turns her back to me as she grabs the final bucket. "I'll probably just lay low and go to bed honestly. I'm whooped. You're paying me time and a half today since it's a holiday, right?"

I don't miss the way she's avoiding my question, but if she doesn't want to answer me, I won't press. Emma has always kept her love life more of a mystery, seeming only to float from one tourist to the next.

"Commitment issues," she told me once when I caught a tourist dropping her off at work one morning. "It's way more fun knowing you'll never see them again."

Emma is totaling up our cash sales from the day when she looks up and says, "Are you sure there's nothing going on between you and Levi?"

"We've already gone over this."

"He's been here for how long now? Almost a month? Has he told you when he's going back?" She stuffs the cash into a bag and then walks into the back room to drop it in the safe before I can answer.

When she returns, I say, "No, he hasn't. We haven't really talked about it either. I think he's staying for you," she says, waggling her eyebrows.

"I think he's staying because he feels guilty for what happened to Adam and doesn't want to leave me alone. I'd bet money that once Adam wakes up, he'll go back to California without giving us a second thought." Once the words are out, I realize that's only what I'm telling myself to keep from getting my hopes up then crashing and burning when he leaves again. After all, he's already left once.

"You don't think he'd really do that, do you?" She grabs a rag and polishes a stubborn spot on the counter where a lily stained it orange.

I shrug. "I'd like to think no, but you never know."

Emma frowns, pausing for a second before saying, "At least try to have fun tonight, okay?"

"One of us has to, considering you're going to bed," I say with a glower.

"And I couldn't be more excited to dive under those covers and snuggle up with a bag of gummy worms. You know, I agreed to work for you because I thought this job would be fun. Turns out, it's more stressful than the time when I was a paranormal tour guide."

"If you keep going to bed with gummy worms, your teeth are going to rot. Also, I still don't understand why you, the person who has to turn on HGTV after seven p.m. because it's the only channel that doesn't play trailers for upcoming scary movies, took that job."

"The pay was good! Plus, the boss was hot. The only reason I quit was because my doctor was considering putting me on blood pressure medication."

"That guy had frosted tips and wore a denim blazer. He was *not* hot."

Emma shrugs, and I follow her to the front door where she locks up and we walk outside. Pretzel gives me an approving lick on the chin when I slide her swim goggles on and strap her to my chest, which feels like second nature now.

"I can't believe I haven't seen a meme of this somewhere on the internet yet." Emma doesn't even bother to hide her laugh, simply shakes her head in disbelief and walks to her car.

After I've dropped Pretzel off at home, I push open the door to Adam's room, the beeping and whirring of the machines hooked up to him still something I'm unable to get used to. There's a stuffed weenie dog tucked beside him, a sign that someone else has visited him recently, and my spirits lift, knowing he hasn't spent the day alone.

I pull a chair out and scoot it to the edge of his bed.

"Happy Fourth," I say, pushing the hair off his forehead and lightly tracing the scar there. "I wish we could watch the fireworks together." I wait for something, any sign he's heard me. If he could only squeeze my hand, anything to let me know he can hear me...but he doesn't. Instead, beeping fills the silence, and I let out a weary exhale.

"I need to tell you something," I say, quietly and take his hand between mine. "I know you can't hear me right now, but not telling you doesn't feel right. Levi has been a good friend to me while you've been gone, and I'm starting to realize I have feelings for him. I've tried to ignore them, but I can't. I know he's your best friend, and I'm so sorry, Adam. But he makes me happy...really happy."

Between my palms, Adam's hand twitches, and my pulse spikes.

Can he...can he *hear* me?

I stare at it, willing it to happen again. "Adam?" I ask. For another hour, I sit there, praying that twitch wasn't some kind of fluke. When it doesn't happen again, I reluctantly push my chair back and give him a kiss on the forehead. I consider telling the doctors what happened, but decide against it, somehow knowing in my heart he heard me.

Before leaving, I push the curtains on his window back in hopes that the firework show somehow makes it to this side of the hospital so he can see.

After visiting Adam, I'm putting the finishing touches on my hair when a knock comes at my door.

"Come on in!" I yell, and then immediately hope to God it's Levi and not some creep. I quickly close the bathroom door and peek out through the crack.

"Oh good, it's just you," I say with a wipe of my brow opening the door wider when Levi rounds the corner.

"What are you doing?" He's wearing a red, white, and blue button-up shirt, and I can't help but notice the top two buttons are undone, leaving a section of his tan, hard, and broad chest out for all to see. I barely catch a glimpse of the tattoo on his pec when he notices me staring and shifts uncomfortably.

"A compass?" I want to reach out and peel back his shirt to get a better look, but from the way he's shifting from one foot to the other, I can tell he's uneasy.

He dips his head and lowers his voice when he says, "I got it in California. I wanted to be reminded that no matter where I am, I always know the way home."

"It's beautiful," I tell him. "Can I see it?"

Shyly, he pulls back his shirt, giving me permission to stare unabashedly at his muscular chest. Unable to resist the urge any longer, I trace the compass lightly with my index finger. His tan skin quivers underneath my touch, and I suppress a satisfied smile, knowing I have that effect on him.

"Why were you hiding behind the door like a weirdo?" he asks when I reluctantly pull my hand back. I shove it into my pocket, afraid if I don't, they'll roam as they please over the rest of his body.

"After I said to come in, I realized you could've been a serial killer." He shakes his head and lets out a little chuckle.

Defensively, I add, "You never know. I'm almost done, though. I just need to swipe on some mascara and I'll be ready."

He's leaned up against the doorframe and there's only a few inches of space between the top of his head and the opening. How have I never noticed how tall is he? He's not wearing his usual ball cap, and he's styled his hair with something that smells piney and citrusy. My pheromones practically squeal.

"Aly?" Levi asks.

"Huh?" I ask, mid-mascara swipe. I'm so close to the mirror, my breath fogs the surface and I swipe at it with a towel.

"I asked why you're making that face?" He's staring intently at my reflection in the mirror with a cocky grin. I immediately snap my mouth shut, which had been wide open in the shape of an O.

"All girls make weird faces when they put on mascara. It's a thing," I say, trying my best to finish without opening my mouth again. I accidentally smear it all over the side of my cheek and glance at him out of the corner of my eye, knowing he saw it all. "Can you just maybe look the other way for like two more seconds?"

He chuckles and turns his back. "One Mississippi, two Mississipp—"

"Done!" I yell triumphantly and shove the wand back into the tube. I rifle around in my makeup bag until I find my trusty tube of ChapStick and swipe some on. When I look up, Levi's gaze is latched onto my mouth. He gives a nervous little cough, then offers his arm. I take it, and flip off the light on my way out. Pretzel is already prancing by the door, no doubt eager to greet Hank, who must be waiting in the Teenie Mobile.

Sure enough, when we walk outside, Hank's sitting in the passenger seat, his nose pressed against the glass, eagerly awaiting Pretzel. After Levi shoves him into the small backseat and Pretzel hops in, we're on our way to his parents' house.

"Did Glenda make it in?" I ask.

"She made it this morning. She's been here for less than twelve hours and has already managed to hide articles about the benefits of power walking all around the house like little Easter eggs. I found one in my sock drawer right before I left, actually."

I let out a low whistle. "Yikes."

"Mom has found her long lost best friend. Dad, not so much. She's dying to meet you, by the way."

We pull up to his parents' a few minutes later. Cars are already parked three deep on both sides of the yard. Someone has strung Edison lights across the driveway and the wrap-around porch. Christmas lights wrap each palm tree, and if this is what the front yard looks like, I can't wait to see the back, where the party is. I step out of the car and slip on Pretzel's leash. The music is already blaring and the sounds of "Take It Easy" by The Eagles floats on the breeze.

"There you are!" I hear when we make our way to the back-yard. Before I'm able to connect a voice with a face, two short, plump arms wrap around me and squeeze. The top of her head rests right below my chin, and I try my best to not let the fact that whoever this is has their face smashed in my chest bother me. Finally, they release their arms and step back, but only a few inches. The unmistakable scent of Bath and Body Works Cucumber Melon lingers.

"You must be Aly." A short, older woman, wearing cat's eye glasses and a Hawaiian print, button up shirt, pants practically up to her throat beams up at me. "I've heard so much about you."

"Glenda?" I try. Seconds later, another woman of the same stature and almost similar outfit joins us and gives Glenda a little hip bump like any cool, best friend would do.

"Hey Tina!" I say, and offer my left arm in a more appropri-ate side hug. She returns it and points to Glenda.

"I see you've met Glenda," she says, and winks. "It's good to see you. I've been meaning to make my way down to your flower store, but the mister has me so busy with keeping his books, it's hard to find any time to escape!"

"No worries at all," I assure her. "Thanks for having me over this evening. This is lovely." I mean that, too. As beautiful as the front yard is, the backyard is even better. More lights have been strung around, and there's even a dance floor near the water's edge. A warm breeze blows off the water, and everything looks and feels magical enough that Walt Disney himself could have created it.

"Help yourself to anything you want," Tina says with a squeeze of my shoulder.

Glenda gives an exaggerated wink to Levi and then whisper-yells, "You're right! She *is* pretty."

"Glenda!" Levi exclaims. "I didn't say that."

"You didn't?" I tease, bumping his shoulder with mine.

"I didn't say that," he huffs and runs a hand through his hair. "I mean...I do think you're pretty. I would just never talk to Glenda about it." She and Tina are poorly suppressing laughs, and he shoots her a pointed look.

"Aren't you glad I'm here?" Glenda asks Levi. Before he has a chance to answer, she's up on her tiptoes, leaving a big, fat kiss on his cheek. Then she and Tina walk away, arm in arm and giggling over shared whispers.

Chapter Nineteen

Levi

"**G**ross," I mutter, then swipe furiously at my cheek with my palm. I turn to Aly and grimace. "So that's Glenda. Don't ask me how she got hired."

"I love her," Aly says with a frown, rubbing at the spot on my cheek I must've missed with her thumb. "I suspect you do, too. Also, remind me to ask her what brand of lipstick that is because it's not budging."

"Knowing her, it's probably expired AVON from the flea market. And I don't *love* Glenda. I tolerate her." My tough guy facade is only centimeter thick, though, and I think Aly sees right through. I *do* have a soft spot for Glenda, and after seeing her and my mom together, I think the reason I hired her all those years ago is because she reminded me of her and eased the sting of homesickness a little.

"Do you want to grab a bite to eat?" I ask Aly, hoping to turn the conversation away from my meddling assistant.

"Sure." We head toward the tables loaded with sides, then stop by the grill, which is manned by my dad. He's wearing an apron that says "Smokin' Hot," and Aly giggles when she notices it.

"You like this?" Dad says, turning left and right before striking a pose with a hand on his hip. Aly's giggles turn to full blown laughter, and my dad finally says, "What can I get you?"

"A hot dog, please." He loads up her plate then turns toward me. Without asking, he slides a burger onto my plate, knowing I think hot dogs are the most disgusting food on the planet.

Aly cocks an eyebrow and looks between the two of us. "Levi wouldn't touch a hot dog if he was paid," Dad explains. "Never could get him to eat them when he was a kid."

I shrug. "Guilty as charged."

"It's good to see you, Aly," Dad adds with a wink.

After munching on hot dogs and chatting with some family and Dad's work crew, the sun begins to sink, and everyone scatters around, trying to find the best seat to watch the fireworks. Aly points to a spot by the water, but I shake my head. "I have somewhere else in mind. Follow me."

I offer my hand and she hesitates only a second before taking it. I wrap my large fingers around her soft, small ones, and I can't help but think they meld perfectly together. I lead her toward the gazebo at the end of the dock that juts out into the marsh. It's quieter out here, and although we're still able to hear Tom Petty crooning from the speakers, it's much softer now. My eyes travel to Aly, who's taking in the setting with obvious appreciation. Her eyes glitter with the reflection of the sunset sinking below the water, and they're so blue, so dark and cool that I wish I could jump into them and float around weightlessly for a small eternity.

"Did you do all this?" she breathes.

I nod, my ears heating with embarrassment. Under the gazebo—which has been strung with more lights—there's a blanket for us and a dog bed at the foot, large enough for both Hank and Pretzel. The dogs have already found it and curled up together, Pretzel being the big spoon. I flip on the light and that's when everything comes to life, more vibrant now with the glow of the lights against the darkness settling around us. I nod, my ears heating with embarrassment.

"This is beautiful," she tells me and sits on the worn blanket, patting the spot next to her. We're sitting so close, our shoulders brush, and if the fireworks don't start soon, I'm going to be the one putting on a show after combusting from the nearness of Aly Bloomington.

When the sun fully sets, the first hint of a firework cuts through the sky with its noisy whine. For a split second, everything is silent until a vivid red explodes across the night, followed by blue and white streaks. I glance over at Aly, whose eyes are wide with excitement and, instead of watching the sky, I enjoy the show from the reflection in her eyes. Slowly, our hands drift closer and closer until our pinkies touch, too. Quietly, she hooks her pinky with mine and dips her head low enough to rest on my shoulder.

She sighs and says, "I love the Fourth of July. I think it's my favorite holiday."

"I would have pegged you for someone who's more obsessed with Christmas," I say.

"I *do* love Christmas. But the Fourth of July...there's just nothing like it."

"What makes it so special?" I ask.

She watches the next few fireworks dance across the sky before saying, "It's summertime, everyone's happy from spending the day out in the sunshine, and everyone seems so carefree, if only just for the day."

Aly's joy is so palpable it's almost enough for me to ignore the ache in my chest. This morning, I received a phone call about a job I had bid on a few months back. It's a complete kitchen and bathroom remodel for a television producer and could be exactly what I need to finally breakthrough in California. It's going to mean heading back soon, and I know I need to tell Aly. Right now, though, she's so happy I can't break the news to her. I promise myself I'll tell her tomorrow.

I unhook my pinky from hers and lean back to rest on my elbows.

When the show is over and the outdoor lights at the house have all been flipped back on, Aly gets to her feet, the sparkle in her eyes from earlier gone. She quickly swipes at them then replaces her glasses, and we silently walk back up to the party.

People are packing up and heading home, and Aly says, "Do you care if we swing by Bloomie's? I need to make a deposit before work tomorrow, and I forgot to grab the bank bag earlier."

"Sure," I tell her, my heart still at the gazebo. It's obvious she's disappointed, but I don't know why. For me, watching the show with her was magical, so I can't figure out why she's upset.

Glenda finds me standing in the middle of the yard while Aly says goodbye to my parents, and stares at me uncomfortably before I finally acknowledge her with a raised eyebrow.

"Looks like you two were pretty cozy." She gives me a goofy smile and makes googly eyes behind her glasses. I roll mine in return. "What did she say when you gave her back the phone?" My eyes dart around frantically in search of Aly and my heart thumps loud enough, I'm sure she can hear it, wherever she is. At my reaction, Glenda's eyes narrow and her hands settle on her ample hips. "You haven't, have you?"

"Shh," I whisper through gritted teeth. "There just hasn't been a good time." It's a flimsy excuse at best, but it's all I've got.

"Boy," she warns. "You're in too deep now to go and screw this up."

"Don't you think I know that? I'm going to fix this. I just don't know how yet."

"Better figure it out soon," she says.

Before I can respond, Aly walks up and stands beside me.

"Everything okay?" she asks, glancing from Glenda to me.

"Yep. Just typical Glenda stuff," I mutter through my clenched jaw.

"It was so good to meet you, Aly, and Pretzel." Glenda gets on all fours and gives Pretzel a kiss on the head. "I hope to see lots of both of you in the future. He's typically way less grouchy when he's got you around. When we're in California and he's not seeing anyone, he's practically intolerable if you know what I mean..."

"GLENDA! For the love," I say, exasperated. Aly stifles a giggle and attempts to give Glenda a quick side hug. Undeterred, Glenda envelops her in a full frontal body hug and gives her a sloppy kiss on the cheek to match.

We finally make our escape and minutes later, we pull up outside of Bloomie's.

"I'll just be a minute," Aly says as she steps out of the car. Pretzel jumps out after her, and I watch through the big, picture windows as they disappear into the back. I'm parked in the middle of the road, and I wait as long as I can until a car behind me beeps, so I circle around the block a few times before finally finding a spot a few stores down. After parallel parking and ensuring the Teenie Mobile's eyelashes aren't brushing the tailgate of the truck in front of me, Hank and I weave in and out of tourists on my way to Bloomie's. King Street is crowded tonight for the holiday, with the locals and tourists alike out celebrating.

Aly didn't seem like she wanted me to follow her in, but after the silent car ride here and her rigid posture in my passenger seat, I know we need to talk. I push open the door, expecting to find her walking out with her bank bag under her arm, but she must still be in the back room.

"Aly?" I call. "It's me. I didn't want to scare you."

"I'll be right out," she calls back in an unusually high voice, followed by a sniffle. I hear the rustle of papers followed by a muttered curse word.

"Everything okay?" I ask, pacing in front of the cash register and running my hands through my hair.

"Mhm," she mumbles followed by another sniffle. I lean against the counter with my forearms, head in my hands, wondering where exactly tonight went wrong.

"Levi?"

I look up to find Aly closer now, silhouetted by the faint light from the back room. I wonder how long she's been here, watching me wrestle with the weight of the evening.

"You didn't have to come in."

"I wanted to make sure you were okay." My eyes travel from her swollen bottom lip to her puffy, red-rimmed eyes.

"I'm fine," she promises, not breaking eye contact, but the splotches on her tear-stained cheeks tell me otherwise. "We can go now."

I inch toward her, slowly trailing my hand along the counter, unsure if what I'm about to do will make the evening better or only more confusing. "What if I'm not ready to go yet?" My voice is husky and foreign to my own ears. Even in the dim security lights, I don't miss the way the skin on her arm prickles with goosebumps when I reach out to tilt her chin up. Her inky blue eyes have filled with tears again, and my frown overtakes my entire face. "Tell me what's wrong."

"Can I tell you a secret?" she asks, her voice barely above a whisper.

"I'll be your secret keeper for the rest of your life if that's what you need, Aly." A glimmer of hope streaks across her face but is gone as quickly. She backs away and my hand drops to my side. She opens and closes her mouth a few times before finally finding the right words. When she speaks, her voice is so quiet, so soft, I strain to hear her.

"Watching the fireworks with you was...magical. Everything I ever dreamed about. And it got me thinking that your time here is limited. I'm surprised you haven't gone back to California already. And I'm so afraid you'll leave and never come back. I'm afraid that you'll only be mine until Adam wakes up and once he does, once you know I'm okay, that'll be the end of whatever this is. I'm afraid of trying this, *us*, and getting so used to having you here, that when it's all ripped away from me, when you never come back to me again, I won't know how to put my pieces back together. I won't let myself fall for you, Levi. I can't. I'm not ready to be wrecked by you."

"I landed a job with a huge client back in California," I blurt.

Aly's eyebrows draw together. "What? When?"

"I got the call this morning. I was going to wait to tell you because tonight was just too perfect, but that doesn't feel right anymore."

"When do you go back?"

"A week or two. It starts in August."

She's silent for so long I'm fully prepared for her to storm away and never speak to me again. Instead, she says, "This is what I was afraid of."

"Aly..." I reach for her and pull her into me, her head resting right under my chin. I breathe in her coconut shampoo and after a couple of seconds, the tension from her body begins to melt away. She softens and finally wraps her arms around me. "I don't know when I'm coming back," I admit, through a shaky breath. "But I know that when Adam wakes up, because he *will*, Aly, I'm not ever going to forget about you. I don't know what my future in California will look like after this job, but I do know that I will never, ever leave you. Not the way I did last time. I'm willing to give this a shot and figure out a way to make it work if you are." I use my thumb and forefinger to tilt her head back so I know she hears me when I say, "I want you, Aly, more than I've ever wanted anything in my life. I want *us*."

"Promise?" she asks shyly, peering up at me through mascara-smudged glasses.

"I promise."

Her lips are only inches from mine, and I can smell the pineapple gum she popped into her mouth on the way over. More than anything, I want to kiss her right now, to taste that pineapple gum, and make the fantasy I've had since high school a reality. Instead, I kiss her softly on the forehead, my lips lingering. When I pull back, she audibly swallows then lifts to her tiptoes.

Her mouth meets mine slowly at first, testing the waters with a gentle caress. When I don't pull back, our kiss turns into something more, something wild and hungry, in seconds.

Finally, I'm giving into the feelings I've suppressed for years. From the way she's kissing me back, it appears she's doing the same. Her hands trail up my back and into the curls at the nape of my neck, and I suppress a feral sound that tries to escape my throat. When she hitches one leg around me, all bets are off, and I hoist the second one up, too, lifting her off her feet. I back her onto the counter and a vase crashes to the floor, but neither of us notices or cares.

Then she pulls back and rests her forehead on mine. We're both a little breathless, and I can't believe I just had the privilege of tasting her strawberry-red mouth.

"I want us, too," she says on an exhale, then dips her head to find my lips once again.

CHAPTER TWENTY

ALY

I'm in the middle of another YouTube video, this time learning how to install new flooring for the bathroom that Levi just finished tiling, when I'm interrupted by Emma's contact photo filling the screen with an incoming call.

"Why are you awake so early?" I ask after answering.

"Good morning to you, too," she chirps. "I was just up and wondering how your date night went. Why are *you* up so early? I know you're an early bird, but whatever you have smeared all over your face tells me you've been up for a while."

I squint at myself in my tiny reflection on screen before remembering there's a huge mirror in the bathroom. Sure enough, caulk covers my forehead and is tangled in the waves of my hair. "I couldn't sleep," I admit.

"You don't look annoyed for once. You actually look…happy? Aly, is that you?"

I try to hide my grin and look heavenward. "Okay, yes. I like Levi. You win. Can you leave me alone now?"

"Not until you give me all the details. And I mean *all* of them." She squints and gives me a dopey smile that makes me crinkle my nose in mock disgust.

"He kissed me in Bloomie's last night after the fireworks, and it was probably the most magical thing I've ever experienced," I confess, my voice easy and floating as if along an invisible breeze. If I were a cartoon, hearts would be popping from my eyes.

"You *did*?" she asks, jumping up and down.

"Did you cut your hair again?" I ask, realizing when her hair flops into her eyes she's got bangs that were not there before.

"I did. I regret it. End of story."

"You usually only get bangs if you break up with someone. Emma, tell me right now. Are those break up bangs?"

"No, they're bored bangs." She bows her head in shame and her shoulders drop. "They'd probably look a lot better if I would've had them professionally done. But you were out last night, I'd already finished my *Gilmore Girls* rewatch, and after a bottle of wine, TikTok really made me think I could do it."

"Oof," I grimace. "I think you should maybe make an appointment."

"They're kind of growing on me. They kind of just scream, 'Mess with me and see what happens. If I'm crazy enough to do this to my hair, imagine what I could do to you,' you know? Anyway, my hair is not the point. This kiss is, and I want details. Nitty gritty, sloppy, saliva-covered details."

"Ew, not happening."

"Was there tongue?" she asks eagerly.

"He's leaving for a few weeks to finish a job," I say instead of giving the details she wants. "And then he's coming back...*hopefully*."

I blow out a puff of air and pinch the bridge of my nose. Unease slides down my spine as I say it out loud, like I gave into my teenage dream without considering the future—which is *not* how it felt in the moment.

"You mean you don't know?" she asks with raised eyebrows.

"He wants to make us work so I mean, yeah, I think so. I hope so." I shrug, realizing how it sounds. I promised myself I wouldn't get my hopes up but here I am—hopes higher than Dolly Parton's hair.

"Well now that I know most of the juicy details, because I know you're not telling me *everything*, I'm going back to bed."

"Emma, we have to be at the store in an hour," I remind her, looking pointedly at my wrist even though my watch is missing.

"Right, so I can sleep for forty-five more minutes," she says defensively.

"You're a mess," I tell her.

"A mess you love," she coos. "See you later!"

"No, see you *soon*—" I start, but before I can finish my sentence, she's ended the call.

As I'm turning the open sign around, the Teenie Mobile parks in a space in front of Bloomie's. Levi uncurls himself from the driver's seat and stretches, clearly uncomfortable in the too-small car. He turns my way and must notice me standing in the doorway, because the smile he flashes me has my knees going weak.

He's wearing his signature black V-neck, ball cap, and faded blue jeans, but somehow, each time I see him, he gets better looking. Or maybe it's the fact I now know what it's like to have his lips against mine, and how his hands feel in my hair...

I snap my mouth shut and do a quick drool check when he reaches the door. He bends down and effortlessly gives me a tender kiss on the cheek, like it's a thing we do, a thing we've done for years. My cheeks heat, and he shoots me a cocky little grin, pleased with the effect he's had on me.

Pretzel, also excited to see him, flies out from her spot under the workbench and paws at his leg before rolling over onto her back. He bends down and scratches her belly before straightening to face me.

"Do you have plans this evening?" Levi asks. Behind me, Emma stands at the cash register, pretending to count the till. Little does she know, I'm fully aware she's "counted" the same stack three times.

I consider his question with a tap on my chin. I can admit I have zero plans and go out with this incredibly attractive man, or I can play it cool.

"Did you have something in mind?" I say, proud of myself for not sounding too eager.

"I wanted to see if you'd like to go on a boat ride with me this evening? We can watch the sunset." A grin spreads across my face at the way his cheeks flush.

"I'd love that," I reply. "Are the dogs coming, too?" He nods then reaches for my hand, giving it a squeeze before he promises to pick me up at closing and turns to leave. I watch him walk away, gaze lingering a little too long on the way his jeans mold to his backside.

I float through the rest of the day, barely able to focus on getting our orders arranged, my mind occupied completely with thoughts of Levi and our date tonight. I feel like I'm in high school again, all day dreams and blushes for the boy I have a crush on.

The day passes slowly, and Emma is no help, taking every opportunity to make fun of what I'm sure is a starry look in my eyes.

Finally, though, it's the end of the day, and a thrill shoots through my body when Levi pulls up right as I'm flipping the sign from *open* to *closed*.

He unfolds himself from the Mini Cooper, the sheer manliness of him completely at odds with the femininity of the Teenie Mobile. It's a study in contrasts, but a testament to how confident Levi is that he doesn't let this turquoise vehicle take away from that.

Emma and I step onto the sidewalk, and I lock the door behind us, then turn to face Levi.

"Have fun, you two," she says with a wink.

Levi smirks at me. "Did you tell her about last night?"

My smile in response is shy, blush creeping into my cheeks. "I might have mentioned it."

His grin grows. "All good things, I hope."

Deciding to mess with him, I say, "Nope. I told her you're a terrible kisser and your breath is atrocious."

He gasps, then pulls back and covers his mouth with a hand.

I chuckle at his response. "I'm just kidding, obviously."

He pretends to wipe at a bead of sweat along his brow and lets out a pent up exhale. "You ready?" he says, walking to the passenger door of the Teenie Mobile and opening it for me.

I get in, and off we go.

A short ride later, we arrive at the Middleton's. When we get out of the car, Levi goes around back and pulls a basket from the trunk. I raise my eyebrows suspiciously, and he gives me a coy smile in return. "You'll see."

When he stretches out his hand, I don't hesitate to curl my fingers around his. It's a gorgeous evening but despite the warm breeze blowing off the water, my arms erupt in goosebumps when our hands come together. He leads me onto his family's boat and I follow the dogs on, taking a seat at the bow while he easily maneuvers it away from the dock and into open water.

It's my favorite time of day during the summer when we finally pull up to a stretch of secluded, sandy beach. When the sun sinks low into the sky, casting everything into a golden hue, life feels a little easier and full of promise.

Levi takes my hand and helps me from the boat, and we wade to shore. He spreads a worn quilt on the sand and drops a picnic basket atop it. The dogs have swam ashore, and are happily running around the empty beach, chasing seagulls and playing tug-of-war with a piece of driftwood that has floated in.

Levi drops onto the quilt and pats the space next to him.

"Close your eyes!" he says after I've taken a seat, and I do as I'm told, giggling when he warns me not to peek. Finally, he tells me I can open them, and when I do, I take in the mouth-watering view of not only two buttery lobster rolls, but him, standing there wide-eyed and eager. I'm not sure which looks more delicious.

"Did you make these?" I ask.

"I did not, and I told Glenda you would absolutely know but she still insisted I take them out of the containers anyway," Levi blushes.

"Glenda helped you?" I ask.

"Against my will," he snorts, then pulls out two solo cups from the basket and fills them with sweet tea. "I *did* make the sweet tea, though. Unless it's terrible. In that case, it was Glenda."

"Thank you," I manage between bites. "For everything."

"If I would've known all I needed to make you happy was buy you food, I would've tried that a long time ago," he jokes.

I shove him playfully on the arm and swallow the last bite of warm, buttery lobster. "Seriously," I say and hesitate before quietly adding, "I'm glad you came back. I know you did it for Adam, and I can't tell you how much that means to me."

For a second he doesn't say anything, simply watches me over the brim of his solo cup. Then he tucks a loose strand of hair behind my ear and leans in for a kiss. I don't allow myself more than a second to think about my buttery, greasy lips or salt-smudged glasses because when his lips collide with mine, It's only Levi, me, and the privacy of this beach.

"Me too," he whispers between kisses.

A yip erupts from somewhere below me, and I pull back to find Pretzel standing on her hind legs, staring at me expectantly.

"What's wrong, girl?" I ask and scoop her into my arms. She nuzzles into me and gives me a small lick on the nose. "I think she misses Adam," I tell Levi.

"She probably does," he says and reaches over to scratch her behind her ear. "What if..." he trails off with a half chuckle before shaking his head. "Never mind."

"What if what?" I press.

"I mentioned it before but it was a crazy idea that would never work." I pout and stare up at him through my lashes as best I can. Eventually, he caves, saying, "I was just going to suggest...what if we snuck Pretzel into the hospital? You know, just so she could see him. It might even be good for him, too. Who knows?"

"You really think we can get away with it?" My mind immediately flashes to Pretzel and me behind bars, wearing matching orange jumpsuits. I know for a fact orange is not my color and would clash horribly with Pretzel's markings. Images of the meme of Pretzel in her goggles strapped to my chest on my Vespa with the headline, "Local business owner and dog currently serving time in county jail," float around my mind as Levi takes Pretzel from me. She's all big eyes and sweet kisses for him. When she rolls onto her back and sticks out her tongue, I can't help but purse my lips in disappointment.

"She's obviously never heard of playing hard to get."

"She doesn't have to," he replies in a baby voice. "But seriously, she's small and doesn't really bark that much. I think we could do it."

His eyes meet mine and his smile is so devilish, so cocky, I melt right there under the southern sunset.

CHAPTER TWENTY-ONE

LEVI

"**A**re you sure the wigs are really necessary?" I ask Aly as I push the curly, blond wig out of my eyes for the millionth time. "And did you really need to give me boobs?" I glance down at the two oranges she shoved under my shirt and notice one is dangerously close to the waistband of my pants. I was serious when I had suggested we sneak Pretzel into the hospital, but *not* when I suggested we do it incognito. Leave it to her to go all out and come up with the most ridiculous disguises.

A typical light and fluffy giggle escapes her, and she immediately covers it with a cough and switches to a huskier chuckle.

"Did that sound real?" she whispers.

"Do you think that's what *I* sound like?" I ask, pointing to myself and accidentally jabbing at the one orange that managed to stay in place. But it rolls down to my waistband, too, matching the other one.

"Fix your..." she gestures to my chest. "All that."

I roll my eyes and reposition the oranges, but something occurs to me. "Aly, I have a beard."

She ignores me and opens the car door. I can't help but shake my head at how ridiculous she looks in a pair of my jeans, which are cinched at the waist, and a too-big flannel tucked into them. Seeing her in my worn shirt *would* be hot if she hadn't pasted a fake, bushy mustache onto her top lip. It looks like a squirrel tail and kind of makes me want to gag. She walks around to the back seat to get Pretzel, who is wearing what looks like a potted plant atop of her head. Aly insisted she'd look like a succulent if anyone happened to peer into her purse.

She trips on my work boots she also insisted on wearing though they're way too big for her and steadies herself with a hand on my bicep.

"Are you sure you don't want to change your shoes?" I ask, knowing the entire roll of paper towels she shoved into the toe of each boots can't be comfortable.

She considers this for a minute with a caress of her mustache then says, "No, I really want to look convincing." *Right.* She hoists the bag with Pretzel onto her shoulder and marches towards the entrance of the hospital. "You coming?" she hollers over her shoulder.

"Do I have a choice?" I say, catching up with her.

She pauses outside the entrance and turns on me, expression serious. "Okay, here's the plan. Don't look anyone in the eyes, keep your head down, and if anyone yells at you to stop, don't. Run. Capeesh?"

"Sounds like a great plan," I say sarcastically.

"Here we go!" She claps her hands and lets out a squeal of excitement and the sliding glass doors open leaving me to follow. She's the definition of suspicious, power walking and tripping through the lobby toward the elevators. Breaking rule number one, I look up and make eye contact with one of the security guards standing by the front desk. He gives me a quizzical look, and I immediately glance down...at the oranges that have once again slid to my belly button.

The elevator dings its arrival, and Aly and I both shove ourselves inside next to a serious-looking doctor in a white jacket and a nurse with a stethoscope around her neck.

"Beautiful day today, huh?" Aly asks the nurse in a husky tone that has my lip quivering with a suppressed smile. The elevator dings again as it reaches the second floor, letting us know we're on the slowest elevator in the world. As nonchalantly as possible, I try to fix my oranges. The nurse replies to

Aly with a quick nod, and I catch her nervous glance toward the doctor, who frowns in suspicion.

I glance at the doctor's name tag and notice he's an orthopedic surgeon.

"Fix a lot of bones today?" I ask in a high pitched, squeaky voice that sounds nothing comparable to a woman. Before he can respond to my stupid question, the elevator reaches Adam's floor at the same time Pretzel lets out a small yip.

Aly and I stare at each other, eyes wide. "Did you really just say *bones?*" she hisses. "As in *Milk Bones?*"

The nurse and the doctor face us completely. I sheepishly shrug my shoulders and avoid Aly's piercing glare. How was I supposed to know that would set Pretzel off?

"Was that a dog?" the nurse asks through pursed lips, hands on her hips.

"If you'll excuse us," Aly says, forgetting her fake voice as she steps around the nurse. I follow her lead and once we break through the doors, we run down a stark white corridor.

"Wait!" the doctor yells, but it's too late. We keep moving, not looking back, until we finally reach Adam's door, laughing hysterically as we burst inside.

Aly's hat is sideways on her head and the tears running down her cheeks have caused her mustache to peel from her face. I straighten her hat, and we both swivel when we hear an "Ahem."

"Emma?" Aly asks, confusion creasing her forehead. Shock crosses Emma's wide-eyed face but is quickly replaced by something more calm.

"Why are you dressed like that?" Emma asks, scanning Aly's disheveled appearance.

Aly lowers her purse with a devilish smile and pulls out Pretzel, who has somehow chewed through the strap holding the potted succulent onto her head.

"No you did not," Emma says, glancing between us. With a nefarious smile, she pries the wriggling dog from Aly and gently sets her on Adam's bed. Pretzel is hesitant at first, unsure of what's going on, then lets out an impatient whine when she nudges his hand and he doesn't move. Finally, she settles, curling up in the space between his arm and ribs.

"I didn't know you came to see my brother." Aly glances from Pretzel to Emma, who's jumpy behavior from minutes before has been replaced with her normally casual self.

"Well yeah, of course I do," Emma replies. "What kind of friend would I be if I didn't?"

"You're the best," she tells Emma and throws her arms around her neck.

Emma glances toward me, gaze locking on my chest. "Your lady bits are a little uneven."

"Quit staring at my boobs, you perv," I tell her before turning around to give myself a quick adjustment. "How long do you think we have before someone walks in?" I ask when I face them again.

"Probably just a few more minutes. Especially if the people in that elevator figure out where we went," Aly answers.

"What happened in the elevator?" Emma asks. Aly and I share a look before she glances nervously toward the door. "You know what? Never mind. I don't even want to know."

"Probably for the best," I say, then glance around the room, taking in the decorations and balloons with ridiculous sayings on them. "Who did all this? Every time I come, they've been swapped out for new ones."

Aly raises her hand with a nervous laugh. "It's actually time to replace some of these. Every time a balloon starts to deflate I replace it with whatever they've got downstairs."

"He's going to love this," I say, taking her hands in mine. "He's so lucky to have you." She beams, and I give her a small kiss on the forehead. I inch toward her mouth when Emma's gagging interrupts us.

Then there's some shuffling outside the door, and we all freeze. As if sensing it's about to go down, Pretzel is immediately up and soaring into Aly's arms like it's a trick they've practiced a thousand times. It's honestly quite impressive. The door opens as Aly is hoisting the bag back onto her shoulder, Pretzel safely tucked inside. A nurse steps inside and glances between the three of us.

"Everything okay in here?" she asks, surveying the room. Aly whistles and bounces on the balls of her feet, Emma stares intently at the *It's a Girl* balloon by the bed, and I'm trying to tuck my blond curls behind my ear with no success. Nothing to see here, lady.

"We had reports of a dog barking and I just wanted to..." She's staring at my oranges now. "Visiting hours are up."

"We were just leaving," I say, ushering the girls out and following them to the parking lot. Immediately, I strip off the wig and pull the oranges from my shirt. Emma grabs one and begins peeling it.

"What?" she says as she slides a slice into her mouth. "It'd be a shame to waste them."

Pretzel pops her head above the opening of Aly's bag, watching us all curiously.

"You're a good girl," I tell her and am rewarded with a few affectionate licks.

"What are your plans for the rest of the day?" Emma asks.

"I think we are putting the finishing touches on Aly's kitchen," I tell her.

"You're welcome to come help if you want," Aly suggests.

"As fun as that sounds, no thanks," she says. "I've got a hot date with my couch and Netflix."

"When my cottage is officially done, and it looks fabulous, I just want you to remember you had no part in it," Aly tells her.

"I'm okay with that," Emma replies.

I let out a small chuckle and take Aly's hand as I walk her around the passenger door of her Bronco. She slides in, and I take my spot behind the wheel.

"I can't believe you're already driving my car and we've only been on what? Two dates?" Aly jokes.

"You have to admit, it's a much more comfortable ride than the Teenie Mobile," I say and ease out of the parking space. The Bronco suddenly backfires and I look around, stunned for a moment.

"That happens a lot," she says with a wave of her hand, as if it's no big deal.

I get it restarted and navigate out of the parking lot.

"Aly, you really need to get that fixed." I flip my blinker on to turn left onto the highway.

"I need to get a lot of things fixed with this car," she tells me. "But with what time and honestly, what cash? Every last dollar I have goes into the cottage or the store. No one prepares you for how expensive being a small business owner is, especially in the early years."

"I can maybe try to fix it for you, but I don't know how much I can get done since, you know...I'm leaving soon." As soon as the words are out of my mouth, I want to shove them back in. I should've known now was not the time or place, especially after just visiting her brother.

"No, it's fine," she tells me. "Honestly, after a few YouTube videos, I can probably fix it myself."

"Aly—" I start.

"Seriously, it's fine," she says, cutting me off. She looks out the window, her shoulders sagging.

"When is Glenda going back?" she asks, fogging up the glass with her breath and tracing frowny faces into it.

"She leaves tomorrow." I hesitate before adding, "She's actually got a few calls since your last post. She's putting together quotes for them."

"Oh," is all she says, and my heart sinks lower than I thought possible. I reach for her hand. Thankfully, she doesn't pull away. Pretzel—who's sitting on her lap—growls, however, which leaves me wondering: am I making the right decision by leaving?

Chapter Twenty-Two

Aly

"You know I've always had a crush on you, right?" I nearly spit out my sweet tea at Levi's confession. He whacks me in the back, which only makes me sputter more.

"You have?" I finally manage to wheeze out. We're sitting on the back porch of my cottage, watching the sun go down, reminiscing on high school and watching Pretzel boss Hank around out in the yard.

"Mhm," he nods. "I realized you were the girl for me during the soccer game against East, when that girl kept kicking you in the shin so you tripped her during the handshake line."

"I had no idea it was going to have a domino effect and the whole team was going to fall," I justify. "How did you know it was me?"

"You were the only one who watched it all go down with your arms crossed and a smug smile," he laughs. "All your teammates were helping them up but not you."

"I asked her politely to stop, and she just kept doing it!" I throw my hands up, defensive, but I still don't regret a single thing.

"That's when I realized it, though," he says. "That's when I realized there was no one else like Aly Bloomington."

"Well, if it makes you feel any better, I've always had a tiny crush on you, too," I say on a cough, trying to cover the words.

"You've what? Sorry, it sounded like you got choked there for a minute." The grin that spreads across his face lets me know he heard me loud and clear. I give him a playful shove and try to ignore my fluttering heart and flushing cheeks.

"You know," he says. "I think Adam knew I had a crush on you and wasn't crazy about it."

"What was your first clue?" I ask. "How he always managed to shove himself in between us when we found ourselves alone, or the times he always did something super obnoxious like suggest a burping contest when I was around you two for too long?"

Suddenly, his eyes darken. "Listen. I've been meaning to tell you I'm sorry for making fun of your glasses," he says, tone serious. "I only made fun of them because I was dying to know what kissing you would feel like, and it was the only way to take my mind off it. If it helps at all, Teenie found out I made fun of you and grounded me for a month. Do you want to know what her punishment was?"

"This should be good." I fold my arms across my chest with a smirk and wait.

"I had to go to knitting class with her every week."

"That doesn't sound too bad. I could see where it probably wasn't your favorite thing, but I could definitely think of way worse punishments."

"Can I tell you a secret?" His voice is barely above a whisper, and his eyes dart around the porch as if Mr. Barnes could be listening—which wasn't too far-fetched.

"Please do," I say, following a bead of sweat that trickles from his forehead into the collar of his shirt.

"I kind of liked it," he whispers.

I feign mock horror and clutch at my chest. "No! You? Enjoyed something other than making fun of me?"

"Remember that red scarf I always wore during the winter of freshman year? I actually made that." He puffs his chest with pride, and I can't help but giggle. "Phew," he says and wipes a hand across his brow. "You have no idea how much better I feel right now. That was really weighing on me."

"I forgive you for making fun of my glasses, Levi. And thank you for trusting me with your dirty secrets. However, I do not forgive you for making approximately a thousand flatulence noises in my presence. That was and always will be disgusting."

"You mean like this?" he asks, tucking his hand into his armpit.

"Don't you dare," I warn.

"Or what?" he challenges. In an instant, I'm tackling him in his rocking chair and fighting for the hand under his shirt. His stomach is rock hard, and I explore a bit too long, pretending I can't find his hand.

"Woah!" he says. "Buy me dinner first!"

Before I can retort the sound of wood splitting pierces the air, and we both stare at each other with wide eyes. In seconds, we're both in a tangled heap on the floor, pieces of dry rotted wood scattered around us.

"I think I got a splinter in a place I didn't know you could get splinters," Levi whines, rubbing his backside.

"I should never have picked these rocking chairs up off the side of the road." I rub at my knee before Levi helps me up and we move to the porch swing.

As soon as he sits, he turns to me with a concerned expression. "Did you pick this up on the side of the road too?"

"No," I laugh. "It came with the house." I tap my chin thoughtfully and add, "Although, the house is roughly a hundred years old. So maybe swing at your own caution?"

"Great," he mutters. We swing in comfortable silence, watching as the sun sinks lower and lower until finally disappearing into the dark water of the harbor.

"Do you ever miss high school?" he asks, scooting closer to lift my legs onto his lap.

"All the time," I answer. "Don't you?"

"I wish I would've realized how easy life was then," he professes. "Back when my biggest concern was what color Abercrombie polo I would be wearing to school that day and not trying to save a failing company." His tone is playful, but I know he means what he's saying.

"I'm trying to think of what the hardest part of my day was in high school," I reply. "Probably fighting off Mrs. Hawthorne every evening. Do you remember her?"

Mrs. Hawthorne had been our very old, very cranky neighbor who never failed to yell at me or Adam at least once a day. We were either being too loud and causing distress to her ancient Poodle, Chancy, or whatever other absurd thing she could think of to scold us for that particular day.

"How could I forget her and her fake British accent? One time I came over to visit Adam and she hit me with her cane because she said I parked too close to her Cadillac...which was across the street."

"One time, Chancy bit me on the ankle when they were out for a walk and she never apologized for it. She just muttered something about getting too close and walked away. I never forgave her for that. From that day forward, I always put our junk mail into her box. It was so satisfying watching her go through two of everything."

"You are so bad," Levi says with wide eyes. I giggle and playfully nudge his shoulder with mine. "When Adam wakes up, do you think he'll be okay with this?" he asks quietly after a beat.

I consider his question, the same one I ask myself at least a thousand times a day. Will Adam be okay knowing the entire time he's been in a coma, his childhood best friend and sister have been seeing each other? "I really don't know," I finally say. "He made it pretty clear in high school he wasn't okay with it."

"Surely things have changed by now, though, right?" he asks. Concern laces every line of his face, and while I should be more concerned about the topic at hand, I find myself pleased that Levi cares this much. "I mean, we *are* almost thirty."

I chew on the inside of my cheek. "Something about it does feel weird, you know? We're out here having the time of our lives together, or at least I am with you, "I tack on sheepishly, "and he's stuck in a hospital room with a million machines attached to him to keep him alive. I feel guilty." I had hoped that finally confessing this would be a weight lifted off my shoulders, but now I feel even worse, as if saying it somehow made it more true.

Levi grows quiet and picks at a splinter in the wooden swing. "I feel guilty every single day," he says quietly. "I'm the one who left him without a word ten years ago, and when he was nice enough to come visit me, when I definitely didn't deserve it, this happens. It feels like a punishment for leaving everyone here in the dust." He tosses the splinter to the ground then raps his fingers against his arm of the swing. His once sparkling amber eyes are now dull and full of sadness. When he speaks, it's so low I almost miss it. "I should be the one in a coma right now, not him."

The weight of his confession slams into my chest like a semi. All along, I've been selfishly thinking I was the only one truly affected by this. How did I never consider Levi's feelings? Behind his strong posture and easy going attitude, he's been struggling with the weight of this *and* carrying it alone.

I still his rapping fingers by curling my hand around his, choosing my next words carefully. "No one should be in a coma right now, Levi. And this is not a punishment." He continues to stare at the ground and chews furiously at the inside of his cheek. "I wish you would've called or come back to visit in the last ten years, but I understand why you didn't. That doesn't justify anyone being in a coma, okay?"

He silently nods and looks out over the yard. There's a cargo ship coming into the harbor, and the consequential waves lap softly at the rocky shoreline. Pretzel and Hank have curled up beneath our feet, only letting out the occasional muted yip as the result of a dream.

I rest my head on Levi's shoulder, wishing I could take his guilt away but knowing the best I can offer is my love and support while he works through this on his own.

And that's when I realize: I'm falling in love with this boy, and have been falling since the day I first met him, with his floppy hair and easy grin. I rub the calluses along his knuckles, noting how perfectly our hands fit together. This *should* be a perfect evening, yet something is off. I can't help but wonder if he feels the same.

Chapter Twenty-Three

Aly

"I think I'm actually busy, Mom, but thanks for the offer," I fib and hold the phone away from my ear, expecting an earful. Sure enough, the unmistakable bark of dad's voice booms through the speaker. Emma shoots me a pitied look as she puts the last of the flower buckets back into the cooler. It's been a long day at Bloomie's, and I *was* looking forward to going home and spending the evening in my newly remodeled bedroom, watching *Friends* reruns. Apparently, my parents have other ideas.

Reluctantly, I move the phone back to my ear and catch the end of my dad lecturing me on the importance of family time. If only he would've given himself that little pep talk about twenty-seven years ago.

"I expect you there at six o'clock sharp, Alyson. Do not be late and do not bring that dog. Your mother had to buy me all new underwear after the last time you let that little rat roam freely around the basement."

"It's Adam's dog, Dad, and I have to bring her. I can't just leave her by herself."

"Figure it out," Dad commands, his tone harsh and full of anything but love. I rub my temples in an attempt to keep my temper in check.

After a few more minutes of lecturing from my parents, I end the phone call and release a pent up breath of air. Emma leans her hip against the counter and raises her eyebrows. "So?"

"My parents planned a family dinner tonight and, for some reason it's incredibly important that I attend."

"I wonder what's going on…" she muses.

"Something about the charity gala, I'm sure. It's still a few weeks away, but they hire people for everything: the planning, the food, the entertainment. They're solely the name on the checks and that's about it. They've never needed my opinion on anything before." I scoop Pretzel up and flip off the lights in the shop. Right as we're walking out the door, a familiar Mini Cooper pulls up in front, and my heart races.

"He really has no shame driving that thing around, does he?" Emma asks under her breath.

"I see it as confidence, and I think it's very attractive, thank you very much."

"Call me if you need me later," she calls over her shoulder and jogs to her car.

Levi unfolds himself from the tiny car, and I decide then that I'll never tire of the way his shirt stretches across his broad chest, hinting at what's underneath. His beard has been neatly trimmed and his usual baseball cap is gone, his hair neatly combed. A soft lick from Pretzel brings me back to Earth and with it, a plan to make this evening not so terrible. He casually kisses me on the cheek, and the spot where his lips touched flushes.

"Why is Pretzel wearing goggles?" he asks in lieu of a greeting.

I point to the Vespa. "How else am I supposed to protect her little eyes?"

"Where does she sit?" he asks, walking around the Vespa and inspecting it like an extra seat would magically appear.

"I...put her in my backpack and wear it backward on my chest," I stammer, embarrassed, and he chokes back a laugh behind a balled up fist. "Whatever. It works. And who are you to judge? You're driving around a car that has eyelashes."

"Touché," he says with a shrug of his shoulders. "But my real ride back in California was a truck, just so you know."

"I love to pollute the air I breathe, too," I say with squinty eyes and the meanest look I can muster.

"Woah, what's got you in such a bad mood?" He backs away with his hands in the air.

"I have a mandatory family dinner tonight at my parents'. It should be fine, though."

"Why is that?" he asks, frowning in suspicion.

"You're coming with me."

"You want me to come to dinner at your parents' house? I think I can count on one hand the number of times I've been inside your house, and it was never once for a family dinner." He rakes a hand through his perfectly combed hair, somehow managing to make it look even better.

"I ate dinner with your parents," I point out.

"But my parents are a lot more...approachable than yours."

"They are," I agree. "But if you came, it would make this unbearable dinner a little more bearable." With puppy dog eyes, I tack on, "Please?"

"I was actually going to see if you wanted to go to dinner tonight," he says, and his polished appearance makes more sense.

"Perfect, so you're free. We'll still be eating dinner together," I say. "Just with some snooty, stick-up-the-butt company."

Riding around in the Teenie Mobile has become second nature to me. Honestly, I've grown quite fond of the eyelashes on the headlights and the purple under glow. I should put a bug in Teenie's ear that if she ever wants to sell it, I call first dibs. But, driving the Teenie Mobile through the wrought iron gates of my parent's mansion and parking next to their fancy cars has me stifling a fit of giggles.

"I knew I should've traded cars with my dad before coming here," Levi mutters with a heavenward glance.

"It's fine," I reassure him. "We didn't have time to trade vehicles anyway."

We decided to leave both dogs at my cottage in one of the back bedrooms that hadn't been remodeled yet, just in case. After dropping them off and making sure the room was as puppy proof as possible, we didn't have time for Levi to swing by his parents and sweet talk his dad into letting him borrow a company truck. Truth be told, Dad would probably frown at a muddy, older model work truck as much as the Teenie Mobile, anyway. I wasn't about to tell Levi that, though.

Levi gets out and walks around to open my door. He gently takes my hand, and I notice how clammy his is.

"Are you okay?" I ask, giving it a squeeze.

"I'm a little nervous," he stammers and, despite the warm, summer breeze, he shivers a little.

"There's nothing to be nervous about," I tell him. "They don't love anyone, not even their two children. So just go into this with the lowest expectations possible, and you won't be disappointed."

When we arrive at the large, antique, carved-oak front door, it swings open before we're given the chance to knock. One of the butlers, dressed in all black, greets us with a warm smile and slow, southern accent.

He shows us to the large formal dining room as if I hadn't grown up here. An obviously catered meal has been dished out onto fine china in an attempt to make it look homemade, which we all know would never happen. A homemade meal hasn't been made here since 2002, when Adam and I attempted boxed macaroni and cheese that ended up exploding all over the kitchen. There's still a dried, crusty noodle on the ceiling, and walking in and noticing that little noodle hanging out, completely out of place in the otherwise sterile and stuffy environment is the only joy this house brings me.

When dad scoots his chair back and walks toward us, Levi audibly swallows beside me and I give his hand an encouraging squeeze.

"Alyson, you didn't tell us you were bringing a guest," he says through a tight-lipped smile, holding out a stiff hand to Levi.

"Do you remember Levi?" I ask him, knowing full well he does not. Dad never attended any high school function, let alone took interest in who our friends were.

"Levi...?" he asks, prompting his last name.

"Middleton. You may know my father?" Levi offers.

"Ah, yes. How is he doing? Still playing in the dirt and sand, building homes for those who can't afford to live downtown, I presume?"

I grimace, and Levi clears his throat, his eyes flashing with anger. "Yes, he's still the owner and operator of the largest construction company in Charleston, if that's what you mean." Dad either brushes off Levi's reply or wasn't even paying attention because he turns around and returns to his seat next to mom.

"Hi, Mom," I say. Her lips are pursed, her face pinched uncomfortably, like maybe her Spanx are too tight.

"Hello, Alyson," she says curtly. She nods toward the other end of the table where there are...*three* place settings. Even without knowing I was bringing a guest, the number the table is set for is strange. My parents aren't the type of people to set a place for my brother as though he was with us in spirit. That could only mean...

On cue, the heavy front door opens and light footsteps echo down the hall.

"Hudson!" Dad cries when he enters the room. Panicked, my gaze darts between my parents and Levi. His jaw is flexed, but other than that, he looks as cool as a cucumber. He reaches a hand over to still my bouncing knee and then stands up to shake Hudson's hand.

"Good evening," Hudson says to all of us. He's wearing a navy pinstripe suit and loafers without socks *again*. I'm not sure if it's the thought of how sweaty his feet must be or how my parents were planning on setting me up for dinner with Hudson this evening that makes my stomach churn. Hudson takes the open seat on my left so I'm wedged uncomfortably between him and Levi.

"Thank you all for coming," Dad says, picking up his wine goblet. Not glass...*goblet*. Because I forgot we're not in the twenty-first century and normal things like solo cups are inappropriate at old southern money-fueled family functions. "We invited *most* of you here today to talk about this year's charity gala." Levi grips his thigh under the table, and his knuckles turn white. "It's coming up at the end of summer, and we expect everyone, who's been invited, to attend." Dad looks pointedly at me when he says this. "As you are all aware, this year will be a little different with the absence of Adam."

'He could be awake by then," I chime in, and Mom shoots me an icy glare.

"Yes," she agrees. "He *could* be. But even if he is, he's going to need his rest. Now, if you'll please let your father finish without any more interruptions..."

Dad clears his throat then continues. "As I was saying, this year is going to be a little different. We were hoping Hudson would be so kind as to fill Adam's seat at the table."

"I would be honored," Hudson says, beaming.

"Great!" Dad exclaims, clasping his hands together in front of his round belly. "It's settled then. You'll be Alyson's date."

"Excuse me?" Levi and I say at the same time.

"My *date*?" I add, disbelief coursing through every vein in my body. How could my own parents try to fill Adam's void with *Hudson?* And use Adam's absence as an excuse for me and Hudson to get together, no less. What little appetite I had vanishes. I push away my plate and stand.

"Please stay seated, Alyson!" Mom cries. "Where are your manners?"

"I'm not going to the gala as Hudson's date. I thought it was obvious I'm seeing someone when I brought Levi here tonight. You're asking me where my manners are while treating Levi like he's invisible since we've been here."

"It was a family dinner, Alyson," Dad hisses through clenched teeth. "How were we supposed to know you'd be bringing someone else?"

I ignore his question and blatant disregard for common decency. "Levi is my boyfriend, and you can like it or not. Hudson and I are not and never will be together, regardless of what excuse you come up with next to try and make it happen." My cheeks flame, and my palms burn from digging my fingernails into them.

Mom coughs nervously, looks to my Dad for backup, then says, "Alyson, in our defense, your dad is right. We *did* only invite you."

Dad nods in agreement. "Frankly, it was rude to invite a guest to a family dinner without our consent."

"Yet you invited Hudson to a family dinner without *my* consent," I point out. I'm trying my best to spare everyone's feelings and show my parents there's a better way to handle things then how they do, but if I have to stay through one more second of this absurdity, I'm going to lose it.

"Hudson, we really do apologize for our daughter's behavior. If you can please look past whatever this is she's going through and see her to the gala, it would mean the world to us," my mom says gently to Hudson, patting his hand.

"You cannot be serious," I mutter. "I'll be at the gala for Adam's sake, but I'm going with Levi."

"You most certainly are not," Dad sputters. "If it wasn't for Levi, we wouldn't be in the situation we're in to begin with."

"That's not fair and you know it," I say, my voice barely above a whisper.

"Let's go," Levi rasps through a clenched jaw.

"If Adam hadn't been gallivanting around, doing God knows what with *him*—" he jabs a finger in Levi's direction, "—then Adam wouldn't be in a coma right now."

"It was a freak accident," I say, tears welling in my eyes. "For you to throw accusations around and show animosity toward the one person who's been there for me through all of this shows just what kind of person you are."

With that, I grab Levi's hand and march down the hallway, tears blurring my vision.

Chapter Twenty-Four

Levi

When we pull up, Aly's cottage is bathed in the deep purple aftermath of a spectacular sunset, and I hate that I had to miss watching it with her. I want to watch *every* sunset with her.

The glow from her front porch illuminates two heads that push back the curtains of the spare bedroom. Dog snouts fog the window, and despite the rough evening, I find myself excited to be reunited with Hank again. That's the thing about dogs: you can be having the worst day in the entire world but to them, it's their best day all because you came home.

Aly doesn't wait for me to open the door for her like I usually do, and the ache in my chest only grows stronger. The entire ride home was full of nothing but "I'm so sorry," and quiet sniffling. I knew her parents treated her unfairly, but I had no idea how bad it was. I have a feeling that wasn't even the worst of it.

Once we're inside, she slumps onto the couch. Before joining her, I let the dogs out and brew some of the lavender tea she loves. A few minutes later, I return with two steaming mugs.

"You okay?" I ask, resting my hand on her knee.

"I just thought they'd be better behaved with you around." She covers her face with her hands, but I gently pry them away. "Could they have been any worse to you?"

"I'm not worried about me," I tell her. "I'm worried about you."

"How could they do that?" she cries. "I can't believe they used Adam's absence as another way to try and push me and Hudson together. What do they see in him? And why can't they understand I'm not interested?"

"Well, he's wealthy for starters," I say. "Isn't he one of the old money Charleston families? He could definitely take care of you."

"What if I don't want to be taken care of? What if I want more in a relationship than old money and a good standing in society?" Her flushed cheeks tell me I've struck a nerve.

"That's not what I'm saying, Aly. I'm just saying they see qualities in him that they don't see in someone like me. Honestly, he'd probably make someone a pretty decent husband."

"If you like infidelity and constantly wondering what your husband is up to, then yeah. I'm sure it's a really nice life because who cares? You've got plenty of money to blow, you know." She uncrosses her legs to stand, but I squeeze her thigh, keeping her seated.

"What do you mean?" I ask, afraid I took her last statement wrong. Surely her dad would've never...

"Dad had plenty of affairs when we were growing up," she says quietly. "It wasn't a secret."

"I had no idea."

"You and maybe only ten percent of the city. The rest of Charleston definitely knew. But you want to know the worst part? It was never a big deal to Mom. She'd just spend more money and eventually get over it."

"That's awful." I know I'm one of the lucky ones who grew up with two parents who were a little overbearing at times but loved me and each other.

"Tell me about it. I don't want that kind of relationship, ever." She settles back into the couch and folds her arms over her chest. Pretzel jumps into her lap and settles into the space between her knees. "Either way, I'm sorry about tonight. I will never ask you to go to another family dinner as long as I live." Her eyes grow wide and she adds, "Except the charity gala. Please go to the charity gala with me."

"I promise I'm okay," I reassure her. "As for the charity gala, if I'm still here..." I trail off, unsure how to continue. I would love nothing more than to be Aly's date, to be her rock during this family event and remind her of her strength when she needed it most. The timing for this next job couldn't be any worse.

"Right," she says, disappointment etched into the corners of her eyes.

"I'm sorry—" I begin, but she interrupts me.

"It's fine," she says and stands, Pretzel yipping as she tumbles to the floor. Aly walks into the kitchen and returns a moment later with a plate of brownies. She offers me one, but instead of accepting, I stand and walk to the front door. "You're leaving?"

"I've got an early start tomorrow helping Dad wrap up a job in Mount Pleasant," I say, bending to kiss her lightly on the forehead.

"Oh," she says, her face falling. "Okay. I'll see you tomorrow, then?"

"Yeah, for sure. I'm sorry I have to leave."

"It's okay." She slides the brownies onto the coffee table, then thinks better of it after catching Pretzel eyeing them and moves the plate to the side table. "Thanks for coming to dinner with me tonight. Again, I'm sorry for how it ended." She rises onto her tip toes and plants a delicate kiss of her own on my cheek. "Be careful tomorrow."

I walk out to the Teenie Mobile, Hank trotting beside me. He folds himself into the back seat, and I crawl behind the wheel. "What an evening," I mutter to Hank as I back out of the driveway.

Remember that toy you always wanted as a kid? You pined for it every second of every day until finally, one Christmas morning, you opened a perfectly wrapped package to find *the* toy. That's what it feels like with Aly. When some people look back on high school, they remember their sports team or late nights shenanigans with friends. I remember those, too, but mostly, I remember Aly. I remember an all-consuming crush on my best friend's sister. A sister who had long, wavy, sandy brown hair, blue eyes, and a tan that lasted well into winter. I remember a free spirited girl with the biggest heart and a smile so contagious, you couldn't help but smile, too. I remember Aly as she is now, but somehow she's become more graceful, more caring, and more beautiful in the ten years we've been apart.

Now that I've got her, I don't ever want to let her go. I went all the way to California, searching for that thing to complete me. Turns out, that missing piece has been here the whole time. I've been missing *her*. But between her brother,

her parents, and my job, I'm not sure how to keep her. I'm not sure if simply wanting to be together is enough.

As I'm lying in bed that night, Adam's phone lights up on my side table, a new text from Aly flashing across the screen.

Have you ever wanted something so bad yet it feels like the world is against you? I miss you so much, Adam. I won't fill you in on the gruesome details of "family" dinner tonight but just know that Hudson showed up and I didn't know he was going to be there. Levi was with me. What a disaster. But I don't want you to wake up to only the venting texts about Mom and Dad from me, so here's a picture of cute lil Pretzel bossing her friend Hank around instead. We miss you so much.

Chapter Twenty-Five

Aly

"Are you sure you're not just overthinking it?" Emma asks.

I'm in the middle of hanging the final set of curtains, the finishing touch on this guest room, and I don't respond for a moment, prompting her to say my name.

"Sorry," I say. "But I don't know? Maybe? I feel like something has been off ever since dinner."

I just finished rehashing the gruesome details of family dinner, the sting is still as fresh as it was last night. I slide one foot onto the top of the dresser and the other onto the window ledge. I'm barely balancing, holding the curtain rod in one hand and an impact drill in the other, when my front door opens.

"Emma, someone is here," I hiss.

"Go see who it is," she says simply.

"I...I can't. I think I'm stuck," I whisper. As if on cue, my fuzzy sock clad foot slides farther and farther away from the rest of my body. "How long would it take you to get here if you left wherever you are right now?" I plead.

"You want me to walk in on a burglar?" she asks. "No thanks. Maybe this will be your lesson to finally start locking your door. We do live in the twenty-first century, you know."

"Emma!" I cry. "I really am stuck. And I know you carry a can of pepper spray on your keychain. Please?"

Although, armed with a curtain rod and impact drill, I realize I could be stuck with worse gear to defend myself against a burglar— if I wasn't teetering on the edge of doing a split.

Before I can prepare myself, the bedroom door flies open and Levi walks in.

"What are you doing?" he asks, taking in my appearance. "And when are you going to start locking your door?"

"I was trying to hang these curtains," I reply, trying to hold up the drill and rod while still balancing. I try to channel my inner flexible goddess and shake the tension from my shoulders. Only when I do, my foot slides another inch further down the window sill and something pops in my hip.

"Didn't I leave a step ladder here somewhere?" Levi asks, scanning the room.

"Now that I'm thinking about it, yes. I think you did."

"Why didn't you just grab that instead of doing...this?" he asks, gesturing at my precarious position. "Also, who wears fuzzy socks in the summer?"

"My feet were cold," I mutter. "If you're not going to help me, can you at least get the step ladder?"

Instead of doing what I asked, he comes over and gently picks me up, standing me upright. It leaves me wondering if his touch will ever stop making my skin tingle and my stomach flip.

Once I'm safely back on my feet, he takes the tools and rod from me and gets to work. Within minutes, the curtains are up and he didn't even have to climb on any furniture to achieve it. God bless his tall, broad shouldered masculinity.

He sets the tools on the dresser, and when his troubled eyes meet mine, I know instantly something is wrong.

"Everything okay?" I quietly ask. He moves to the edge of the bed and pulls me between his knees, leaning forward until our foreheads are pressed together.

"I've got to leave tomorrow," he whispers.

"Tomorrow? Why so soon?" I ask, a little louder than necessary. Blood rushes to my cheeks and my heart sinks into my stomach, making me a little queasy.

"The owner of the home we're starting on wants to add a few more projects, and the only way we can make it work is if we get started as soon as possible," he explains.

"Do you know when you'll be back?" My hands tremble, and he takes them into his own, softly kissing the back of each, then cradles them against his chest.

He sighs and avoids my gaze as he answers. "I don't yet."

I want to trust him, to understand why he's doing this, to believe he's planning on coming back and staying for good, but he already left us once. I want to push back from him, to remind him that he's got a good job here, a family here...*me* here. I want to kick and scream until he understands that we've already waited so long to be together, and I don't want to wait any longer.

I'm not ready for this summer to be over. I'm not ready to watch him board a plane and have everything I've gotten used to over the past couple of months taken from me. I'm not ready to wake up in two days only to be reminded that he's gone. I'm not ready for anticipation and excitement to be replaced by something empty and hollow.

I'm not ready.

But instead I take a deep, shaky breath, and lay my head in the crook of his neck. His heart is pounding, the blood pumping through his veins so hard that I know he didn't want to tell me as much as I don't want him to go.

"I'm sorry, Aly."

We sit like that for a few minutes longer, Levi stroking the back of my head, until a cold, wet nose nudges right above the edge of my fuzzy sock.

Pretzel stands on her hind legs, eyes pleading, and Hank's not far away.

"How can we separate these two?"

He forces a laugh and then strokes his beard thoughtfully. "Let's make the rest of this day the best day ever, for them."

"What do you have in mind?"

"This! This is perfect!" Levi says, eyes wide with excitement as he holds up a visor and matching fanny pack. "They have one in green and one in blue. What color do you want?"

"Blue, obviously."

"Obviously?"

"It matches my eyes."

"Right, of course. Let's see if we can find those super obnoxious state flag shirts too."

As soon as we check out, we immediately put on our new gear.

"Do I look touristy enough?" I ask.

"You look like a massive cheeseball," he chuckles. "It's perfect."

I grin then untie the dogs from the lamp post. When Levi suggested we dress up as tourists and do all the touristy things, I couldn't say no.

Afterall, I've never been on a dolphin sightseeing tour.

"Excuse me, sir, but we don't allow pets," the guy checking tickets at the gate says. I hurry to cover the fanny pack currently housing Pretzel in an attempt to keep him from noticing another dog. Levi adjusts his visor and looks down at Hank.

"You can't make an exception, just this once? He's a really good boy and you won't even notice he's there," Levi says. The guy points to the sign like he's done it a million times and sure enough, "No pets allowed," is fourth on the list. Levi lowers his voice. "Please, man. It's my last day in town and I just want to make it special for my girl. Don't make us miss this. She *loves* dolphins. They're like...her thing."

I try not to giggle, though him calling me his girl makes me warm and tingly inside.

"Sorry, man, I don't make the rules." He's already peering behind us, ready to usher the next set of tourists through.

"Who does, then?" Levi asks and slyly pulls a crumbled bill from his fanny pack. I can't tell what denomination it is, but it's enough to make the man perk up.

"Today, I do. Looks like there are a few seats open in the back." He takes the bill, unfolds it, and holds it up against the sunlight for inspection. "Enjoy your ride!"

Levi gives me the biggest, dopiest grin I've ever seen and hooks his thumb toward the boat. "Ready?"

I follow him and Hank as we file into our seats. When no one is looking, I unzip my fanny pack and let Pretzel stick her head out. Once we're on the water and the boat gains speed, Hank and Pretzel raise their faces to the wind, tongues lolling as they pant happily. I snap a picture and immediately send it to Adam.

"I think it's definitely the best day ever for them," I say to Levi, raising my voice above the noise of the engine. He threads his fingers through mine and nods in agreement.

Minutes later, we halt in the water and the same guy that checked our tickets takes his position at the front of the boat. Then his nasally voice comes over the loudspeaker. "Okay ladies and gentleman, if you look to the right of the boat, we've got a pod coming towards us. It looks like there's maybe twelve. Please remember to keep your hands, feet, and other objects inside the boat, and please do not feed them. Feel free to take all the pictures you want, though."

People from the other side of the boat squeeze onto ours and crane their necks, searching for the dolphins. Levi gets up and moves to another spot to make more room for the actual tourists, but I stay put, and Hank remains at my feet. Within minutes, the dolphins swim up to the side of the boat to squeals of excitement from the tourists, phones held out to capture the creatures. Levi surprises me by pulling out a disposable camera and snaps a few pictures, too.

"Where did you get that?" I ask.

"I added it at check out while you weren't looking. I thought it might be a fun surprise and make us look extra touristy."

"I didn't even know they made those anymore," I say.

Then, someone shouts, "Oh no!" and I look over to find a middle aged woman wheeling her arms, frantically grabbing at the air.

"My phone!" she screeches, her arms flailing knocking the chips from her husband's hands.

"My snack," he frowns. At the mention of the word "snack," two sets of dog ears perk up. *Oh no.*

"Levi! Grab Hank—" But before I can finish the warning, Hank has his front paws on the railing, eyes trained on the bag of chips floating in the ocean.

"Don't do it, Hank," I plead. He turns and gives me a look, but right as I reach for his collar, he's is in the water, swimming next to the dolphins and happily licking at the soggy bag of chips.

Wide eyed, I turn to Levi. "What do we do?" I ask, but his gaze is focused on my midsection—on my fanny pack.

My heart sinks to my stomach for the millionth time that day as my hands move to the fanny pack, knowing what I'll find.

Pretzel is gone.

"Where did she go?" I cry, frantically scanning the area around us until I notice her a few rows back, front paws on the railing.

"Pretzel!" I shout. She turns, spares me what can only be described as a withering glance, then hops into the water after Hank. When Levi and I push past the crowd to the railing, it's in time to catch Pretzel climb onto Hank's back.

"This is...not good," Levi stammers. "Not good at all."

An hour later, the four of us stand on the dock, soaking wet, watching as the boat takes off to finish the tour.

"You think he was serious about that restraining order?" Levi asks.

"I'm going to go with yes," I mutter and turn to begin my walk of shame back to the Bronco.

"We said we wanted them to have the best day ever," Levi says after we've loaded up. "And they look pretty happy to me."

Once I climb behind the wheel, I peek into the back. The pups are curled up, fast asleep, with cute little puppy dog smiles plastered on their faces.

Chapter Twenty-Six

Aly

A foghorn jolts me from my slumber. The space in bed beside me is empty, and my heart sinks in Levi's absence. I slide my feet into some house slippers and shuffle into the kitchen.

The smell of rich coffee greets me; the sides of the pot are still warm, so he must've left recently. I pour myself a cup, and as I'm reaching for the creamer in the back of the fridge, a note on the counter catches my eye.

Wanted to get in a few last East Coast waves and didn't want to wake you. I'll be back around nine. - Levi

My heart catches on the word *last,* but I refuse to think about what it means. I have three hours before he's supposed to be back. I could join him—after all, I love a good early morning surf session, too. But he must've wanted to go alone this morning, to clear his head before going back to California. Otherwise, he would have woken me.

Instead, I decide to shower and come up with a plan for us to enjoy our last few hours together.

After tidying the house and showering, I curl up on the unmade bed in my robe, my wet hair wrapped in a towel. Both dogs are sound asleep at my feet but when I pick up my phone, Pretzel stirs then lays her head on Hank's back. Her eyes are heavy with sadness, like she can tell something is up.

I'm thinking we'll start the day at my favorite brunch spot, then maybe squeeze in one last cheeseball tourist event, like a haunted ghost tour.

I pull up the text thread with my brother and start typing.

Today is Levi's last day in town for a while, so we made the most of yesterday with a dolphin tour. Both Pretzel and Hank ended up in the water, and we were kicked off the boat, so keep that in mind for future reference. I'm pretty sure anyone with the last name Bloomington or Middleton is banned from there. Anyway, miss and love you!

I hit send, and that satisfying tri-tone fills the silence. Across the room, a phone beeps with an incoming message, and I realize Levi must've forgotten his phone when he went surfing.

"Aly? You up?" Levi pokes his head in the bedroom and...*that's funny.* He's holding his phone.

"Yeah! I'll be right out," I reply.

"I wanted to show you some pictures I took of the sunrise this morning," he says, grinning down at his phone. "What's wrong?" he asks when he finally meets my eyes. "I'm sorry I didn't wake you this morning. You were sleeping so peacefully."

"I just keep hearing this buzzing across the room and I don't know what it is," I say. "I thought you left your phone here, but obviously not."

Something unrecognizable—fear, maybe—flashes across Levi's face so fast I almost missed it. Now I'm more confused than ever. Levi clears his throat, his eyes dart around the room, and I get up and approach him.

"It's probably nothing. Why don't you come into the living room?"

"I just want to see what this is first," I say. I first noticed it when I texted Adam, so I type out another simple message and hit send.

Hi.

Immediately, there's the buzz again, and I toss the pile of Levi's clothes from last night across the room. At the very bottom are his jeans with a lump in the pocket.

"Aly," he says quietly. "Wait. Please let me explain."

I ignore him, reach into his pocket, and withdraw the phone.

The navy blue case. The lock screen of Pretzel as a puppy. Adam's *phone.*

"Why do you have this?" I whisper, keeping my back to him. Surely, there *must* be a logical explanation for why he has Adam's phone. When he doesn't immediately answer, my heart sinks further than I thought possible. "Answer me, please," I croak out. Hot tears stream down my face.

In an instant, he's in front of me, reaching for me.

"Please tell me," I beg, holding up my hands to stop him. He sighs, his shoulders slumping, telling me everything I need to know. "Did you read them?" I ask, my voice quivering. "Did you read the messages I've been sending him?"

His head falls to his hands then he grips his hair at the roots, knuckles white in frustration. Still, he doesn't answer me.

"Did. You. Read. Them?" I ask again, growing more irritated.

"I wanted to tell you," he says.

"That's not an answer."

Slowly, he nods, and I'm certain the floor beneath my feet has turned to quicksand. I brace myself against my dresser, blinking rapidly to clear the haze creeping into the edges of my vision.

"All of them?" He nods again and a choked sob escapes me. "Why would you do that?"

"It's not that I wanted to," Levi starts, and I find myself wishing he'd leave. I clench my fists as he continues. "But when I got home from the hospital, I realized they got his phone mixed up with my stuff. I didn't mean to *keep* reading them, but every time I tried to get the phone back to you, something came up."

"Something came up? *Something came up?* You can't seriously tell me there wasn't a single moment the entire time you've been here where you could've given the phone back?"

My eyes burn with unshed tears and right now, I don't care if Levi's flight is in five minutes or five hours. The ache of what he's done settles on my chest like a heavy weight, and I want him as far away from me as possible.

"I really did try," Levi says pathetically.

For a split second, I consider hearing him out. He's not a bad guy; I know he's not. But then I think of Adam, and I'm blinded by rage. Levi's chin quivers, and I force myself to look away. He doesn't deserve my pity right now.

"You had more than enough chances to tell me. But you didn't."

"Please let me explain," he pleads.

Still avoiding his gaze, I point to the door. "You need to leave."

He opens his mouth, then closes it with a shake of his head. In a fit of rage, desperate to get him out of my home and my sight, I say the opposite of everything I've been thinking all summer. "Stay in California for all I care."

With a curt nod, he turns and leaves, Hank moping behind him.

"Aly, are you sure you're okay?" Emma asks, standing an arm's length away, like she's not sure if she fully trusts me at this moment. In her defense, I'm not sure *I* fully trust myself.

"Never better," I murmur through gritted teeth. "Are your safety glasses on?" I watch out of the corner of my eye as her hands fly to her face to check.

"Yes, but are you sure this is the best idea? I don't know if it's...safe." She backs up a few more steps from me and the hammer casually strung across my shoulder like I was born for this. I *feel* born for this. Something is getting destroyed today.

"It's gotta go, Em," I say. "Today."

"You don't want to wait for, you know, a professional?"

"I'm going to pretend I'm not insulted by your lack of faith in me. I watched a YouTube video earlier, so I'm basically a professional. Do you want to go first?" I ask, offering the hammer. She shakes her head vehemently.

"Can you just tell me what happened? We can talk through this instead of you potentially destroying your home. There are better ways to go about this." Her face softens and for a second, I consider it. Then the image of Adam's phone in Levi's pants pockets makes me mad all over again.

I take a swing to one of the support beams on my old back porch, the *thunk* of contact satisfying. Already, I feel better. I swing again, grinning as the wood splits. "Sure. We can talk about it while I destroy what's left of this porch."

Emma yields another step, one eye squinted, the other on the wood that splinters further with each strike of my hammer.

"I swear you told me Levi leaves today. Why aren't you at the airport with him?"

I move to the other end of the porch and take aim at those beams, too. "Levi *is* going back to California today and hopefully *never* coming back." *Whack.* "Ever." *Whack.* "Ever. Ever. Ever." *Whack. Whack. Whack.*

"Why?" Emma asks tentatively.

"He's a liar." *Whack.* "A two faced, lying, jerk." *Whack. Whack. Whack.*

"Aly!" she screeches, pulling the hammer from my grip before I can swing again. Gently, she settles my hands on my shoulders and spins me to face her. Then she sits on a worn porch step and pats the spot next to her. "Tell me what happened."

My chin wobbles uncontrollably, and I blink furiously to keep from crying.

"You know how I've been texting Adam to give him little updates so he doesn't feel like he's missed out on a bunch when he wakes?" She nods. "I honestly didn't know where his phone was. I assumed either Mom or Dad had it, or the nurses had it ready to give back when he woke up. But actually, Levi had it."

"Why is that a bad thing?" Emma asks, searching my face.

"He's been secretly reading all the text messages I've sent to Adam." I cover my face with my hands and let out a muffled, albeit satisfying, scream.

"Did you say anything you regret?" Emma asks.

"No, I meant everything I said, but that's not the point. The point is, he was never supposed to read them. They were supposed to be private between me and my brother. He had every opportunity to tell me he had Adam's phone, and he never did. Don't you think that's kind of scummy?"

"It is," Emma agrees. "But I don't think he tried to deliberately hurt you either, Aly. There has to be a good reason why he kept it, don't you think?"

"Who's side are you on?" I ask, glaring at her while searching for the hammer she took from me.

"Yours, obviously. I'll always be on your side. But I'm just saying, I think if you talked to him, saw his side of things, it might make you feel better."

"What will make me feel better is ripping down this eyesore and setting it on fire."

Emma sighs, and reluctantly hands me the hammer. Then, she takes off around the house toward the shed.

"What are you doing?"

"Looking for another hammer, I guess," she says, throwing her hands up in submission.

I knew we were best friends for a reason.

Chapter Twenty-Seven

Levi

"Excuse me, could you point me to where I can pick up my dog?" I ask a gate attendant. With a phone to her ear, she shoots me a dirty look. A well timed howl erupts from behind me, and I whirl to find Hank's crate being pushed by another attendant. Pawing manically at the door, he lets out another pitiful cry that sounds more like it would come from Pretzel than a ninety pound German Shepherd. Some guard dog he is.

"Is that your dog?" the attendant asks, eyebrow cocked.

"Nope," I say and give her a little wave before following Hank.

"Excuse me," I say to the man pushing his crate when I catch up with them at baggage claim. "I can take him from here."

With a grateful nod, he steps away, muttering, "Thank God," under his breath.

"It's okay, buddy," I tell Hank and bend to peek through the crate door. Instantly, he perks up and licks my fingers through the wire door.

When the luggage carousel squeaks to life, I straighten and watch for my bag. Next to me, Hank whines in his cage, his way of begging to be let out after being cooped up for the cross country flight.

"Shh, bud," I say soothingly. "We're almost home." I feel bad lying to him, but he's a dog; what does he know?

My bag passes through the flaps, but before I can reach for it, there's a loud *boom*. I turn in time to see Hank throwing himself against the door, and before I can stop it, the lock springs. Sensing his freedom, Hank shoots past me, launching himself onto the conveyor.

Hank runs circles on the baggage claim, happy as a clam to be stretching his legs. Without hesitation, I climb up after him, hurdling suitcases both soft and hard. Other travelers gape in shock and awe as I chase my dog. Hank is close enough now that I can reach for his collar, but as soon as I extend my hand, the carousel stops, knocking me off my feet. Hank and I tumble gracelessly to the ground, taking a pink, hard sided suitcase with us.

"Hey!" someone yells. "What do you think you're doing?"

I push Hank off me and find two security guards running toward us.

I offer a weak chuckle and sheepish smile. "Sorry about that. We don't fly often, and *someone* gets a little anxious, if you know what I mean," I say, hooking my thumb at Hank, who sits pretty at my feet. I take the opportunity to return him to the crate, doing my best to secure the nearly-mangled lock. "Dogs," I add with a head shake and a jesting elbow to one of the guards. Both wear matching expressions of disgust. "We're just going to go now."

Stacking my bag atop the crate, I briskly push Hank to the nearest exit. Surprisingly, security doesn't follow.

As soon as we're outside, I kneel so I'm eye level with the crate. "Why?" I demand.

All I get in return is an unrepentant glare.

"Stop whining!" I say to Hank—who has been giving me puppy dog eyes from the couch all day—for the tenth time.

"What's got you in a foul mood?" Glenda asks, sitting next to me and taking a bite of pizza.

"You're here uninvited, for starters," I mutter.

Glenda either doesn't hear or chooses to ignore me. Around a mouthful of cheese and pepperoni, she says, "She found the phone didn't she?"

"Why are you here again?" I ask, taking the second slice of pizza off her plate and adding it to my own.

"I knew this was going to happen, and I thought you'd need company," she says simply, and I'm reminded why I keep Glenda around.

"She found the phone," I confirm. "And it didn't go well."

"Well, can you blame her for being upset?" Despite the fact that she's right, all the fondness I experienced for her a moment before evaporates.

"No, I can't blame her. But I *did* try to give the phone back. The timing was just never right."

"Did you talk about it?" Glenda asks, eyeing the slice of pizza I stole from her. I cover it with my hand, then lick it for good measure.

"No, we didn't. She told me to leave and stay in California for all she cared. So here I am." Hank whines again, and I blow out a puff of air. "Hank also really misses Pretzel, and every time he whines, I'm reminded of what a complete screw up I am."

"I think you're being a little dramatic," Glenda says. "But I also think you should give her time to process what you did, then go to her and apologize. Didn't I overhear something about a big party at the end of summer? Go surprise her and tell you're sorry. It'll be just like the movies."

"Glenda, that's only two weeks away. I can't finish this job *or* expect her to forgive me in two weeks."

"About that," Glenda says, avoiding my gaze. "The clients called yesterday and want to cancel the extra kitchen project. They said they under-budgeted and can only afford the spare bathroom now." She glances at my pizza again, and then steals it from my plate.

"You just watched me lick that," I say, fighting the urge to gag as she stuffs it into her mouth anyway. "They canceled the entire kitchen project?" She nods. "A spare bathroom will only take a few days," I say, my heart sinking.

"That gives you more time to pack and think about how you're going to tell your girl you're sorry," Glenda says.

"I guess now is as good a time as any to talk about your future with the company," I say wearily.

"Don't worry about it," Glenda says and pats my knee.

"Do you already have something else lined up?" I ask. "I'd give you a reference, you know. As much as you irritate me, I'll do whatever I can to get you a good job when this is over."

"Oh honey," she says. "Don't worry at all. I'm coming to Charleston with you."

"You're coming...with...me?" I repeat, confused.

"Teenie and I are starting a business together. We're not sure what yet, but we'll figure it out. Charleston is full of possibilities."

"Where are you going to live?" I ask, afraid of the answer.

"With your parents, of course."

"There's only two bedrooms."

"Right, so you'll be on the couch. But it'll only be temporary. Hey, why don't we make it a game? See who can find a place first?" Glenda asks, her cheeks rosy with excitement.

"Glenda," I say, exasperated, her name like a curse word. "It's getting late. I think it's time you head home."

She checks the watch she wears religiously on her left arm. It's the gold kind with a stretchy band and numbers the size of Texas. "It's only seven," she says. "The night is still young. And what if you need me?"

"I won't need you," I say with a pointed look at the door.

"About that..." Glenda says. "I sort of already sold my house."

"*What?* Why? Where are you going to stay?"

"With you, of course," she repeats.

I sigh and sink back into the couch cushions, wondering where exactly I went wrong.

Chapter Twenty-Eight

Aly

"I really wish you could give me some advice right now."

I sit on the edge of Adam's bed and watch the steady rise and fall of his chest, reassured that, even if he isn't awake, he's still here with me.

"I've made such a mess of things, and I don't know how to fix any of them. My porch is a disaster. Emma and I tried to demolish it, and that went about as well as you'd expect. My heart is in no better shape." With a sigh, I add, "Levi and I got into a big fight and I told him to leave and go back to California." A tear glides down my cheek and falls to the floor. I sniffle and wipe at my eye with the back of my hand. "He really hurt me, Adam. I wish you could tell me what to do."

The door opens with a surprised, "Oh." My mom softly shuts the door behind her and joins me on the other side of Adam's bed. "I didn't know you would be here."

"I'm here a lot, actually," I say defensively.

Mom sighs and sets down the bag she's brought with her. "I didn't mean it like that, Alyson. You just startled me, that's all." She digs into the bag, pulls out a bumper sticker that says, "Proud Weenie Dog Dad," and sets it on the table beside him.

"What is that?" I ask.

A natural blush peeks through all the Chanel makeup she is wearing. "I saw it at a boutique today and thought Adam might like it."

"Did you bring that, too?" I ask, pointing to the stuffed wiener dog I found on the Fourth of July.

"I did."

I chew on this information before answering. "Why?"

Mom glances around the room before her eyes finally meet mine. "I know how much he loves that dog. And...when he wakes up, I want him to know I care. He's my son. I love him."

I'm surprised to find tears welling in my eyes. "I'm sure he'll love them both, Mom." And knowing Adam, he really will. The second he's able, there's no doubt he'll be proudly flashing that bumper sticker all over Charleston.

"I care about you too, you know," she says. "And I'm proud of you both."

Unable to say anything, I simply nod and turn to face the other wall to wipe the tears that have fallen. I feel her hand on my back before she encompasses me into a hug.

"I can cover for you if you want to take the day off," Emma says tentatively as soon as I step into Bloomie's.

"Do I look that bad?" I ask, glancing at my reflection in the shop window. A piece of hair stands straight up, and I pat it down.

"You look...tired," Emma says carefully.

I *am* tired. After my fight with Levi, I haven't slept very well, and visiting my brother this morning left me even more emotionally drained.

"I'm fine," I reassure Emma. "Just a long night of tossing and turning and hoping a wild animal didn't come through the hole in the side of the house."

"I told you we should've let a professional take your porch off," Emma says, crossing her arms. "And it's not even that big."

After only a few minutes of hammering yesterday, Emma found out she actually really loves demolition. However, one wrong swing left a hole in the siding large enough for a bear to fit through.

When the bell above the door tinkles, I turn to greet the customer.

"Good morn—" I say, falling silent when I realize it's Hudson.

"Good morning, Aly," he says smoothly and glides to where I'm standing. I can't help but glance down at his feet to see if maybe, by some small miracle, he's wearing socks today.

He's not.

"How is our favorite flower shop owner?" he asks, and I cringe when he takes my hands. If he notices, he pretends he doesn't because he keeps holding them. His hands are actually very soft...*too* soft. I tug out of his grasp and shove them into the front pocket of my apron.

"I'm good, Hudson," I say dryly. "What can I help you with?"

"Let's see. What can *you* help *me* with?" He rests his finger on his chin, and it takes everything in me not to roll my eyes. He's so dramatic. "How about I pick you up Friday night around six and we go out together?"

"Friday night? That's the night of the gala," I say.

"Exactly. Don't tell me you're still set on taking that boy who drives a Mini Cooper with eyelashes."

I almost tell him, *of course I am,* but then I remember Levi isn't here, and he's not coming back. Especially not after our fight. My stomach sinks at the memory, but I shove it to the farthest corner of my mind.

"Well?" Hudson asks.

"I'm not going with anyone," I say firmly.

"So, if we bump into each other at the gala and sit together, it wouldn't hurt. Is that what you're saying?" Hudson asks.

I consider that. I guess, *technically*, it wouldn't hurt anything. I would be saved from Mom and Dad's wrath, the night would go a lot smoother, and as long as he didn't pick me up, it couldn't be considered a date. I'd also have my own way home in case things got to be too much.

I tap my index finger against my lower lip before answering. "No, I guess that wouldn't hurt anything."

"Great. So it's settled. I'll see you then," he says, and bends to kiss me on the cheek, his wintergreen breath lingering. I'm so tired, so mentally exhausted, I don't even move after he's gone. Distantly, I hear the bells on the door jingle, and Emma snaps her fingers in front of my face.

"What was that all about?" Emma asks. "Why did you just agree to that? How did he even know Levi was out of town?"

"He probably doesn't even know that Levi left," I say, which I know doesn't answer her question. That's simply how Hudson is, showing up and flexing every chance he gets. He probably would've asked me with Levi standing right here. "And why shouldn't I have agreed? Levi's not here. Hudson isn't *that* bad. We've probably made him out to be a lot worse than he is."

"Aly, he doesn't wear socks with his loafers. And don't get me started on how small his feet are. I know for a fact I saw those loafers for sale at Ann Taylor Loft."

Come to think of it, I'm pretty sure I looked at the same pair. "I can tolerate one evening with him if it means I get my parents off my back for a little while. Besides, it can't be any worse than going alone."

Emma sucks in her lower lip and gives a noncommittal hum.

"It'll be fine," I say, unsure if I'm reassuring her or myself.

When I get home, Pretzel is tucked under the covers of my bed. She looks so pitiful, and I know if she had thumbs, she would've turned on a sappy break-up film.

"Do we need to watch a rom com?" I ask. She side-eyes me, then lets out a small yip. "I'll be right back," I tell her and run to the kitchen. I grab all the chocolate I can find, a box of tissues, and the carton of Milk Bones. I scoot in beside her and toss her a bone, which she happily licks up. Even though it's seventy-eight degrees and the middle of summer, I press play on *The Holiday* and snuggle next to Pretzel.

"Do you miss Hank, girl?" I ask as I scratch behind her ears. At the mention of Hank's name, her ears perk up and she looks around the room for him. "I miss him, too," I whisper and wish for the millionth time—for Pretzel's sake of course—that dogs could FaceTime.

Pretzel snuggles herself deeper into the crook of my arm, and I can't help but wonder what would've happened if I would've had to go through these past few weeks without her. And to think, at the very beginning of our relationship, she took every opportunity to cause trouble for me. And now, she's snuggled up next to me; the shift is almost unthinkable. We've become a team.

I snap a picture to send to Adam, and his phone lights up on my nightstand with my incoming text. I push aside all thoughts of Levi, open another chocolate, and burrow deeper into the covers. Pretzel and I are simply two heartbroken girls, cuddling our sorrows away.

CHAPTER TWENTY-NINE

LEVI

"I think that's the last of it, don't you?" I ask Glenda.

"You tell me," she replies. "You're the one who packed everything."

She's been watching me carry boxes to a moving van for the past three hours, and giving her unsolicited opinion on everything instead of lifting a finger to help. I guess I shouldn't be too upset. She's the one driving the moving van from California to South Carolina.

"Are you sure you're up for this drive?" I ask. Not only has she agreed to drive the entire thirty-five hours, but she's also taking Hank along with her since I recently found out the hard way he's not the best flier.

"Oh yeah," she says, waving a dismissive hand. "I was a truck driver before I met you, you know."

"Your resume said you were an office manager for an eye doctor," I say skeptically.

"Is that what she put?" Glenda said absently as she stroked Hank's head. "I told Teenie to make it sound believable, and I guess it did the trick."

You know those moments in the movies when a record scratches and everything comes to a standstill? That's what happened to me.

"Teenie?" I ask. "As in...my mom?"

Glenda's hand flies to her chest with a gasp, and when she turns to me, her eyes are wide as saucers behind her glasses.

"Shoot!" Glenda says. "You were never supposed to know!"

"Know what?" I ask through gritted teeth.

With a world-weary sigh, Glenda says, "Your mom and I have known each other for years."

"What?" I sputter. "How?"

"I used to live in Charleston, you know." My eyebrows raise clear to my hairline, but before I can ask more questions, Glenda continues. "Your mom and I met at Stitch and Sip."

"You were..." My hand flies to my mouth. "Oh my gosh. *That's* why you looked so familiar when I interviewed you."

Glenda nods solemnly.

"What were you going to do if I didn't hire you?"

She shrugs. "I would've found some other way to weasel into your life."

"So how did you end up out here?"

"I wanted a change of scenery," she says simply, and I chuckle at how on brand that is for her, to move clear across the country on a whim. "And when you moved out here, your mom asked me to keep an eye on you."

"So you two have been in cahoots this entire time?" I ask.

"Yep!" Glenda says happily, then walks over to the moving truck, and for reasons unknown to me, opens one of my carefully packed boxes.

Finally, everything makes sense. How woefully under-qualified Glenda is for her job. How fast she and Mom became best friends. Why Glenda had always had her nose stuck so far into my business.

I make a mental note to do more extensive research before actually hiring someone next time, then remember, there won't *be* a next time. I'm closing up shop in California and heading home to work for Dad again.

When I called to ask what he thought about me moving back, his response was, "About time. We've got a big project in Mount Pleasant that I could really use your help on next month."

And that was that. So, I finished the last remodel in California as quickly as I could, found a renter for the warehouse, packed up, and here we are.

"Did you ever apologize to that girl? What was her name? Amy?" Glenda asks, rifling through a box. She pulls out a pair of my underwear, the ones with unicorns on them, and lifts them up for me to see.

"Her name is Aly," I snap and grab the underwear from her. "And quit going through the boxes I just spent days packing up."

"Testy," she whistles. "I take that as a no."

"I tried. I've tried calling her, texting her, everything I can think of. She must've blocked my number."

"I probably would've, too," Glenda says, examining her nails. Today, they are bright red to match the shirt she has tucked into her stretchy, yellow pants that are pulled up to her chin, per usual.

"What else am I supposed to do?" I say, thinking of the YouTube video I watched on box breathing to keep myself from getting worked up around Glenda. Unfortunately, all the video accomplished was reminding me of Aly and her love for DIY videos.

"Tonight's the night of her family's big shindig, right?"

I look down at my watch to check the date. How could I have forgotten?

I nod, and Glenda says, "Well, are you ready or what? You've got a girl to get back, and I've got a thirty-five hour drive with a dog that snores louder than you do. Let's get this show on the road. I've been waiting hours for you anyway."

"I've been a little busy packing and loading this truck," I say through gritted teeth, then do some mental math. If my flight leaves in two hours, I'll land in Charleston an hour before the gala starts. If I don't have any delays, and as long as traffic is on my side, I should be able to make it in time to find Aly. I *might* have a shot at getting my girl back.

"Get in!" Glenda says and scoots her seat as close to the steering wheel as she can. Hank jumps in between us, and we're headed to the airport.

"Good luck getting your girl back!" Glenda yells over her incredibly loud fiesta music. Why that's her station of choice, I have no idea. She shakes the top half of her body along to the music, and I try to erase that image out of my brain but I'm afraid it's seared there for the rest of eternity.

"Be careful, please," I tell her. "Let me know as soon as you make it to your first stop tonight. And please don't forget about Hank."

"I could never forget about Hank!" she says. My anxiety lessens, but only for a moment until she adds, "His gas is terrible."

"I'll see you soon, okay, buddy?" I say, scratching behind his ears and giving him a kiss on the head. "Hang in there. Thirty-five more hours until you can see Pretzel." At this, he perks up, and I give him one more scratch under the chin.

"See you soon!" she calls over the mariachi band. I throw up a wave and head into the airport, wondering if Hank will ever forgive me.

Once I'm through security, I locate my gate. They've already started boarding, but only the first group of passengers. I wait patiently for my turn before taking my place in line. The flight attendant checking my ticket looks down at it then up to me before blurting, "You're the hot contractor, aren't you?"

"Excuse me?"

"The hot contractor! On Instagram! I knew you were from California, and I wondered if I'd ever get to meet you!"

"Oh," I say, taken aback. I catch her staring at my midsection, growing more uncomfortable when her gaze lingers too long. I'm waiting for laser beams to shoot from her eyes and burn off my shirt, and several people behind me sigh impatiently. "I think we should probably...wrap this up," I tell her through a strained smile.

"No worries," she says with a wink. "I'll be on the flight, and we can chat then." She blows me an air kiss and I'm so surprised, I trip over my own feet. She reaches out and grabs my bicep, giving it a tight squeeze before letting go. "See you soon," she says with a little wiggle of her eyebrows.

"I am so uncomfortable right now," I mutter to no one as I walk down the jet bridge and onto the plane. After I find my seat, thankfully between a middle aged man and an older lady, I sit down and crack open my book. I've barely made it into the first chapter when I hear, "There you are!" and I look up and find the same flight attendant, who apparently doesn't know what personal space is.

"So how come you didn't answer my message?" she asks, as if there aren't two other people in this row.

"Your message?" I ask, my eyes darting around for help. Where do those oxygen masks come from again? Maybe I can fake a panic attack. Maybe this lady's crazy eyes will send me into one, and I won't need to pretend.

"Yeah. My message. I asked you out on a date, and you read it but didn't reply." Her tone changes from sweet and a little too high pitched to accusing and full of ice.

"I guess I didn't see it," I say.

"You read it," she repeats. "And didn't reply." She fishes out her phone and scrolls for a few seconds before shoving the phone into my face. I take a second to read the message and my face burns bright red at her choice of words. No wonder Aly ignored it.

"I don't operate my Instagram," I tell her, wondering if that's the correct way to say it. "Someone posts for me."

"Oh, so you're a fake," she says. "Does someone do your contracting work for you, too?"

"No, that's all me," I say. I'm blessedly saved by a voice over the speakers, asking us to take our seats.

The flight attendant shoots me a smug look and whispers, "You missed out," before returning to the front of the plane.

"I'm glad I'm not you right now," the man beside me grumbles and flips the page of his newspaper. I pick up my book again but set it down after reading the same paragraph ten times. I close my eyes, lean against the headrest, and think of a plan to get Aly Bloomington back.

My last flight lands with a thud and screech against the tarmac, and I wait as patiently as I can while the other passengers slowly deplane. Finally, it's my turn, and I grab my carry on and hurry up the aisle, keeping my head lowered to avoid crazy pants.

I've got a girl to find, apologize to, and profess my undying love for. Time is of the essence.

I hail a cab outside the airport and when I slide in, he looks at me expectantly.

"Where to?" he asks, and it hits me that I'm not exactly sure where this gala is.

"To the gala?" I reply, hoping that's enough. How many galas are happening in Charleston tonight?

"Address or get out. We gotta keep things movin' man."

"Take me to King Street, then," I say.

As we cruise away from the airport, my brain buzzes. If I were hosting a fancy, rich-people gala, where would it be?

In no time, the cab pulls up to King Street and I hop out.

"Thanks," I hastily say before he peels off. I jog down to Bloomie's and of course, the sign says closed early for an event. *But where?*

I'm pacing in front of the shop when my phone buzzes in my pocket. "Did you make it?" Glenda asks when I answer.

"Yes, but I don't really have time to talk right now," I tell her, frantically searching for any sign of where Aly might be.

"I made it to my stop for the night, thanks for asking," Glenda huffs. "And your dog is fine, too, in case you were wondering."

"Glenda, do you by any chance know where this gala is?" I ask, panic creeping into my voice. What if I don't find her in time and my whole plan is ruined?

"I do. But until you learn some manners, I'm not telling you," she says, then murmurs to Hank, "Do you want to tell your hateful hooman hi?"

I take a deep breath and massage my temple with my free hand. "Glenda, how was your drive?"

"It was great! Thanks for asking," she replies cheerily.

"That's great! Where is the gala?" I try again.

"I think you can do better," she says. I hear kissy noises, and now I know for certain Hank will never forgive me.

"Did you see anything exciting on your drive today?"

"Oh yes! Lots. Hold on, I'll send you a picture." Her voice gets far away and after some furious tapping in my ear, my phone vibrates again. A picture of Glenda's face fills the screen, and I can barely make out the Grand Canyon in the background.

"That's great! The Grand Canyon, huh?" I say, feigning enthusiasm. I quiet my tapping foot and take another deep breath.

"One more," Glenda says, and my phone vibrates again. This time it's a picture of Hank sitting in front of a random gas station.

"That's...great," I say. "Thanks for those."

"Now, would you like to know where the gala is?" Glenda asks.

"More than anything."

"It's at her parent's house. Where else would it be?"

"A convention center, a restaurant, literally anywhere but there."

Glenda ignores me and says, "Welp, I found a real fun motel on the side of the road in Arizona. You know, like the ones you see in murder mystery documentaries? Anyway, Hank and I have a bubble bath to get into."

"I don't think Hank really likes bubble baths," I say. "And I would *not* subject myself to whatever is in that bathtub."

"Call you tomorrow!" Glenda says and hangs up.

I slide my phone back into my pocket, say a prayer for my poor, sweet, undeserving dog, and take off toward Aly's parents' house.

As I round the corner of their street, out of breath, the large mansion comes into view. The wrought iron gates are open and cars I can't even pronounce the names of pull up, spilling people in tuxedos and ball gowns onto the drive. I look down at my own attire of black tee and jeans and mutter a little curse. How can I get in there?

I sneak up the sidewalk while brushing my hands across my shirt in an attempt to get the airplane wrinkles out when I see it: Aly's Bronco.

Bingo.

Up ahead, a woman with long, wavy, sandy brown hair in a floor-length yellow dress stands with her back to me, and I know without a doubt it's her.

"Aly!" I call, but she's too far away. "Aly!" I holler again. She stops momentarily and turns her head, looking around, but continues on after being unable to locate the voice. I run after her, but I'm stopped when a man in all black walks up to me.

"Can I help you?" he asks with an amused expression on his face. He's wearing dark sunglasses and has a mic in his ear.

"You can," I say, my eyes trailing Aly. If he keeps me here any longer, I'm going to lose sight of her. "You can let me go."

"Not happening," the security guard says.

"No, it's fine I promise. I know her," I say and point to Aly behind his shoulder.

He turns around and gives Aly a once over. "Aly Bloomington? The daughter of the owner and CEO of Bloomington Boat Works? I'm sure you do." He looks me up and down and smirks. Aly moves further and further away, and a man joins her. He's tall, wearing a tuxedo, and my heart sinks when I realize it's Hudson. He links arms with her, and they disappear behind the gate.

"You know what?" I say to the bodyguard. "You're right. Sorry for your trouble."

I turn and walk in the opposite direction, confusion and hurt gripping at my chest.

CHAPTER THIRTY

ALY

"You look hot," Hudson says and links his arm through mine. I crane my neck, sweeping my gaze over the crowd, and he says, "What are you looking for?"

"I just thought I heard my name," I say. "I must be going crazy."

"Oh, look! It's the governor. Let's go say hi," Hudson says and steers me toward the man. There's a squeaking noise with every step Hudson takes, and I look down in confusion.

"Hudson?"

"Smile, okay? Sometimes you have RBF, and I really need to make a good impression on the governor."

"RBF? Are you kidding me?"

"What? I didn't mean anything by it. I just wanted to make sure you smile."

I plaster on a fake smile. "Can I ask my question now?"

"If you make it quick."

"Why don't you ever wear socks?"

Before he can answer me, the governor notices Hudson and strides over.

"Hudson!" he beams and shakes his hand. "Here with *the* Aly Bloomington, I see. Congrats, my friend. I'm sure her father is proud."

"Her father is over the moon that we are finally together," Hudson replies without missing a beat.

I open my mouth to protest, but Hudson steps on my foot.

"That's great to hear. I wish you two the best of luck and will be looking in the mail for our wedding invite soon." He shoots me a wink, and I swallow the bile in my throat. As he walks away, I turn to Hudson.

"What was that?" I ask. "We are most definitely *not* together."

"We are tonight, aren't we?" he asks, caressing my cheek with the back of his hand.

I turn my head to avoid his touch. "That doesn't warrant a wedding invite in the future. Why didn't you correct him? Or let me correct him without you stepping on my foot?"

"Oh, Aly," Hudson says indulgently, like I'm a silly child, and links his arm through mine again.

I tell myself it can't be like this all night. Surely Hudson will calm down and we might actually have a decent evening.

But things only get worse.

"Waiter? Waiter!" Hudson says once we're all seated at the head table under one of the large white tents in the backyard. A waiter jogs over, eager to please.

"My steak is medium, and I asked for medium rare. Also, my potatoes are too cold."

"Hudson, you asked for medium. I heard you," I say, fighting the urge to throw the whole plate in his face.

He ignores me and lifts the plate up to the waiter. "Can you get me what I ordered and make sure it's *hot,* please?" The waiter scurries off and I take another bite of my potatoes that are plenty warm, and delicious at that.

A knife clinking against a wine glass quiets the room, and I look over to see my dad standing, a mic in hand.

Here we go, I think.

"Thank you all so much for coming tonight as we celebrate our fifteenth annual charity gala. I just received word on the amount of money received from this year's donations and I'm pleased to announce we beat last year's record by fifty thousand dollars!" Cheers burst out but quiet after a few seconds.

"As you all know, the past few months have been more than difficult for us following the accident of our son, Adam. We wish he could be here and are thankful for your continued prayers. We are also thankful for our daughter." He points to me and I smile awkwardly into the crowd. "And her more than fantastic, supportive boyfriend, Hudson." Cheers assaults my ears again, and all the blood drains from my face. "With that, I would like to announce my retirement at the end of the year. As sad as I am to take a step back, I know the family business will be in great hands. Hudson, do you mind joining me?"

"What did you do?" I whisper-yell at Hudson. Again, he ignores me and walks up to join my dad, taking the microphone from him.

"Good evening, everyone!" Hudson croons. "I am thrilled to be here tonight and even more thrilled to have been considered, let alone given the wonderful honor of filling Mr. Bloomington's shoes."

"You earned it!" Dad says and slaps him on the back. The crowd claps and Hudson waits for it to die down before continuing.

"I promise to take care of not only your business but your daughter as well. Thank you, sir, for trusting me with both."

My once delicious potatoes have turned sour in my stomach. I hastily push away from the table and run inside, searching for the nearest restroom. As if a wave has crashed over me, everything becomes crystal clear.

Hudson needed to prove to my dad we were "together" before he ever got the business handed over to him. Dad did all of this without even considering Adam. My mind spins, and I pray they haven't signed the papers yet, making this official. How could Hudson have done this? And my dad, too? My brother, the man who *should* be at the helm of the company when Dad retires, is in a coma, yet everyone is acting like he's already dead.

With shaky hands, I pull out my phone to call Emma but find my screen littered with a slew of missed calls and texts from her already.

"Emma?" I ask when she answers after the first ring.

"Aly, where have you been? I've been trying to reach you all evening."

"What's wrong?" I ask, panic rising in my chest.

"Adam is awake," she says happily, and I can tell she's been crying. "How fast can you get here?"

With shaky legs, I rush outside, climb into my Bronco, and peel out of my parking spot. Naturally, the engine misfires like a gunshot, and I hope it makes Hudson scream like a baby in front of everyone during the remainder of his stupid little speech.

"Come on, come on!" I yell when I hit a red light, banging my fists against the steering wheel, as if it'll turn green any quicker.

I turn on my flashers and speed to the hospital, miraculously finding a parking spot near the front. I peel off my heels and run as fast as I can into the hospital.

"Shoes are required, miss!" the security guard calls after me as I tear through the lobby, but I ignore him, praying you can't catch typhoid fever through your feet as I climb the stairs two at a time. I push those thoughts aside when I reach Adam's room and burst through the door.

I've never seen a more beautiful sight.

There he is, sitting up in his hospital bed, smiling, as if he was expecting me, knowing I'd roll in on two wheels. I run to his bed and fling my arms around him. When I hear him chuckle softly, I pull back and look into his face.

"I missed you so much," I tell him, my eyes welling with tears.

"I couldn't let you sit through another charity gala without me. I had to pull through for you, you know?" His voice is gruff but strong.

"How'd you know that was tonight?" I ask, confused. He points to my dress, then gestures to Emma.

"Well, for one, you dress up exactly once a year. And two, Emma told me."

"You don't know what kind of disaster you just saved me from," I say and give his hand a squeeze. It's fragile and pale, but warm, and my heart pounds with the sudden realization that Adam is *awake*. *My brother, my best friend, my twin is finally* awake.

"How are you feeling?" I ask.

"Like I got hit by a truck," Adam jokes, and that would be more funny to me if it weren't true, if that weren't the very reason he'd been in a coma for months.

"Can I get you anything?" Emma asks from the other side of the bed. "I think I might head out before too long." Adam shakes his head and looks at her curiously.

"Thanks, but I think I'm okay," he says "Will you be back? I'd like to finish our conversation."

Emma nods and avoids my gaze. I'm too caught up in the moment to wonder what that's all about, and instead lean down and squeeze Adam's neck again.

"Did you call Mom and Dad?" I ask, turning to Emma.

Emma shifts uncomfortably on her feet, and Adam answers for her. "I asked her not to call them until you got here." He smiles and my heart surges at the simple gesture of my twin knowing exactly what I need.

"Thank you for everything." I wrap my arms around Emma and walk her to the door. "I'll call you tonight, okay?" Emma nods and leaves, and I turn back to my brother.

"We have so much to catch up on," I say, wondering where to even begin.

"I want to hear it all," he says, but I can tell from the slight droop in his eyes his energy is flagging.

"How about I tell you everything tomorrow?" I ask.

"Deal," he says, his eyes fluttering closed. Then he blinks them open and stares at me. "Hey Aly?"

"Hmm?" The buzzing and whirring of the machines he's hooked up to is oddly calming, causing me to get a little drowsy, too.

"I had the craziest dream while I was asleep that you and Levi brought Pretzel in here. Isn't that funny? It seemed so real. I could almost feel her next to me."

"Adam," I say, chuckling softly. "We did sneak her in here, and she did crawl up onto your bed."

"You did?" he asks, relief flooding his face. "I knew it seemed too real to be a dream. Levi was with you, wasn't he? I remember his voice."

"He was," I say carefully.

"Tell me about it tomorrow?" he asks.

"Tomorrow," I promise as he lays his head back on the pillow and falls fast asleep.

Chapter Thirty-One

Levi

It's been one whole week since my entire world crashed down around me. Seven days of misery induced by the image of that slimy greaseball Hudson wrapping his arm around Aly and walking her through those gates like she was his. All week, I've been wrestling with that. How could she hate the guy one minute, and the next, attend one of the most important social events in Charleston on his arm? I was supposed to be the guy standing next to her, my arm wrapped around her, whispering jokes into her ear all night to keep her smiling in an otherwise tense situation. I was supposed to protect her from anything and everything that could've possibly gone wrong at that dinner. Instead, I'm the guy tossed to the side with not even so much as a second thought.

After the way she found Adam's phone, I can't say I blame her. If I could go back and give her the phone at the very beginning, I would. I wouldn't chicken out every time I tried. I wouldn't read any of those private text messages.

So yeah, I could see why she was upset, which only made me more angry with myself. Looking back, I realize Aly would've given me a chance if I would've come clean from the beginning. How could I have thought that giving her the phone would've screwed all that up?

I get up off Mom and Dad's couch and turn off *Sleepless in Seattle,* which has been playing on repeat all week. Mom comes in and stands in front of the TV, hands on her hips.

"Are you going to shower this week? Maybe get off the couch? At the very least, watch something different? Your dad and I have had all we can take of Meg Ryan and the way you smell."

"Thanks for the tough love." I press play on the movie anyway while simultaneously sniffing my armpit. *Yikes.* With a disappointed shake of her head, she walks back into the kitchen, she and Dad sharing whispered words. It's still dark outside, which means it's either early morning, or late night. In my rom com and ice cream induced haze, it seems I've lost track of time.

"I think he's heart broken, Tom. What do we do?"

"He needs to toughen up and get back to work. That's what I think." Dad makes no attempt to hide his gruff tone, and the screech of his chair being pushed back from the table fills the silence.

"Oh, Tom! Could you be a little more sensitive?"

"Nope. I gotta get back to work." A soft smack sounds from the kiss he plants on Mom's cheek, then he's in the living room. He bends to put his boots on and, when they're laced, he turns to me. "Have you tried talking to her?" he asks quietly. I shake my head, too tired to go into detail.

"You know where she works, don't you?" he asks with a raised brow then slips out the door.

With a sigh, I turn off the TV. He has a point. I have to make at least one more attempt to apologize. If she accepts, great. If she doesn't...well, I don't want to think about a life without Aly.

Searching for my phone, I finally locate it wedged between two cushions and check the time. It's seven in the morning, and Bloomie's doesn't open until nine, but I know there's a fair chance she's already there, preparing for the day. Summoning the courage, I pry myself off the couch and slide on my tennis shoes

"Um, Levi?" Mom asks, standing in the doorway to the kitchen, eyeing me warily.

"Hmm?"

"A shower never hurt anyone." She points behind her to the bathroom. "I just restocked it with fresh towels. You better enjoy a bathroom to yourself while you can, anyway. Glenda called and said she'll be here this evening."

"Right," I said, managing a smile. "It's about time she brought my dog back."

"I think she's grown pretty fond of Hank. She sent me a picture of them in matching pajamas last night."

"She sent me the same picture. Hank looks miserable. He'll never forgive me."

Mom bites her lip to keep from chuckling, and I shuffle past her to the bathroom.

I park a few blocks from Bloomie's and unfold myself from behind the steering wheel. The distance between the car and the door to the shop passes too quickly as I rehearse my speech to Aly. When I go to open it with a shaky hand, the door swings open and a red-faced Aly comes flying out.

"What do you want?" she snarls, hands planted on her hips. I know anger isn't a normal emotion for Aly, but her finger wags my face, and I'm going cross eyed trying to follow it.

"I, uh," I say, taking a few steps back to focus. "I wanted to—"

"To offer puppy support?" Her voice escalates with each word, and people along the sidewalk stop and stare.

"Puppy support?" I repeat.

"Don't play dumb with me, Levi," she sputters. "Puppy support. Like child support but for puppies."

"I'm not following," I say. "Can we go inside? Maybe get off the sidewalk?" Someone across the street has pulled out their phone, and I'm sure they're videoing. If we don't move fast, we'll be the next viral internet sensation.

"You don't want the world to know what your dog did to my precious, innocent, angel Pretzel? She just turned two, Levi! She's only a teenager!" Her cheeks are flushed bright red, and her blue eyes have darkened to the color of the nighttime sky. Her hair is haphazardly piled on top of her head, a few pieces escaping to fall down around her face. I shake my head to clear my mind. Now is not the time to think about how beautiful she looks.

"Is Pretzel...with puppy?" I ask, finally putting the pieces together.

"With *puppies*," she corrects. "Four of them."

"And are you sure Hank is...you know..."

"The father? Of course he's the father! What are you trying to say about Pretzel?"

"Nothing!" I splutter and move toward her.

"Don't you dare," she says, backing up. "How do you even have the audacity to show up here after everything you've done?" The anger has disappeared from her eyes, replaced by pain, like a wounded animal. There's a scratch at the door, and I look down to find a waddling Pretzel with a swollen belly, pawing to come outside.

"Not now," Aly says to Pretzel. "I know you're excited to see him, but I'm not."

"Ouch," I mutter. "Can we at least get coffee or something? Talk about this? About us?"

She sighs and glances at Pretzel again.

"I don't know," Aly says. "I'm still pretty upset, Levi."

"I know you are," I say, "And I've never been more sorry for anything in my life. Please, let me explain everything to you. Give me a chance." I reach out my hand, but she ignores it.

"We do need to figure out what to do with the puppies," she says hesitantly, tapping a finger to her chin. "They're your grand dogs, and I can't deny you rights to see them." I let out a small chuckle, and she flashes me a look full of disgust. "Should we ask Pretzel if she thinks this is funny?"

"No, you're right. This isn't funny. I'm sorry. A million times over, Aly." I shove my hands into my pockets and wait for her response.

She glances down at her watch and then says, "I have an hour before we open. Let's walk down to the coffee shop." She opens the door to scoop up Pretzel, and I follow a few doors down to the coffee shop.

We place our orders and settle into a booth in the corner, both nursing our coffees before I finally speak up.

"I don't know where to begin," I start, "but I know what I did was wrong. I was given every opportunity to come clean and give you his phone back, and I didn't. For that, I will never forgive myself, and I'm not expecting you to, either."

Aly chews on her lower lip and looks down at Pretzel, who is curled in her lap. I suck in a deep breath and continue. "I should never have read any of the messages between you and your brother."

"You shouldn't have," she snaps.

"But Aly," I say, the words bubbling beneath the surface, ready to explode. "I've had a crush on you since the day I met you. When I moved away, I thought I'd never see you again. When I saw your name pop up on that screen...it wasn't right. I know it wasn't. But I missed you so much..." I trail off.

"Then why did you leave again?" With hollow eyes, she peers at me from behind her smudged glasses, and I know these past few weeks have been as hard for her as they were for me.

"I thought I needed to prove myself. I thought if I stayed here, I'd look like a coward for running from my failing company. I thought a lot of things that weren't true," I confess. I place a sweaty palm on my bouncing knee, stilling myself. "I'm sorry again, for everything." I try to meet her gaze, but she's still staring at Pretzel and absently rubbing her growing belly.

"I'll let you know when she has the puppies," she says quietly, finally meeting my eyes. "When is your flight back to California?"

"I'm staying, Aly. For good."

"You are?" Her chin quivers, and I finally feel like I've reached a breakthrough with her. Not a large one by any means, but it's something.

"I'm not losing you again. I'm here and I'll be waiting for you, however long that takes."

Aly glances out the window then down at her watch. "You should know that Adam is awake."

"He is? That's great!" Relief courses through my veins, and the crushing weight finally lifts off my chest. "Is he home or still in the hospital?"

"You're his best friend. You should know."

My stomach drops. "You're absolutely right. I've been so selfish, Aly."

I wish I could say something, anything, to make her understand what she means to me but I can't find the right words. Instead, I reach down and scratch Pretzel under the chin, then rise to leave.

"Bye for now, Aly."

Chapter Thirty-Two

Aly

Watching Levi walk from the table, shoulders down, face distorted in agony, was almost enough to make me stop him. Almost. I've forgiven him, and I wish I had the strength to tell him.

But the sting from Levi's actions is still present, and even though it's dulled, the embarrassment that my innermost thoughts were out there on display for the guy I've been pining over since our childhood hasn't lessened.

I sit in the coffee shop a few minutes longer with Pretzel, finishing my coffee, before finally getting up and heading back to Bloomie's. The lights are on and the flowers are out, meaning Emma must already be in.

"Where have you been?" she calls from the back room. She comes out a few seconds later carrying a bucket of daisies. "We had a special order for fifteen daisy arrangements that need to be delivered today, by the way. I think the ad we ran on Instagram really helped."

"That's great," I mumble absentmindedly, staring out the window.

"What are you looking for?" she asks, following my gaze. "Why do you look so...pale? It's not flu season yet, is it?"

"I just saw Levi," I confess. I shut my eyes tightly, ready for the blow from Emma. Instead, I'm greeted with silence. I crack one eye to find her staring at me, arms folded across her chest.

"And?" she asks.

"He apologized."

"So are you two..." She pauses, looking for the right words. "Okay?"

"I didn't accept his apology," I say.

"Hmm," Emma says, pulling a daisy from the bucket and twirling it between her fingers. "Why not?"

"I'm not ready. What he did was wrong, and it still hurts."

"It was wrong, yes. But he confessed to every part of it, didn't he?"

"Who's side are you on?" I say, stomping my foot like a child.

"Have you talked to Adam about it?"

"I gave his phone back to him the other morning and told him what had happened. He agreed it was a real crappy thing to do, but you know how Adam is. He doesn't let stuff like that bother him."

I pull a vase from the shelf and fill it with water so we can get started on the arrangements. We work side by side until I catch Emma staring at me from the corner of my eye.

"What?"

"Nothing," she says and turns back to her arrangement.

"What?" I repeat, facing her fully, my voice rising in agitation.

"It's just that...you saw Levi for what? An hour this morning? And you already seem different. Like there's a light back in your eyes that wasn't there when he was gone."

I pause and suck in a breath. That can't be right. "What? No. There's no way. I'm still hurting. I'm still upset with him. It's probably just the three cups of coffee I had this morning."

"I'm just saying," Emma says, the corner of her lips curving into a smile.

Work flies by thanks to fourteen new online orders and the last of the summer tourists stopping by to browse. Within no time, I'm locking the door and putting what's left of the fresh flowers back into the cooler. Pretzel and I say our goodbyes to

Emma for the weekend, then head to see Adam. My plan is to keep her in my backpack and pray she doesn't bark. Today should be Adam's last day in the hospital if his vitals stay steady.

When we finally arrive, I walk down to his room, thinking I could probably find it with my eyes closed at this point. As I round the corner, familiar voices trail down the hall.

"I don't know what to tell you, man. You know how stubborn she can be," Adam says above the chatter coming from other rooms.

"I can't stop thinking about her." A second, muffled voice says, and I can't quite make out who it is. "I'm sorry for trying to go after her without your permission."

Adam's laugh rings out, warming my heart. I creep closer, my nosiness getting the best of me.

"You don't need my permission. I should be apologizing to you for getting in the way every time you tried to make a move on her in high school. Heck, now I probably wouldn't trust anyone with her *but* you. She's my sister, though, you know? I had to make sure she was okay. I didn't realize what she meant to you then or now."

I freeze in my tracks.

"She means a lot to me, man." Levi pauses and then awkwardly clears his throat. "I...I love her."

Those three words send my head spinning. The hallway walls whirl around, closing in on me, Adam's room getting farther and farther away.

Get a grip, Aly. Boys have told you they loved you before.

But not Levi.

Levi loves me.

And then...the world goes black.

"Can you hear me?"

I blink open my eyes to a nurse standing over me, waving an ammonia stick in front of my face, the smell so terrible I want to slap it out of her hand.

"Yes," I say and roll onto my side, then all fours. Instantly, I scan the area for my backpack and can't find it anywhere. Panic rises in my chest when Levi pops his head out of the room.

"I've got your backpack. It's safe and sound with Adam," he says with a wink. My heart rate begins to return to normal, and I'm thankful he knew to grab it and Pretzel before anyone found her.

"Can you stand?" the nurse asks and offers a hand. "I can get a wheelchair if you feel like you need it."

"I'm fine," I say, ignoring her hand and standing woozily to my feet. "Thank you."

"When you landed, you made a strange noise. Almost like a yip. I knew it must've hurt," the nurse says, with concern. "Have you eaten today?"

I think back on the three coffees I had earlier. "I haven't."

"What room are you headed to? I'll bring in some crackers and juice." I point to Adam's door, and she nods before turning away.

"You okay?" Levi asks.

"Never better," I mumble, my cheeks turning crimson.

"What happened?" Concern lines his face. Instead of answering, I walk toward Adam's room.

A million thoughts race through my mind. I can tell him I heard his confession to Adam, but that would be admitting to eavesdropping. Or, I could pretend like nothing ever happened, but then I would be doing exactly what Levi did to me with the texts. Karma has a real funny way of biting you in the butt.

I spin on my heel to face him. I take his face between my palms and look him straight in the eye. "I forgive you," I tell him.

"Aly, I'm so sorry," he starts.

"No, stop. I'm not done, I say, holding a hand up to shush him. "I love you, too."

He reaches his hands up to mine and gently holds them there, tilting his head to lean in and kiss me. For three whole seconds, I forget I'm in a hospital, surrounded by the smell of ammonia and bleach, with my brother mere feet away.

Someone clears their throat right when Levi delivers a teasing bite to my lower lip. We peel back from each other to find Adam, arms crossed, looking every which way but the two of us. "Do you think you two could do that...somewhere else?"

I giggle, and my cheeks flush. "Are you sure you're okay with me loving your best friend?" I ask him quietly.

"Yes, but please just...don't do that in front of me," he says. Pretzel pops her head out from under the covers beside Adam, as if she's been hiding her eyes too.

Levi clears his throat and looks down, the tips of his ears red with embarrassment. "I guess it's probably a bad time to talk to you about how Hank impregnated your dog then, too, huh?"

"No, probably not," Adam says with a smile. "You're not off the hook for that one yet."

The first puppy makes her debut early on a Saturday morning. Pretzel is already exhausted, but I have a feeling it's more from Glenda and my mom constantly obsessing over her than from giving birth.

"She needs water!" Glenda exclaims, then proceeds to bring her a bowl and set it next to the two Mom has already put beside her.

"Do you think she's hungry?" Mom asks no one in particular.

"I think she'll let us know if she needs anything," Aly replies and strokes Pretzel's ear. Pretzel gives her a soft lick of appreciation.

With Adam still recovering, Pretzel has been staying with Aly. I flash back to all the times she was a little terror for Aly and how far they've come since. Now, they're two peas in a pod.

"Oh! Another one is coming!" Glenda says and scooches down beside us to get a front row seat. "Have you told them the news?" She asks us, glancing toward my mom, who's making her way in with a bowl of food.

"What news?" I ask.

"We're taking one of the puppies," Mom says. "And we're going to make him or her a mascot for our next business adventure."

"Business adventure?" Aly asks hesitantly.

"Picture this," Glenda says. "A food truck parked down by the waterfront. We sell nothing but the best hot dogs. Tourists will flock to us. I think it's the greatest idea we've ever had, don't you, Teen?"

"Yes!" Mom says, clapping her hands together excitedly. "But we haven't even told them the best part. You want to tell them the best part, Glenda?"

"Oh! Right! Yes, the best part. We're going to name it..." Glenda smacks a drumroll off her thighs and announces dramatically, "Gleenie's Weenies!"

"Gleenie's Weenies!" Mom echoes. "Isn't that so cute? Because we put Glenda and Teenie together to make Gleenie, and then weenie rhymes with it?"

Aly is doubled over in hysterics at this revelation, and I'm so lost for words, I can only shake my head.

"Gleenie's Weenies," Aly chokes out, tears streaming down her face. "Only you two."

After Pretzel gives birth to her last puppy, Glenda and my mom walk off to discuss business plans, leaving me and Levi alone with Pretzel and her four perfectly adorable puppies. They each have long bodies that match Pretzel's, and broad heads and sharp muzzles like Hank's. It's too early to tell if they'll have droopy ears like Pretzel or tall, pointy ones like Hank, but their markings are a mix of both their mother and father.

"Are you going to miss Pretzel?" I ask.

"Of course I'll miss her," Aly says. "But I know how excited she is to be back with Adam, and I really feel like this time we were forced to spend together did some good for us. Plus, I'm definitely taking a puppy." She reaches over and strokes the smallest one. All four puppies are nursing, and Pretzel looks like she's on the verge of falling asleep.

"Which one?" I ask.

"Mmm, I think I like that one." She points to a little puppy with similar coloring and markings to Pretzel's. "She's the only little girl. She reminds me of her mommy."

"Do you have a name picked out?"

"Peanut. Or Biscuit. I can't decide quite yet."

Hank pads around the corner and sniffs at his offspring.

"Now you show up," I scold playfully. "I thought I raised you better."

He looks up with sorrowful eyes, and Pretzel gives him a glare that makes even me a little nervous.

Aly lays her head on my shoulder, and I'm filled with a sense that everything is exactly how it should be. A month and a half ago, I was afraid Aly was never coming back to me. If she hadn't been eavesdropping in the hallway of the hospital that day I told Adam I loved her, I'm not sure things would've played out the way they did.

But I know one thing is for certain. I've *finally* got my girl, I've got my best friend, and we've got our pups, all in the best place in the world.

Home.

Aly and Levi have gotten their happy ending, but this isn't the last you'll see of them. Stay tuned for Emma and Adam's story next!

Acknowledgments

I can't say thank you enough to The Pancakes for helping me with this book. Between staying up way too late on our "writer's retreat" and bouncing ideas off each other for this book to starting a podcast together and everything in between, you all are the best and I don't know what I ever did without you. You each mean the world to me and I'm so grateful for our friendship.

I also can't say thank you enough to Amanda Chaperon for being the best editor I could ever ask for. You went above and beyond to make this book what it is today, and I will never be able express my gratitude enough. I truly believe you are the best editor in the world.

To my beta readers, you all saw this when it was a messy first draft and still powered through! Your feedback and ideas were so incredibly helpful and I'm thankful for each and every one of you.

To my husband, thank you for always supporting me and listening to my crazy ideas for scenes. I love you so much and I'm so grateful that I get to call you mine. Also, if a wiener dog puppy happens to show up at our house one day named Pretzel, I apologize in advance.

To my entire family, thank you for always supporting me. I don't know how I got so blessed to call you all mine. Erica, I added that wedgie adjustment in just for you!

Writing this book was so much fun and I'm so thankful for everyone who continued to encourage and support me along the way. I love you all!

Kelsey Whitney is a romantic comedy and coastal fiction writer living in the mountains of West Virginia with a heart for the coast. You can generally find her with her nose in a book, whether that's on the beach or snuggled with her dogs on her front porch and a glass of lemonade. You can also enjoy Kelsey's debut coastal fiction, *In The End*.